THE
IMMORTAL
FALLS

OTHER BOOKS BY ANNA DURAND

THE IMMORTAL FALLS

Undercover Elementals, Book Eight

ANNA DURAND

JACOBSVILLE BOOKS JB MARIETTA, OHIO

THE IMMORTAL FALLS

Copyright © 2024 by Lisa A. Shiel
All rights reserved.

ISBN: 978-1-958144-41-1 (paperback)
ISBN: 978-1-958144-42-8 (ebook)
ISBN: 978-1-958144-43-5 (audiobook)
ISBN: 978-1-958144-90-9 (library audio)

Manufactured in the United States.

Jacobsville Books
www.JacobsvilleBooks.com

Publisher's Cataloging-in-Publication Data
provided by Five Rainbows Cataloging Services

Names: Durand, Anna.
Title: The immortal falls / Anna Durand.
Description: Marietta, OH : Jacobsville Books, 2024. | Series: Undercover elementals, bk. 8.
Identifiers: ISBN 978-1-958144-41-1 (paperback) | ISBN: 978-1-958144-42-8 (ebook) | ISBN 978-1-958144-43-5 (audiobook) | ISBN: 978-1-958144-90-9 (library audio)
Subjects: LCSH: Gods--Fiction. | Time travel--Fiction. | Magic--Fiction. | Romance fiction. | Paranormal romance stories | BISAC: FICTION / Romance / Paranormal / General. | FICTION / Romance / Time Travel. | FICTION / Romance / Fantasy. | FICTION / Romance / Action & Adventure. | GSAFD: Love stories. | Occult fiction. | Fantasy fiction.
Classification: LCC PS3604.U724 I44 2024 (print) | LCC PS3604.U724 (ebook) | DDC 813/.6--dc23.

PROLOGUE

Janus

I HOVER IN THE AETHER, FORMLESS, ISOLATED, EXISTING IN a state of perpetual limbo while the rest of the world has moved on without me. I endure, yet I cannot speak to or touch any realm. The Four Winds trapped me in this state, for reasons I doubt I will ever understand or that they will ever explain. I float about like a ghost who is never seen or even felt.

I am…nothing.

Why did The Four Winds allow seven of my fellow gods to destroy me? The balancing power in the Unseen realm has never done such a thing to any other being unless that being committed an atrocity beyond comprehension.

But I have never committed any such act.

My only tether to the real world has become a form of torture. The Four Winds must have believed that forcing me to watch as the only ones I have ever loved moved on with their lives would provide some sort of insight. After three thousand years in limbo, I feel no more insightful than before my destruction. I have been tethered to my descendants for so long that I often find myself watching them as if they were characters in a play, not the remnants of my family.

For more generations than even I can count, I've kept watch over my progeny—not by choice, but by the edict of The Four

1

Winds. And I have learned a great deal during this time. Nothing that illuminates the reasons why I was erased from the Unseen. But I have noticed a pattern.

In every generation of my descendants, only one child is born, always a female.

Why? I cannot ask for clarification because I do not exist.

Yet I can see, hear, and sometimes even detect aromas. Nothing that has been done to me makes any variety of sense. The Four Winds have never tortured another being in this manner, so far as I know. For the first three hundred and twenty-nine years of my detention in limbo, I cursed The Four Winds and assumed they did this to me because they are, in fact, agents of the darkest powers. Whoever or whatever they might be.

What am I left with? *Mortem obire.* I have died, yet I live on, while the ones I loved no longer exist except in my dreams. My descendants are strangers to me.

Generation after generation after generation...I remain alone and invisible.

Pain spikes into my chest, hard and cold, swiftly fading away. I know what this is. I've experienced it so many times that I stopped counting after the first thousand instances. Yet I feel that frigid, piercing pain every time it happens.

I squeeze my eyes shut, though technically, I have no eyes. Shutting my incorporeal lids cannot stop me from witnessing this event. So, I open my eyes and watch as another of my descendants dies. She lies in bed, barely coherent yet seeming at peace, while her friends and family speak words of comfort. As tears trickle down their cheeks, my incorporeal mouth goes dry. I swallow against a lump in my throat that does not exist, yet I feel it constricting. I even wipe intangible tears from my eyes.

Why must I watch this? Why? How can I deserve such cruelty?

If I still had a corporeal form, I know my throat would tighten and tears would sting my eyes. So many deaths...

And yet, my descendants continue to procreate. They are... happy.

Countless generations have lived full lives, and I have kept watch over them for all this time. Yet none will ever know I exist.

More years...more generations...

I have kept track of the decades and centuries and millennia, always hoping The Four Winds would release me so I might enter the spirit realm and enjoy my perpetual afterlife. After three thousand years, it has finally happened. Not in the way I had imagined, however.

A jolt shakes me with such force that I almost feel as if I were standing on solid ground. Yet I remain in limbo, disembodied, untouchable. Seconds later, a wave of temporal energy slams through me.

Have I been restored? Have The Four Winds released me?

I am yanked out of limbo and unceremoniously dropped onto a solid surface. My vision is blurry, yet I can hear and smell the world around me.

Et sanguinem infernum. I believe I am…free.

For a moment, I simply lie here reveling in the solidity of my body. The earth beneath me feels cool and a touch damp. As I gaze up at the bright orb that hovers in the sky, I feel my lips curl into a slight smile. I cannot recall the last time I felt any physical sensation. I leap to my feet and spin in a circle, taking in my surroundings. I stand in a forest. And I seem to be inside a large cavity in the ground.

How strange.

I attempt to leap out of the hole, which I estimate is approximately six feet in depth and ten feet in width as well. Yes, this is an oval cavity. Leaping out of this hole is no problem for a god such as I. So, I bend my knees deeply and jump.

But I miss the rim of the depression, tumbling to the bottom. "*Futuo!*"

Snarling a Latin curse does nothing to help me get out of this hole. I am a god. By what sorcery has someone prevented me from escaping this dank depression? How dare anyone do such a thing to me.

"Whoa-ho, look at that," a strange male voice declares. "Get over here, Ennea. You're missing the show."

The footfalls of another being approach, but I still cannot see either of the creatures.

"Holy guacamole," a female exclaims. "You caught a naked guy in the woods. Maybe he's Bigfoot."

The male being snorts. "Bigfoot is hairy, and he doesn't exist."

"How would you know, Tris? You aren't an expert on everything or even most things."

"We can't just leave this guy down there. What if he's a bad dude?"

Very little of what these creatures have said makes any sort of sense, and I've had enough of their inane banter. I thrust my arms up, waving them about, and shout, "Cease your speaking and assist me."

A red-haired male approaches the rim of the chasm and gazes down at me with a curious expression. "What's a naked Italian guy doing in a hole in Michigan? If you're a lost tourist, jeez, man, you really took a wrong turn."

The female now approaches the rim as well and gazes down at me with a furrowed brow—until her attention wanders down my body. Her lips quirk, and her green eyes sparkle. "Maybe we can keep him, Tris. He's one smokin' hot stranger. Look at those muscles and that big—"

"Shut up, Ennea. Did you ever think he might be a demon or one of those kerkopes freaks?"

Did this creature actually compare me to those vile beasts? I hoist my chin and glower at the irritating red-headed creature. "I am a god, you idiot. More precisely, I am the Roman god Janus, and I control gateways, doorways, beginnings, transitions, endings, and time itself."

"Uh-huh, sure you do." He looks at the female. "You ever hear of this Janus guy, Ennea?" When she doesn't respond, Tris waves his hand in front of her face. "Wake up. This is no time to be gawking at the nudist. We just had a freaky earthquake, remember?"

Ennea turns toward Tris and sets her hands on her hips. "I'm older than you, so show a little respect for your elder." She peers down at me, but no longer seems as fascinated by my *mentula* as she had been. Now, her expression seems wary. "Did you say your name is Janus? The Roman god?"

"Yes." I virtually hissed the word. It took a ridiculously long time for these creatures to grasp the situation. "I demand to speak to the Janusite."

I had been aware of what the oracle Bob had done, creating the Janusite prophecy a century ago. It foretold of one descendant in my lineage who would, upon coming of age and finding her way to a certain geographic location, become invested with my powers. No one asked me how I felt about Bob's ridiculous plan. Lindsey Porter is that descendant. She still holds my powers, and I want them returned to me. After all these millennia, I deserve to be restored to my former glory.

Ennea hugs herself. "This is starting to creep me out."

"Just now it's starting to bother you?" Tris huffs. "One of us has to go tell the gang about this. Wanna decide the rock-paper-scissors way?"

"What, are we toddlers?" She gives Tris a light shove. "You go. Get Lindsey and Nevan. I'll watch this guy."

Tris jogs away.

A moment or two later, he returns with Lindsey and Nevan as well as Brennus, the raven shifter and former right hand of the now-deceased sylph king, Notus.

Tris points toward the chasm where I am trapped. "It's over there."

Brennus pushes past the others while Nevan holds Lindsey back. "Wait. Please, love, let Brennus survey the area first."

I have liked Nevan since Lindsey first met him, despite the fact he is a sylph. I had watched their unusual courtship during my tenure in limbo. He has protected Lindsey, no matter what the cost to himself.

Brennus appears at the rim of the depression and squints down at me.

I lift my chin. "I demand to speak to the Janusite—to Lindsey."

The raven shifter grunts, then jogs back to the others.

A moment later, Lindsey and Nevan approach the chasm in which I am trapped.

I'm forced to tip my head back to see them. As my gaze lands on Lindsey, I snap my spine straight. To see her in person, staring down at me...I was not prepared for the way it affects me, and I manage to speak only three words. "Lindsey Astrid Porter."

She bites her lip as her brows furrow. "Um...yes. Who are you?"

Fighting back my dismaying anxiety, I puff up my chest and lift my chin once again. "I am Janus. And I want my powers back."

She snaps ramrod straight, puckering her lips. "Excuse me? Janus was destroyed a long, long time ago. His powers got scattered to The Four Winds. Why on earth would I believe you are Janus? I don't suppose you've got some identification."

"Identification?" I spoke each syllable with care, having no idea what the word means.

Nevan slings an arm around her waist. "Gods don't have driver's licenses."

What in the worlds is a driver's license? Clearly, I missed a great deal while in limbo, despite watching over my descendants. I wasn't privy to everything they did.

Lindsey rakes her suspicious gaze over me as she speaks to Nevan. "Don't tell me you're buying this 'I'm the god Janus' crap."

"Perhaps not. Or perhaps yes."

"Thanks for the ever-so-helpful wishy-washiness." Lindsey flaps a hand toward the chasm in which I am trapped. "How do we find out if he's legit?"

Nevan shrugs.

Lindsey squints at me. "Do something godlike."

"Since my powers currently reside in you, I cannot do anything remotely godlike."

"Don't get snippy with the woman you're trying to convince to buy your story."

I remember well how long it took for Lindsey and her friends to accept that I am the god Janus. We all fought together when the harpy Aello tried to destroy the time stream, but the battle cost Lindsey dearly. Nevan was destroyed in the final battle with Aello and her cohorts. After everything the Janusite had suffered, never once complaining but always doing what must be done, she deserved a happy ending. Despite everything, she turned my powers over to me instead of keeping them so she might use their magics to resurrect her husband.

Six months later, Nevan was returned to her.

Yes, The Four Winds finally deigned to return Lindsey's true love to her. Nevan is now a mortal. He and Lindsey are the parents of a little boy, Liam. I visit them as often as I can, though not as often as I would like. Since my resurrection, I have been quite busy. Pesky elementals often try to breach the portals that I control.

They never succeed.

As far as I know…

CHAPTER ONE

Felicia

WELCOME TO THE WESTERN WISCONSIN MUSEUM OF HIS-
tory and Mysteries," I tell the group of people that stands before me. I point to the badge pinned to my polo shirt, which has the
museum's logo on it. "My name is Felicia, and I'll be your guide on
this tour of the Badger State's most fascinating artifacts, historical
records, and much more. Any questions before we begin?"

A guy who looks like he just graduated from high school raises
his hand.

I nod to him. "Please, ask away."

"Will we see Mothman today?"

"No, the Mothman legend is from West Virginia." I wag my
brows. "But you never know, you might see Bigfoot or the Lake
Pepin water monster. We have quite a variety of stories about mysterious creatures here in Wisconsin."

The kid grins. "Cool."

An older man aims his disdainful expression at me. "Listen, lady,
if this tour is going to be all about that kind of hooey, I want a
refund."

"Don't worry. We'll be looking at a lot of bona fide history too." I
happen to enjoy talking about the paranormal, but it's not my job to
explain my interest in mysterious creatures and places. So, I'll stick
to the script. "If there aren't any more questions…"

The fourteen people in my group stay silent. That's my cue.

I start walking and wave for my group to do the same. "Follow me. Our first stop will be the Mysteries of the Past exhibit hall."

The tour takes one hour and forty-five minutes. I always put in a bit of padding to ensure everyone gets the most out of their ticket price and has the chance to use the restroom as needed. I've never lost a visitor because I keep track of them like a mama bear watching out for her cubs. When the tour concludes, everyone thanks me for making it fun and informative. My group genuinely loved the tour and the way I kept things moving. I receive plenty of praise for my narration of the exhibits too.

This was my last group of the day. Now I get to go home—alone, just like always.

As I climb the steps to my front door, my next-door neighbor waves and smiles. I do the same and even call out, "Your petunias are looking fantastic, Mrs. Moore! Can't wait to see the zinnias come up."

She grins.

Maybe I can't make myself happy, but at least I can give an elderly woman a compliment that makes her feel good.

I shut the door behind me and lean against it, suddenly exhausted. Sure, I had a long day at work, but I shouldn't be wiped out this much. Maybe I'm just tired of my monotonous life. Breakfast, work, lunch, work, go home, dinner, fall asleep in front of the TV, drag myself to bed.

As I stuff a handful of cashews into my mouth, I wonder for the thousandth time why this is my life. Lonely. Bored. In desperate need of something to shake up my world. When I was younger, I thought nothing could stop me from making my dreams come true. But it never happened. A long series of bad dates eventually led me to the man I believed was my Prince Charming, but even that turned out to be not what I'd expected.

Come on, universe, cut me some slack, huh? Maybe a fairytale life is too much to expect, but at least give me a good man. Please.

A forty-two-year-old woman shouldn't beg the cosmos for a boyfriend. It's pathetic. I should resign myself to spending the rest of my existence alone. That's my lot in life, apparently.

I shut off the TV, heave myself off the sofa, and drag my feet toward the bedroom. Along the way, I glance at the photos on the wall. My parents, who passed away more than a decade ago. My brother, who died in a car accident a few years back. My grandparents on both sides of the family passed away even longer ago. I have cousins, but they hate me for reasons I've never understood. My aunts and uncles are gone too.

A weight settles in my chest, and my eyes burn just enough to trigger a few tears that trickle down my cheeks.

Snap out of it, woman. It's the divorce making you maudlin, that's all. Forget about that jerk of a husband. Blake Vincent doesn't deserve you.

"Damn straight," I tell any ghosts that might be listening. "It's time to rip up that final divorce decree and move on."

Yeah, it's always that easy.

I change into my nightie and pick up the divorce papers. No more whining in my head. Time to exorcise the ghost of my marriage. I grab the papers and dig around in the nightstand until I find the lighter I keep there in case of a power outage. I have a candle in there too, but right now, I don't need that. I grab the metal ashtray that serves as a key holder and crumple the papers onto it. Then, I set those papers on fire.

And the smoke alarm goes off.

Oh, shit. I grab the water glass from the table, about to douse the flames, but then stop myself. I wanted to get rid of Blake for good, so why not let the fire erase our marriage? When the embers are all that's left, I finally douse the flames.

Good riddance, Blake Vincent.

That night, I sleep better than I have in a long, long time. Maybe I did actually exorcise that jerk. Blake might've been hot in bed—unbelievably hot—but I should never have married a man for earth-shattering orgasms. Besides, there had always been something unsettling about the sex. I swear sometimes it felt like he was trying to stake a claim or brand me or...I don't know. Most men love sex and want it often, but my ex-husband had an unusually powerful lust for screwing me. Toward the end of our relationship, it wasn't even romantic.

That's why I filed for divorce two years ago.

After a few more days of work, I have nothing to do over the weekend. That's hardly unusual. But this weekend, I vow to stop acting like I have nothing left to live for and do something to fix my life. How?

By taking a vacation.

I spend the weekend figuring out where I'd like to go. The usual tourist hot spots don't appeal to me. I need to explore a new place with new sights. Since I've never liked cities, I settle on a rural area in the Upper Peninsula of Michigan known as the Keweenaw Peninsula. It's a tiny finger of land bisected by a canal. With a bit of research, I find out the Keweenaw has plenty of paranormal mysteries and historical ones too. Yep, that finger of land is just my style.

On Monday morning, I tell my boss I desperately need a vacation. He gives me the time off without complaining at all. In fact, he tells me that I'm the hardest-working member of the staff and I've earned a break.

Ten days later, I drive away from my hometown of Cravemire, Wisconsin, and head straight to the Keweenaw. The trip takes more than six hours, but that's because I stop occasionally to appreciate the scenery or stop at a kitschy store. Since I started my trip early this morning, I don't need to rush to get to the bed-and-breakfast where I'd booked a room for the duration.

Wow, the scenery here is gorgeous. I might never go home.

At last, I pull into the gravel parking lot of the one destination I had specifically wanted to visit—Rock the Keweenaw, the Copper Country's Geology Superstore. The name alone made me curious. But when I'd looked up the website, I discovered photos of the interior and exterior that showed some intriguingly kooky stuff, like a garden of whimsical statues inspired by mythology. Yes, I definitely need to get a close-up look at that.

I've just parked my car when my phone rings. When I snatch it up, I groan. "Ugh, Blake, leave me the hell alone, would you?"

Talking to myself as if my ex-husband were here seems like a bad sign. Yeah, it means I'd reach through the phone to strangle him if I could.

My phone keeps ringing, so I give up and answer. "What do you want, Blake?"

"I was worried about you, honey. When I stopped by your house this morning, the door was locked. You didn't answer when I called out to you."

"Of course my door was locked. That's what people do when they aren't home."

"But you changed the locks on me."

I fight a strong urge to swear a blue streak. "You don't live there, never did. I bought that house after the divorce, numbskull."

"You shouldn't have done that, Fliss." His voice has turned softer, yet almost menacing. "I don't like being shut out. And besides, I know precisely where you are at every moment of every day."

A chill slithers up my spine, and my throat tightens. "I am not your property. Fuck off, Blake."

I jam my thumb down on the phone screen, cutting the call off. It rings again within seconds, but I block his number. I've done that before, but somehow, he always manages to get unblocked. Buying a new phone hadn't helped.

No more letting that bastard ruin my life.

I shove my phone into the glove compartment, then jump out of the car and head for the corrugated metal building that houses Rock the Keweenaw. The barn-red paint job is adorable. The second I walk through the door, I feel a rush of sweet relief that makes my knees weak, though it only lasts a moment. That call from Blake upset me more than I realized, I guess.

A pretty brunette waves at me, grinning broadly. "Come on in! Welcome to Rock the Keweenaw."

Though I see a few people wandering among the rows of trinkets, they don't pay any attention to the woman behind the counter.

I hustle toward her and set my arms on the countertop. "Thanks for the cheerful greeting."

The woman raises her brows. "I guess those other shops aren't very friendly."

"Well, to be fair, this is the first place I stopped."

"Are you from the UP?"

"No. I live in Wisconsin."

"That's a beautiful state to be from." She winces and smacks her forehead. "I didn't introduce myself. How rude of me." She holds out her hand. "I'm Lindsey O'Roarke, formerly Lindsey Porter until I married my hottie husband. He's Irish."

"I'm Felicia Vincent." Why am I still using Blake's last name? *Note to self: Change your frigging driver's license.* "It's great to meet you, Lindsey." I glance around the shop, noticing the racks of jewelry. "Hey, are those necklaces real gemstones?"

"Sure are. We've got semi-precious and precious. Take your pick."

I shuffle over to the display and cautiously sort through the necklaces. When I glance back, Lindsey is watching me while smiling. She probably wonders why I'm treating necklaces like they might explode in my face. I can't explain it. Blake's call probably has something to do with it.

Lindsey trots over to me. "Need some help deciding?"

"Uh, sure. I'm leaning toward amethyst, but I know absolutely nothing about gemstones."

"No problem. Let me enlighten you." She nabs a silver chain that has a single polished lavender stone attached to it. "This is amethyst. It's believed to have all sorts of healing qualities. There's even a myth that one of the Titans gave Dionysus an amethyst stone to keep him from going insane."

I snort. "Sounds like my ex-husband needs one of those. He's gone off the rails lately." I wince. "Jeez, I really didn't mean to blurt out all of that to you. Sorry."

"Don't worry about it." She drapes the necklace around my neck, and it hangs down precisely in the center of my sternum. "Amethyst is reported to have many excellent properties, including stress relief and pain relief, as well as spiritual soothing, mental acuity, even skin rejuvenation."

"That sounds wonderful. Give me ten of these necklaces, and maybe it'll dial back the years."

Lindsey laughs. "I like you, Felicia. If you ever decide to move to the Keweenaw, let me know. We could hang out together every day."

"I'd love that."

Just as we return to the sales counter, the rear door of the shop flies open, and two extremely tall and extremely hot men walk inside. They have a brief discussion. Then the dark-haired one drags the blond one closer to the counter.

The dark-haired one grins. "Lindsey! Guess what? Janus finally fell in love—at first sight, no less. It's a bloody miracle." The man points at me. "And she's the one."

Chapter Two

Janus
Seventeen Minutes Ago

THE PANORAMA BEFORE ME SHOULD TAKE MY BREATH away, but I've lived far too long to take joy from anything. Mountains like none on Earth unfold into the distance, beyond the horizon, and further still. This is the Unseen realm. Its occasional beauty is often interrupted by violence and apocalyptic disaster. Why can't elementals learn to avert war and settle their differences with words instead of weapons? I grow tired of watching them destroy each other for no permissible reason.

No one who has lived as long as I have can remain sane. Yet I do not feel deranged. How many creatures have self-destructed in my presence? Too many.

As I sit here atop the highest mountain in the realm, I begin to ponder those questions. The longer I study this world, the wearier I grow. My legs dangle over the cliff's edge, yet even if I leaped off this mountain, I would not die. I am immortal. Indestructible. A god above all other gods.

My life sucks.

Futuo. Now I'm using the language of the modern mortal world. Those words do seem appropriate and the best description of my existence. It sucks. No one has yet explained to me precisely what it means for something or someone to "suck," and I know only that the term represents unpleasant things.

A pounding erupts in my skull, three times precisely.

I release a long, groaning sigh and hiss, *"Deodamnatus."*

Clearly, I will receive no peace on this day—or any other. An elemental is calling me, and I know which one it is. Rising to my full height, I take a brief moment to assert my usual demeanor, then whisk myself to the portal in Michigan. The doorway remains closed. The being who summoned me here is tapping the toe of one shoe on the pockmarked floor of the cave. Beyond him, I see the waterfall cascading down, concealing the cave and the portal.

Despite the thunderous noise of the waterfall, I will be able to hear the leprechaun Triskaideka when he speaks. And he will speak. At length. He always does. The magics that dampen the roar of the water will do nothing to silence him.

Tris folds his arms over his chest and lifts his brows. "What took ya so damn long, Janus? My wife is pregnant, and she's waiting for me to bring her food." He holds up a plastic sack and shakes it, creating a rustling sound. "Riley has a craving for clams and peanut butter. Don't ask me why. She started crying when I told her that sounded totally gross, which is why I had to pay my penance by shopping for disgusting foods in the mortal world."

Why can Tris never be succinct? I turn sideways to the portal, and without speaking a word or making any gesture, I activate the doorway to the Unseen. "Go now, little leprechaun, before I decide to destroy you, simply to stop you from speaking."

"Damn, you're in a crappy mood. Do gods get PMS?"

I release a loud snarl and flap my arm toward the portal. "Leave immediately. Do you think I have nothing better to do than listen to your inane commentary?"

"You sure are in a mood today, aren't you?" When I bare my teeth, about to snarl at him again, he throws his hands up. The plastic sack slides down to his wrist. "Okay, okay, forget it. I'm going."

Finally. *Stulte.* But I shouldn't curse the leprechaun as an idiot. It would be untrue.

As he approaches the shimmering portal, Tris glances back at me over his shoulder. "You know, Lindsey will find out about how you're acting today. She always knows."

Triskaideka leaps through the portal, and it telescopes shut behind him.

I shuffle over to the cave wall and sag against it. The sound of water dripping somewhere inside this chamber becomes quite irritating after a moment, and I teleport myself into the woods to escape the noise. Standing at the edge of the waterfall pool, I watch the river disgorging its contents into the depths. The swirling water and the foam it creates draw me into a semi-trance state, and my eyes gradually drift closed.

Memories unreel in my mind.

A woman's face. She smiles with a depth of affection that makes my chest ache. Nothing could ever erase her from my mind, not even if the multiverse exploded.

"Don't go diving in headfirst, Your Majesty. Might get sucked into the vortex."

"*Futuo.*" I spin around to glower at the incubus who spoke to me. "Leave, Maximus. I don't care for your humor."

"I prefer to be called Max, Your Majestic Godliness. And you should try saying 'fuck' instead of the Latin version." He saunters up to me. "I fell into that ruddy pool once, but that was because Harper shot me in the back. Ah, the good old days. My wife doesn't threaten to murder me the way she used to do. I guess having a baby softened her up."

"What do you want, salamander? I wish to be alone."

"Thought you preferred the term incubus." Max squints at me, raking his gaze over me from head to toe. "Something's different about you, mate."

"Yes. The difference is your irritating behavior."

"No, it's something else." The salamander studies me with his lips puckered and rubs his chin. Then he suddenly grins and slaps my arm. "This is bloody wonderful. I finally have something to harass you about. Can't believe it took me so long to realize what happened."

I clench my teeth and snarl, "Leave my sight immediately."

"Repeat after me. I am the Roman god Janus, and I'm an uptight arse who can't accept that he's not Italian anymore."

I clench my fists now. "I am on the verge of pummeling you into the dirt."

"Come on, mate. You can't be that oblivious." Max thumps his fist on my chest. "You are not Italian anymore. Your accent has changed. The Unseen decided it was time to make you American."

"What? No, you are insane."

"Afraid not. If you don't believe me, let's go ask Lindsey. You trust her. If I'm having you on, she'll know it right away."

I stare at Max for a moment, unable to comprehend his claim. Has my accent changed? The Unseen governs all the beings in that realm. But I am a god. We are immune to such things.

Aren't we?

Max pats my arm in an almost sympathetic manner. "Why don't we zip ourselves to the rock shop? Lindsey can settle this, ah, disagreement."

"I would prefer to walk to the shop."

"Whatever you want, Your Highness."

"Do not call me that. I'm a god, not a king."

"Sure thing, Your Holiness."

I groan and give up. "Let's walk."

Fortunately, Max doesn't speak while we're ambling down the dirt path that leads to the shop. Perhaps it was inevitable that my accent would change. I have spent a great deal of time in the mortal world ever since I met my descendants, Lindsey and her family. Her father is not directly related to me. But her mother is. When Lindsey was the Janusite and held my powers within her, she could have abused that privilege. But she refused to do so. Yes, I have become quite fond of Lindsey and her family. That includes her husband, Nevan, a former sylph.

Perhaps I shouldn't fight what the Unseen wants.

I stop at the end of the trail, where the rock garden begins. It slopes down toward the corrugated-metal building that houses the rock shop. Statues of creatures that most mortals assume are mythical appear here and there throughout the garden.

Max grins at me. "You're relaxing already. And we haven't even gone into the shop yet."

"Be silent," I snap. "We must conceal our true nature now."

"Oh, do you really think mortals might be a little upset if they see a naked incubus and a toga-wearing god traipsing through the garden? I never would've guessed."

I resist the urge to punch him in the jaw, though I can't stop myself from grinding my teeth again. "You worry about our attire or lack thereof, but it's our skin color that would frighten mortals. Yours is red. Mine is gold."

"Right. I see your point."

We both glamour to present a false appearance and seem human. As we wander through the garden of statuary, I begin to hear voices coming from the parking lot and a few somewhere within the garden. We smile and nod to the mortals who pass by us, though I do that strictly to avoid seeming…out of place. Max genuinely enjoys consorting with humans. I feel uncomfortable among them.

Perhaps that's why I'm seen as aloof and arrogant.

When we reach the back door of the shop, Max swings it open for me. "Not doing this because you're a god. It's just polite."

He spoke softly so no one else would hear.

I stride into the building, where half a dozen customers loiter among the bins of rocks and shelves of merchandise. As we approach the far end of the sales counter, I see Lindsey behind the counter, talking to a woman.

And I freeze.

That woman, she is a goddess in mortal form. My breaths shorten, and a strange tingle sweeps over my skin. I know the woman is not literally a goddess. But her beauty has transfixed me in a manner I've not experienced since the days of the Roman empire. Her hair is a glistening shade of amber laced with gold, and her eyes are an entrancing and rare shade of turquoise blue.

I inch closer, halting near the closest end of the counter.

Max claps a hand on my shoulder and whispers, "If you keep staring at that bird like a serial killer who just found his next victim, somebody's likely to get hurt."

I am indestructible. I want to say that, but my voice refuses to function.

The salamander sighs and rolls his eyes heavenward. Then he smirks and shouts, "Lindsey! Guess what? Janus finally fell in love—at first sight, no less. It's a bloody miracle."

Lindsey's eyes go wide. She stares at me for a moment, then grins. "That's wonderful! Who is she?"

Max points at the mesmerizing woman. "That bird right there."

CHAPTER THREE

Felicia

I GLANCE BACK AND FORTH BETWEEN LINDSEY AND THE strange man. What did that weird British guy just say? My brows shot up and my jaw dropped the second he pronounced that his friend is in love with me. What kind of con are these people trying to pull? I've never met the big, muscular man they seem to be talking about. Lindsey had seemed like a nice, friendly shopkeeper, but now I might need to reevaluate my opinion of her.

I glance at the stranger sideways, backing away a smidgen. "I've never seen this guy before. And I definitely am not going anywhere with him. He can't have a thing for me. We're total strangers."

Lindsey reaches across the counter to pat my hand. "I'm sorry, Felicia. We didn't mean to freak you out. It's just that my, um, uncle doesn't date much. You're the first woman who's caught his eye in a long time." She shakes her head. "A *really* long time."

"Uh-huh." I didn't fail to notice how awkwardly she referred to that strange guy as her uncle. Is she actually related to him? He seems too damn young to be Lindsey's uncle. Cousin, I might have believed. "I think it's time for me to leave. Thanks for the information about amethyst."

"I wish you weren't leaving, but I understand why need to." Lindsey grasps my hand to place an amethyst necklace on my palm. "This is a gift. Please accept it."

"Okay. That's very kind of you."

I turn to walk away.

"Wait, Felicia."

That deep, sexy voice brings me to a halt. A warm, shivery sensation rushes over me, and I suddenly can't catch my breath. What is happening to me? *Move, damn feet, move.* But my body ignores my command.

The man who had been gawking at me has now come up beside me. "Forgive me. I did not mean to upset you, and I shouldn't have stared at you so rudely without at least introducing myself. I am Janus."

What a strange name. But I'm not stupid enough to say that out loud. "I'd like to say it's nice to meet you, but…"

"I understand. May I at least escort you to your conveyance?"

Am I hallucinating? He couldn't have just used the word conveyance to describe my car. I might think he's from another country and that's why he used a bizarre word, but he speaks with an American accent. Or maybe Canadian. Either way, nobody in their right mind would use the term conveyance.

The British guy hurries over to us and whispers something to Janus.

I've never heard of anyone whose first name was Janus. The man standing a couple of feet away doesn't look like anyone I've ever seen either. He has the most unusual shade of golden-blond hair that seems to glisten as if it's actual gold. But his irises…they shimmer with the same unusual shades of gold as his hair. Something in his eyes, and the way he stares at me, makes every hair on my body shiver erect.

Maybe he's an alien.

Baloney. I don't believe in that nonsense.

And I need to get out of this place. So, I start hustling for the nearest exit while Janus and his buddy whisper to each other. I'd thought this shop was a cute, kitschy tourist trap that might have something I'd like to buy as a souvenir. The amethyst necklace Lindsey had shown me was gorgeous. But the strange man with golden eyes unsettled me in ways I can't even describe.

As I reach my car, I fumble to unlock the door with my key fob. Why is my hand shaking? I'm not scared. I'm…confused. By what? Not sure. But I need to escape from this place as quickly as possible.

Finally, I open the door and climb inside. But I fumble again, this time while trying to do up my frigging seatbelt.

Someone knocks on my window.

I jerk and yelp, swerving my gaze to the person who had scared the living daylights out of me. But seeing his face doesn't ease my, um, unease.

Janus is staring at me.

His look of contrition makes me feel like a jerk. Hey, wait, he's the one who stalked me into the parking lot and banged on my window. No sympathy for the weirdo, period.

"May I speak to you, Felicia?"

That earnest expression is my undoing. I roll the window down. "What is it? I have someplace to be."

I don't, but that's none of his business. My politeness instinct kicked in, and I've never been able to fight that.

"You are very kind, Felicia." He seems so relieved that I begin to feel like I'm a jerk and he's the aggrieved party. "I realize my reaction to seeing you was inappropriate and may have upset you. That was not my intent."

"Uh-huh. Thanks for the apology, but I really need to get going." My body disagrees. Warmth flushes my skin, and I experience a bizarre urge to lean out the window and kiss him. A total stranger. I've lost my mind for sure. "Well, goodbye."

I start to roll up the window.

He sets his hand on the glass, preventing the window from moving. "You are the most beautiful, intriguing, mesmerizing woman I have ever encountered. I would appreciate it if you would allow me to see you again."

"I have to go home. My boss only gave me a week off."

I push the button that's supposed to roll the window up, but after three tries, I surrender. He's too strong. Yet somehow, despite Janus wedging the window halfway open, the mechanism doesn't make any noises like it should if it's being forced downward. Janus isn't struggling to control the window. He simply has his hand resting on it, casually.

Then he eases the window down all the way.

I intend to grab my purse and pull out my can of pepper spray, but my muscles refuse to function and so does my brain.

Janus leans through the open window—and kisses me.

The second his lips meet mine, I lose all control over my body and my mind. I moan softly, parting my lips for him, virtually begging him to thrust his tongue into my mouth. The scent of him does inexplicable things to me, like he's given me a drug that makes me want him so badly that it's embarrassing. I can't close my eyes, transfixed by the eerie gold of his irises. I coil my tongue around his, and finally, my lids flutter shut.

He slides a hand into my hair, tipping my head back, deepening the kiss.

What the fuck is wrong with me? Kissing a stranger?

Janus peels his lips away so slowly that I moan again.

As I open my eyes, I still can't look away from his golden irises.

He smiles in the sweetest, almost sad way as he brushes hairs away from my eyes. "I wish to see you again, *dulcissima*, but I will not bother you. If you should wish to see me, I will find you."

Janus walks away.

I watch him in the rearview mirror until he disappears into the rock shop. Why am I breathless? Like I've just said goodbye to my true love. I don't even know Janus. He might be a serial killer.

But damn, he knows how to kiss.

After a minute or two, I drive away. My mind keeps forcing me to glance back in the rearview mirror, as if I want to see Janus again so badly that I can hardly stand it. Now that I'm on the road again, heading south, I start to feel more like myself with every passing mile. Whatever hoodoo had taken me over for a few minutes has disintegrated now. And I can enjoy the scenery again, like I'd been doing before I ever saw that rock shop.

Woods full of tall pine trees flank the road at either side. An eagle swoops low overhead. I smile and relax, getting back into the groove of driving. Not sure what impulse compelled me to vacation here in the northernmost region of Michigan's Upper Peninsula. I live in Wisconsin. Michigan is quite aways from home. I've never been a huge fan of collecting rocks, but something inside me urged me to visit Lindsey's shop. It was almost like…fate.

Bullshit.

Up ahead, I see a sign for a rest stop. I could use a little fresh air and would love to stretch my legs, since I didn't get a chance to explore the trails behind the rock shop. The little rest stop seems like the perfect place to do that. No other cars are in the parking lot. That's even more perfect. I pull into a space and shut off the engine. Then I get out and stretch my entire body. *Oh, that feels good.* Driving for two hours had started to give me muscle cramps.

A little wooden building, labeled "restroom," sits right beside a dirt path. The trail is marked with a small wooden sign that says, "This way to the falls."

Hmm, a waterfall. That sounds lovely.

The weather has cooled a bit, though it's still very pleasant. I grab my denim jacket and stash my phone in the pocket. Then, I stroll down the trail. Birds I can't identify serenade me because I've never bothered to learn their names. Now, I wish I'd bought a guidebook of Keweenaw wildlife. *Oh, well.* At least I have the scenery all to myself.

Rumbling up ahead assures me I'm almost to the waterfall.

Lindsey had told me the rock shop also has a waterfall, but it's back in the woods a little ways and hard to see from the parking lot. I'd wanted to visit that spot, but the Janus incident sidetracked me. I'm sure this waterfall is just as gorgeous as the one I missed out on.

Suddenly, the trees part, revealing the falls.

I stop at the edge of the pool, in awe of the beautiful scene before me. The waterfall itself isn't very high, maybe ten feet, but it stretches out at either side with slender rivulets that drain down into the small pool at the base. Mist rises up from the water as it pounds down into the pool. As I draw closer, a faint rainbow forms amid the mist, growing brighter gradually.

"There she is. Shall we take her now?"

I freeze at the sound of that gravelly, hushed voice. It sounds male, though pitched at the middle range rather than a deep timbre. The hairs on my arms and at my nape prickle and lift. Goosebumps raise up and down my arms.

Something bad is coming.

Why did that thought pop into my mind? I don't know, but the truth of it hits me like a blow to the head. I stumble backward, suddenly dizzy, and bump into a wide pine tree. My pulse thunders in my ears. A cold sweat breaks out on my brow.

"Oh, I think she's noticed us. Won't help her."

Another voice that's just as creepy sniggers, "No help for the mortal, no help at all."

"Even the Almighty One can't save her."

Chapter Four

Janus

"DON'T WORRY, THE WOMAN WILL COME BACK," Nevan tells me. The fact that a former sylph who is now human believes I need to be comforted is galling. But Nevan isn't done yet. His Irish accent never bothers me, but today, it does. "Would ye like to hold Liam? There's nothing like a cuddle with a baby to brighten up anyone's day. Besides, he's your descendant."

"Liam is not a baby anymore. He's a toddler." I know this because Lindsey explained it to me. Otherwise, I would have no idea what a toddler is. "The last time I held your child, he spat up on me."

Nevan thrusts the creature at me. "Give it a try."

I cautiously accept the child, who begins to babble, interspersed with saying my name. He cannot pronounce it properly, though, and calls me "Jah-Jah." Perhaps I dislike holding Lindsey and Nevan's child because doing so reminds me of what I had lost all those millennia ago.

My throat thickens. My eyes burn.

I thrust the child at Nevan. "That is enough cuddling."

The child smiles, and something in his eyes reminds me of…something I swore never to think of again.

Fortunately, Nevan takes Liam.

A slithering chill winds its way through me, from my skin down to the essence of my being. I freeze. Something else has taken hold of me too, something dark and oily, filled with the essence of dark magics.

Felicia.

Her name echoes in my mind, and the air has taken on a strange dankness, akin to a warning of an impending storm.

Lindsey comes out from behind the sales counter, halting inches away from me. "What's wrong, Janus? You look like you've seen a ghost."

"I feel something. It's vague but—" A shot of dark energy slams into me with the force of a cannonball. I stagger backward. "I do not know what—"

"Janus!" Lindsey reaches for me, but she is too late.

I tumble to the floor on my back. My spine arches. A roar erupts from me.

And then the agony vanishes.

But I know what has happened. Perhaps "know" isn't the right word. I sense that something dreadful has occurred or will occur at any moment, and I have no time to waste on explanations or goodbyes. I whisk myself straight to the location from whence the dark energies had originated.

I find myself in the forest, near a small waterfall, and I immediately remove my glamour. Now dressed in my toga, with a gold torque encircling one of my biceps, I visually search for the source of my painful premonition. I can sense that I'm still on the Keweenaw Peninsula, not far from the shop.

"Get your hands off me, you slimy monsters!"

Rustling ensues.

I recognize that voice. Racing toward the vicinity of that exclamation, I discover the source and halt. Felicia is pinned to a large pine tree by two of the vilest sorts of creatures in the Unseen realm.

A pair of kerkopes have caged her.

The monkey-like beings boast humanoid bodies and the wings of a giant bird, though their spines are permanently bent. Their black skin and talons ensure that no one, not even a mortal oblivious to the supernatural around them, could mistake these kerkopes for anything else.

I can just see Felicia's head. The monkey creatures tower over her.

"Oh, what soft flesh this one has," one creature says. Then he flicks his tongue like a serpent, making a slurping sound. "She will taste dee-lish-uss with barbecue sauce."

How dare that vile creature speak to a woman in such a manner. How dare either of them harass Felicia.

I fly across the distance to the beasts and seize them by the throat, one in each hand, throttling them. "Why have you surrounded this woman? What is your purpose? Tell me now, or I shall destroy you both."

"Ohhh, it's the mighty Janus," one creature says while I'm choking him. "We're so frightened of the god who wears a dress."

"Don't forget the sparkly jewelry," the other creature adds.

I squeeze their throats even harder. "What is your purpose here? Tell me now, or I shall cleave your heads from your bodies."

Felicia aims a hard stare at me. "Does anyone care what I think? I'm the one who got attacked by these creepy, slimy monsters."

Kerkopes are not slimy, but that's hardly relevant right now.

I need to know the motivations of these creatures, but that will require quite severe methods of procuring the information. So, I tell Felicia, "Close your eyes. You will not want to watch as I torture the truth out of them."

"Don't treat me like I'm a child. I refuse to shut my eyes, which means you should just get on with it."

Oddly, her stubbornness arouses me. But I ignore my carnal desires and focus on the foul creatures. "Since you will not co-operate..." I slam one creature down on the ground, on his back, and pin him with one foot on his chest. I keep my hand around the other beast's throat and squeeze until blood gurgles out of his mouth. "Who sent you to abduct this woman?"

The beast who's pinned beneath my foot thrashes to no avail. "Don't tell the god anything. You-know-who will destroy us if we spill the beans. Keep your mouth shut, Stiodel."

His friend bares his fangs at the other creature. "Shut *your* mouth, Freknel, you imbecile. You just told the god my name, so I tattled yours."

Stiodel can barely speak with so much blood pouring from his throat. It's almost impressive that he manages to speak at all.

I stomp my foot on Freknel's chest, making him snarl and thrash. "Last chance. Who sent you?"

Stiodel spits at me.

I pull in a deep breath and shout loudly enough that the trees quiver, "Who sent you?"

My words reverberate through the clearing with such power that the sound of the waterfall is drowned out.

Stiodel has gone pale beneath his black skin. His eyes are bulging now. "I want to tell you, but if I do, he will destroy me."

Freknel snarls again. "You coward."

I hoist Stiodel higher. "You will die either way. Might as well betray your master in the meantime. It's your nature, after all. Kerkopes are the lowest of the low creatures in the Unseen."

"Our master calls himself Silenus."

Everything inside me seems to turn to ice. I drop Stiodel and take one step backward, removing my foot from Freknel's chest. "Your master cannot be Silenus. He was destroyed eons ago."

The kerkopes shuffle backward away from me.

"Believe what you will," Freknel says. "But we know the truth. Darkness is coming, and our master desires a sacrifice. That's all the knowledge we have."

I believe this grotesque creature. Kerkopes are not known for lying. They are also famously cowards. And I believe that they know nothing more than what they've told me. I wave my hand toward them. "You may go."

The pair disappears.

Felicia stares at me with wide eyes. "What are you? I could believe you're just an incredibly strong man—until you hollered so loud the earth shook."

Never have I attempted to explain myself to a mortal. But now I must. "I am a god. More precisely, I am the Roman god of beginnings, endings, transitions, gateways, doorways, and time itself."

She stops blinking. "Oh. That's, um, interesting."

I take a step toward her.

Felicia raises a hand. "Please don't come any closer. I need some space after being attacked by vulgar creatures and finding out the sweet young man I'd met at the rock shop is actually a Roman god."

Young man? I won't explain to her how ancient I am, not yet. She will need time to accept the truth of what has occurred in this clearing, much less of what I am.

I move closer. When she doesn't shy away, I take another step. Then another. Finally, I stand an arm's length from her. "Will you permit me to accompany you to your conveyance? I assume it's in the parking area."

"Um, okay. I guess that wouldn't hurt. Those monkey things might be hanging around in the woods."

"They would not dare challenge me again."

"Yeah, I believe that."

As we stride down the trail, I experience a strange urge to hold her hand. It would be inappropriate, though. I barely know this woman. Her aplomb during the kerkopes attack reminded me of Lindsey, who never shied away from danger. Now that she's a mother, she has reined in her tendency to run toward certain death.

I walk with Felicia all the way to her conveyance. Then I open the door for her, offering my hand to assist her. Rather than accepting my help, she folds her arms atop the open door and gives me a strange look. "You were wearing normal clothes the first time I saw you. Everything about you looked normal. Well, except for your eyes and your massive muscles. But otherwise, you seemed like an average guy."

"But I am neither normal nor average."

"No kidding." She scans me from head to toe, licking her lips. "Why do you wear a toga? I'm guessing that's your usual way of dressing."

"It is." I step closer, settling a hand atop her own. "I must see you again. When we kissed, it stirred something within me, and I believe you felt it too. We need to explore—"

"Oh, no, sweetie. There will be no exploring. I'm grateful you got rid of those winged freaks, but that's the end of it. Time to say goodbye, Janus."

"Why?"

She smiles a touch, shaking her head. "For one thing, you're too damn young for me."

"Too young? That is preposterous."

Felicia lifts her brows. "Come on, sweetie. You can't be more than twenty-five. I'm forty-two, and I have no desire to become one of those lecherous older women who prowl for young studs to seduce."

I have no idea what any of that means. All I do know is that I cannot walk away from this woman yet. But her statement about my age is preposterous. "You are mistaken, *dulcissima*. I am not twenty-five years old."

"Maybe you're twenty-nine or thirty. Either way, I won't go down that road. Goodbye, Janus."

"Felicia, wait. I am not as young as you believe. I'm far older than you, more ancient in fact than any living human."

"Uh, sure you are." She jumps into the conveyance and slams the door.

I watch her drive away, frozen in this location, as the woman who has transfixed me races down the road and out of my sight. I could teleport myself into her vehicle. But that might frighten her so much that she loses control and dies in a horrible accident. No, I cannot allow that to happen.

My only recourse is to attempt to forget about her. A god and a mortal should never consort with each other. I know this un-equivocally, for I experienced the devastation wrought by such a union firsthand. I lost the woman whom I had loved more than life itself. I lost Vita.

The Four Winds took her away from me.

CHAPTER FIVE

Felicia

I SHOULD BE FOCUSED ON THE ROAD, SO I WON'T DRIVE off into a ditch or run into a moose. But my mind won't let me do that. Images of Janus flash through my thoughts over and over. His eerily beautiful eyes. The strange way he speaks. The sincerity in his voice and his expression when he begged me to spend more time with him. Oddly, he never uses the word please, yet somehow he conveys that statement without actually saying it.

I've just gone past a mile marker. Guess that means I'm one mile from the waterfall I'd just visited. Nope, I will never go back to that place. Freakish monkey men with wings? No thanks. I'll steer clear of any waterfalls from now on. Well, I can't reasonably avoid every waterfall on the planet, or even all the ones in the Upper Peninsula.

No more wandering down lonely paths in the middle of nowhere. That's for sure.

I notice a building up ahead and slow down to look. It seems like a restaurant based on the neon sign that declares it to be "Theo's Taverna, The Best Food on the Keweenaw Peninsula." I do feel hungry. As I slow down, preparing to turn into the restaurant's driveway, my mouth begins to water, and I swear I can smell the aromas of food even with the windows rolled up. That's odd. But I'm so hungry I don't care.

Only two cars are parked in the lot.

I pull into a space right in front of the door, then grab my purse and waltz into the restaurant. And I freeze, overcome by the delicious aromas. Damn, my tummy is grumbling like I could gobble up any kind of food right now, even anchovies which I hate. How strange that I wasn't hungry at all until I saw the sign for this establishment.

When I glance around, I don't see many people here. An elderly couple sits in a booth in the far corner. A middle-aged man occupies a small table a little ways from the old couple.

An attractive man approaches me. "*Kalispera*. That means good afternoon. May I escort you to a table?"

"Sure, why not."

I follow him toward the opposite end of the restaurant, and I can't help feeling like something is off. This guy is good looking and friendly, but his smile makes me uneasy. He spoke a Greek phrase, yet he's American. That's no surprise. I am in the UP of Michigan, after all, not Athens. I hadn't noticed this place when I drove to the rock shop earlier, though I must have passed by the restaurant.

How could I have missed it? Maybe I just forgot after the insanity at the waterfall.

The man gestures for me to sit down in a curved booth. "My name is Theo." He hands me a menu. "May I get you a glass of water while you browse the menu?"

"Yeah, sure. I'm Felicia, by the way."

"A pleasure to meet you." He clasps my hand, kissing the knuckles tenderly, and gazes into my eyes with an intensity that sends a shiver up my spine. "I'll return in a moment to take your order."

He waits one second too long to release my hand and walk away, considering that he's a stranger. Maybe that shouldn't bother me, but I can't help it. After my experience with the monkey men and the literal god, I don't know up from down anymore.

Janus had been so sweet…

Forget about the young stud. You're too old for him.

But according to Janus, he's too old for me. That's impossible.

I need some good hot Greek food to ease my worries. The aromas in this restaurant remind me of all the times my dad whipped up a hearty Italian meal for our family. That smelled a lot like this, which I guess isn't surprising since Greece and Italy are in the same general region. I try to ignore my niggling doubts as I skim the menu and pick out the foods I want to order. The first item that catches my eye is keftedes, or Greek meatballs. Souvlaki also appeals to me too, though it sounds like the Greek version of shish kababs. I want dessert too, but I can't decide which one to choose.

Theo appears beside me, leaning over my shoulder to peer at the menu. "Are you having trouble selecting your foods?"

"Yes. The stew does sound delicious, but I suppose it would be too much to order keftedes and chestnut stifado."

"Nonsense." He leans closer, and I can smell…him. The scent is intoxicating, and it's making me a touch lightheaded. "Greek food is the most sensual fare you will ever consume. And you must have dessert too. No meal is complete without it."

"Not sure which dessert I should try."

"Take them all." His lips brush my cheek as he speaks. "Once you sink your teeth into a bite of baklava, the flaky pastry and tantalizing flavors will arouse your taste buds. A hint of lemon will awaken your senses, along with the slight taste of cinnamon and drizzles of rich chocolate. And of course, your meal isn't complete without fresh figs and warm, toasted hazelnuts."

"I shouldn't eat that much."

He kisses my knuckles for the second time, now tracing his tongue over them, making me shiver again. "Devour all of it, Felicia. Hold nothing back and set your desires free."

I yank my hand away, suddenly certain that he's doing something to me, something wicked and treacherous. "You know what? I really need to get going. Forgot I'm supposed to meet an old friend at twelve thirty. Maybe I'll stop by here another time to try your food. Goodbye, Theo."

When I move to stand up, he grips my shoulders and pushes me back down. He won't release me no matter how much I struggle. "You can't leave yet, Felicia. *Gia pánta kai mia méra*, you belong to me."

"Like hell." I grab his balls and twist them hard. But he doesn't even wince. "Let go of me, you bastard."

Theo chuckles. His smile conveys humor and menace in equal quantities. "Don't worry, darling. I can wait until you've simmered long enough. Of all my talents, cooking is my favorite. I will watch you ripen, then return to feed you the juices of your own desire. You will be mine, *omorfia mu*."

Whatever he just said, I swear the words themselves have slithered inside me.

Theo rises and steps backward. "Go on, darling. Our fornication is inevitable."

I cautiously slide out of the booth and try to keep as much distance between me and this creep as I can. He doesn't interfere when I head for the door and rush outside. But I catch him observing me through the window. He smirks and winks, then waves at me.

And I get the hell out of there.

When I glance back at the restaurant…it's gone. *Shit, shit, shit.* What have I gotten myself into this time?

Maybe I drive a little too fast, and maybe I have no clue where I'm going, but I don't care. My hands shake, but not so much that I can't keep them firmly on the wheel. My teeth chatter. I don't feel cold, though. My pulse races, and I grow a touch lightheaded. Who is Theo? What is he? Why does he want to torment me? He appears only slightly older than Janus, but then, Janus told me he is not young but very ancient. Theo might be older than he seems too.

By the time I do get hungry, I'm afraid to go into a restaurant.

That's ridiculous. I probably imagined everything that went down in Theo's Taverna. Hell, I probably imagined the restaurant itself. The building had vanished, after all.

I keep driving and leave the Keweenaw Peninsula behind me. I don't stop until I've crossed the border into Wisconsin. My vacation was supposed to last for ten days, but I don't feel up to exploring anymore, not after my disturbing encounter with the being who called himself Theo. As dusk fades away, I abruptly realize I don't know where I'm going. I try to bring up a map on my phone, but I can't get a signal. Where am I? No frigging idea.

Damn, damn, damn.

I pull over at a little gravel turnaround spot and try to calm down. Deep breaths. Exhale slowly. I shut my eyes and perform my relaxation routine, the one that always calms me down. No chance of that tonight. But as the seconds turn into minutes, at least the panic is subsiding. *Whew.* What a horrible day this has been. Once I'm home, all of this will become nothing but a bad dream.

After who knows how many hours on the road, I need to stretch my legs. So, I risk getting out and walking back and forth for a couple of minutes. Then I literally stretch my legs—and my arms too. *Much better.*

"Felicia."

I yelp and spin around. "Janus? What on earth are you doing here?"

He shrugs one shoulder. "I do not know. Something compelled me to come to this location."

"You don't know everything? I thought that was a god's MO, being all-powerful and all-knowing."

"That is not what a god of the Unseen is like."

Goosebumps crop up on my arms, but it's not because I'm afraid of him. I probably should be, but I can't muster any fear when I'm with him. Instead, the chilly air is causing this reaction. My nipples have tightened for the same reason, and Janus can't stop staring at them.

I snap my fingers in front of his eyes. "Wake up and stop gawking at my tits."

His eyes bulge for a second, then he winces. "I regret my behavior."

"Why is it that you never say the words please or sorry? That's what everyone else does."

"I am not a mortal. For a god of the Unseen, to speak such words would be dangerous."

"Uh-huh. That sounds like a lame excuse."

"Perhaps it is." He shuffles around in a circle, then gazes up at the starry night sky before returning his attention to me. "We are not in Michigan any longer."

"I know that. This is Wisconsin."

He snaps his body ramrod straight, lifts his chin, and gazes down at me with a haughty expression. "You are lost. I have never been lost, therefore I shall assist you in returning to the rock shop."

"Oh, no. I am not going anywhere near the Keweenaw Peninsula ever again. I'll be much safer somewhere else. Anywhere else."

His brows crinkle. "Safer? You have no need to fear me."

"Never said I felt unsafe with you." I probably should, but for some strange reason, I don't feel that way with Janus. He seems like he genuinely wants to help me, so I guess I should tell him what happened. "I had a creepy experience after we said goodbye earlier. It freaked me out so much that I just had to get as far away from the Keweenaw as humanly possible."

He tips his head down to study me. "What is a 'creepy experience'?"

"Something disturbing."

34

"Tell me about it."

Oh, why not. Things couldn't get any weirder or more disturbing. "I bumped into a strange man who tried to seduce me."

CHAPTER SIX

Janus

I SHOULD NEVER HAVE LEFT FELICIA ALONE, ESPECIALLY not after sunset. That's when the worst creatures emerge from the Unseen. My job is to prevent those with evil intent from breaching the portals and swarming the mortal world. Yet I failed. Two kerkopes assaulted Felicia, and an unknown male harassed her as well. "Tell me about your 'creepy experience,' *dulcissima*. Perhaps I can help you understand what occurred."

"Oh, what the hell." She hugs herself as if the memory has given her a chill. "I was driving away from the waterfall, and I started to get hungry. So, I pulled over, where there was a restaurant. Something seemed off about the place, but I needed to eat." She shakes her head. "What an idiot, huh?"

"No, you are not mentally deficient. What transpired inside the restaurant?"

"Rather not talk about it, but I'll do it anyway." She rubs her arms in a vain attempt to banish a chill that I'm certain originates inside her. "The place was called Theo's Taverna, a Greek restaurant. I went inside, and this very attractive young man introduced himself as the owner, Theo. But there was hardly anyone there, just a few people. Things got even more bizarre after that. Theo was, um, trying to…seduce me with Greek food."

My spine snaps ramrod straight again, though this time it happens because I am genuinely disturbed by her description of those events. "Did you consume any of the food?"

"No. I panicked and ran away."

I let my posture relax a bit. "That is quite fortunate."

"Do you think he planned to poison me?"

"I cannot say since I have no knowledge of any elemental called Theo. Perhaps he intended to abduct you and take you into the Unseen." I rub my jaw. "There are few creatures in the other world whom I do not know, at least tangentially. For the kerkopes and this other being to enter the Unseen without my permission… It is unheard of. This Theo is completely unfamiliar to me."

"Maybe he used a fake name."

"That is possible. I must return to the scene of your encounter to search for clues." I grasp her elbow. "I shall teleport you to the home of Lindsey and Nevan. It's outside the boundaries. They will take care of you while I do what I must."

"No way. I'm staying with you." When I open my mouth to object, she seals two fingers over my lips. "I'm the only witness. You need me with you to figure out what's going on."

As much as I would prefer to send her elsewhere, I know she's right. Felicia is indeed the only witness.

She removes her fingers from my lips. "What is a boundary? I assume it's not a fence or a wall. Must be something supernatural."

"Indeed it is. There are invisible boundaries throughout the mortal world designed to protect your kind. No elemental may cross a boundary, for they will be destroyed if they do so."

"We must be inside one of those. You haven't blown up or whatever being destroyed means."

I seem to have trouble remembering that Felicia is a mortal, and I speak as if she knows all that I know. She doesn't, though. "I am a god of the Unseen. That means I cannot be destroyed by the usual means." Once I was destroyed, but I do not care to discuss that with her. I dislike mentioning it at all. Besides, we have other matters to deal with that require all our attention. "May I pull you close to me? Strictly to transport us both."

Does whisking us away require me to hold her close? No. I can't explain why I am pretending that we must travel this way.

Felicia swallows hard, and the movement is visible in her throat. "Okay. You can, um, pull me close."

I sling an arm around her waist, tugging her snugly against me. The warmth and suppleness of her body pressed to mine awakens desires I haven't known for such a long time that I'd nearly forgotten how it feels. The scent of her, sweet and feminine, makes my breaths shorten. But when she links her hands at my nape, I battle against the urge to kiss her again.

Instead, I whisk us away.

We land in a grassy area alongside the highway that seems wide enough to have accommodated a restaurant. However, no such establishment resides here.

"Told you it was gone," Felicia says. Then she bites her lip as she gazes up at me. "How did you know where to go?"

"You leave a trace of you behind wherever you travel. All mortals do. Many elementals also leave such traces."

"That's fascinating and spooky at the same time."

"I must investigate this area now."

Though I release her from my hold and back away two paces, she reaches out to clasp my hand. "I can't just stand here while you poke around. We stay together, okay?"

"As you wish."

With her fingers threaded between mine, I begin to explore the vicinity. Remnants of powerful magics tease my senses, though I have trouble distinguishing what sort they are. A god such as I should know the answer immediately. No elemental is strong enough to erase virtually all signs of the spells or incantations employed by the being in question.

"You look perplexed, Janus. I thought a god must be omnipotent."

"Unfortunately not." I swivel my head left and right, then rotate in a circle while still keeping hold of her hand. I sniff the air but detect nothing I can describe. When I kneel to touch the earth, a sharp electrical shock races up my nerves. *Et sanguinem infernum.* It cannot be."

Felicia kneels too. "What is it?"

"Dark magics. The blackest sort." I rub my fingers in the earth and lift them to my nostrils, breathing in the odor. "These dark magics are like none I have ever encountered."

She stares at me with wide eyes. "And you can't figure out who did this. Gotta admit I'm scared right now. Too scared to worry about what language you were speaking a minute ago."

"It was Latin, and I said 'bloody hell.' I learned the phrase from a salamander but translated it into my native tongue."

A deep, masculine chuckle echoes through the clearing.

I draw Felicia closer to me. "I am Janus. You do not wish to anger me, for I am a god. My powers eclipse yours."

"Do they?" The voice emanates from everywhere, but the being who speaks remains hidden. "We'll see about that, Janus the Almighty."

"Who are you?"

The being chuckles again. "You will find out when the time comes. But first, you must suffer. Felicia is the key to my vengeance."

"You will regret harassing this woman, for I will rip your body apart limb by limb before I hurl you across the nearest boundary."

The being laughs with such fervor that the sound vibrates my eardrums. "You cannot stop me, puny god."

"Theo?" Felicia says. "Is that you? I recognize your voice."

"Though Theo is the name I've taken for the moment, it is not who I am. Only when the time is right will I reveal myself." The crunching of boots on pebbles alerts me to the being's location, yet I suddenly find I cannot move. "I am the dark power that will annihilate you and the entire Unseen."

Theo has spirited himself away. I felt his departure. And the potent magics I'd sensed vanish in a heartbeat.

Felicia clings to me. "Am I wrong, or are we in serious trouble?"

"Yes, we are indeed in serious trouble. I must take you to a safe place immediately."

A beam of pure white light lances down from the heavens and stabs into the earth a short distance away from us. The light beam remains in that spot as four beings walk out of it and approach us. They wear white robes, and their feet hover several inches above the ground. A slight breeze wafts around them but does not touch us.

"Why have the four of you come?" I ask. "You rarely leave the Unseen."

"That is true," says Miriella, one of two female members of The Four Winds. "But an unprecedented event has occurred. A being we cannot identify has gathered enough magics to tip the balance of power in their favor. You understand what this means."

Felicia raises her hand. "Uh, I don't understand what it means."

Miriella aims a serene, if patient, smile at her. "You are new to the realities of the Unseen. A shift in the balance of power means a shift in the balance of magics. The dark energies have overtaken the light ones."

"I still don't get it."

"Janus does. He may explain. We have come to give you a warning." Miriella spreads her arms wide. "Follow the clues. That is all we can tell you at this moment."

The Four Winds retreat into the cone of white light, then both the light and the four beings vanish.

"Okay, Janus, explain. That white-haired chick told you to."

"When dark power overtakes light power, an apocalypse is imminent, the sort that might rock the multiverse. All the worlds could be affected."

Felicia scuffles backward away from me. "Oh, hell, no. I don't want anything to do with an apocalypse. I've had my fill of creepy shit. I'll walk all the way back to my car, if necessary, but I am not going anywhere with you."

"Do you not understand the meaning of the word apocalypse? It means there will be nowhere to hide from the devastation."

She continues backing away from me. "Uh-uh, I'm done. Bye-bye, adios, ciao, in whatever language you want, I'm saying this crazy interlude is over. I'm going home to sleep for three days and forget this shit ever happened."

"You cannot go anywhere."

"Like hell. I have feet, hands, and a mouth. That's all I need to find my way home."

She has retreated so far that she risks stepping backward onto the road.

I rush toward her at lightning speed, tugging her into me.

Felicia scowls. "This is turning into a kidnapping. Maybe I should have stayed with Theo. He's creepy, but at least he didn't hold me hostage."

"He would have if you hadn't run away, I'm certain of that. He was trying to ensorcell you, which means he would have taken complete control of your mind."

"Then why did he let me go? For all I know, you're working with him."

I can't stop myself from grinding my teeth. "First, you say Theo is superior because he allowed you to leave. Then, you suggest I'm conspiring with him. Both cannot be true."

"Sure they can." She rubs the back of her neck. "I've had enough, and I'm leaving. Can you at least send me back to my home?"

"Where is that?"

"Cravemire, Wisconsin. Do you need my address?"

"No. Goodbye, Felicia."

I wave my hand, and she vanishes. Simply to be certain, I cloak myself and teleport to her home. As she climbs the steps to her stoop, she wrinkles her brows as she notices the object I had left there for her. She picks up her handbag as if it might choke her to death, turning it this way and that until she at last seems to accept that a demonic hand won't leap out to assault her.

But just as she unlocks the door to her home, she hesitates. Her gaze swivels toward me. No, she cannot see me. Yet somehow, she must sense me. That is impossible. When she finally walks into her house, I whisk myself away. But questions plague me.

Who is Theo? And what does he want with Felicia?

Chapter Seven

Felicia

DID I SLEEP LAST NIGHT? OH, HELL NO. AFTER JANUS teleported me back to my house without any explanations or a goodbye, I made myself a cup of chamomile tea, hoping that would relax me. It didn't work. The memory of Theo and his vanishing restaurant, followed by the creepy things he said to me and Janus later, kept me from getting any shuteye. After that experience, I couldn't convince myself to change into a nightie or even take my boots off. What if I need to run? If Theo can teleport the way Janus does, then I have zero chance of protecting myself. Running won't do any good.

I woke up this morning with a crick in my neck, a bad taste in my mouth, and my feet aching because I wore my boots all night. *Ugh*. My makeup was smeared on my pillow too. Nope, I didn't wash my face last night. After a few minutes, I force myself to get up and wash off all the grime, even the kind that's only in my mind. Sure, I feel weird about it, and I take the world's fastest shower. But no creatures from another world accost me, so at least I'm clean now.

Now that I'm wearing fresh clothes too, I feel brave enough to walk out into the living room.

Sheesh. When did I become such a coward?

Yesterday, that's when.

As I shuffle across the living room, I realize I can't go on like this. So, I stop and take a few slow, deep breaths. The monsters from another realm aren't here. I'm alone. I've never been a coward, and I need to stop acting like a damsel in distress. If Janus or Theo shows up, I'll behave like an adult.

Theo gives me cold shivers. But Janus... He gives me the warm, sensual kind of shiver.

No, I do not want to see him again. I'm done with supernatural insanity. I'll stick to the real world from now on.

Thankfully, I still have nine days of my vacation left. That's plenty of time to chill out and recover from the world's craziest holiday. I won't need to try to pretend nothing happened when I go back to work because everything will be normal again.

After making myself a hearty breakfast that includes enough food to feed a football team, I decide to take a walk. I love morning strolls, especially when it's a little foggy out. The world seems quieter and more private under those conditions.

My ex-husband hadn't cared about my privacy.

Don't think about that jerk.

As if on cue, my cell phone rings. The caller ID says "unknown." Yeah, that's incredibly helpful. After my divorce, and the harassment from Blake that followed, I stopped answering anonymous calls. It might just be a telemarketer who wants to pester me, so I swipe left to decline.

Then someone knocks on my door.

I shuffle over there and peek through the peephole.

One amber eye peers right back at me.

"Shit!" I shout as I jump backward.

"Open the door, Fliss. We need to talk."

I lay a hand on my chest. My pulse is still racing. "Go away, Blake, or I'll call the police."

He chuckles. "That's adorable. You think the authorities will run to your rescue. It's all right, darling. I can wait until you're ready, no matter how long that takes. Your new lover won't last long. Then you'll come running back to me."

What lover? I haven't had sex in two years. And he must be insane if he thinks I want him back.

"Until then," Blake says. Then I hear footsteps fading away.

I count to one minute, a second at a time, then peek out the peephole again. No Blake. Thank goodness. Time for that relaxing walk.

While I amble down the sidewalk, heading for a nearby park, I try not to think about anything and just enjoy the quiet. That's all I want. A nice, normal, easygoing walk.

I've just reached the park, where the fog is a little thicker. The streetlights are on, despite the fact it's past sunrise. The fog shrouds the city, and I've always loved strolling through the park during this kind of weather. It's quiet now. No people around. But I can hear waves lapping against the shore.

This is perfection to me.

"Ah, there you are, darling."

I freeze. My heart thuds. *No, no, no, not him again.*

Theo slides his arms around my waist from behind. "Running away from the restaurant was rude, Felicia. But bringing that *koprìas* Janus into our private time was quite annoying."

Koprìas? What on earth does that mean? It sounded like an insult of some sort.

I struggle but can't escape his hold. It's gentle yet impossible to overcome, which makes no sense at all. "Let me go, you repulsive dirtbag."

"What charming insults you come up with. But I'm afraid I can't let you go. You must be mine, with or without your consent."

"If you assault me, I'll find a way to kill you."

He brushes his lips over my ear. "I won't need to force you in order to get what I need. My seduction in the taverna was working."

"I got away from you then."

Theo chuckles. "No, darling. I allowed you to leave."

He's lying. He must be. If Theo let me go, that means…I don't have any control over this situation.

Fuck that. No one controls me.

I slam my elbow backward into his gut.

Theo laughs again. "You are a spunky one, eh? I like spirit in a woman—so I can break it and make her my slave."

I can't get enough leverage to grab his balls and twist them. Neither can I ram my boot down on the top of his foot, since he's much taller and my boot dangles several inches above his ankle. Flailing my legs won't help either, I'm sure. Might as well give it a try, though.

Then I get an idea. It combines two elements and, if I have any luck at all, it might give me the slender edge I need.

I flail my legs while ducking my head to clamp my teeth down on his arm.

Theo chuckles.

Oh, I'm really getting sick of this jerk. Since I've had no luck with trying to escape, maybe it's time to act like a damsel in distress, as much as I despise that trope. I pull in a deep breath and scream, "Janus!"

Theo plasters his lips to my ear. "Go on, lover, scream away. I hadn't intended to invite Janus to our party, but I can adjust my plans. This will work out even better."

Janus appears in front of me.

My heart rate shifts into overdrive. I'm glad to see him, yes, but only because I pray he can get this jackass off me. I'm not excited to see Janus. That would be insane.

The god's brows knit together. His gaze flicks back and forth between me and Theo several times, then it lands on the creep who has his lips on my ear. Janus fists his hands. "Release her. Immediately."

The seething hatred in his deceptively calm voice sends a hot shiver tingling up my spine. Damn, there's nothing sexier than an enraged god.

Theo clucks his tongue. "Desperate to have this woman, aren't you? How sad that a god has fallen so low."

"I will not converse with you. Release her now or suffer my wrath."

"Oh, I'm so terribly frightened of the god of time. What will you do? Disrupt the time stream simply to stop me? I don't think the Unseen would like that at all."

Janus flicks his finger.

And suddenly, I'm standing behind him staring at his back from six feet away.

He rushes at Theo, strapping his arm around the jerk's neck only to slam him down onto the ground. While Theo seems briefly stunned, Janus begins pummeling him with a ferocity that I'm positive only a god could achieve. Blood pours from Theo's mouth, yet he starts laughing with maniacal glee.

I have no idea what to do. I can't help Janus, but I'm terrified that Theo might have enough power to severely injure the god. Is that possible? I know nothing about the Unseen and what a god from that world can do.

Jeez, when did I accept that the supernatural exists?

The moment I first saw Janus, that's when. I hadn't wanted to believe it, but deep down, I knew it was true.

Janus gives up on pounding Theo's face and instead shakes him violently. "Who are you? What do you want? Why are you determined to abduct this woman? I demand answers now, or I shall rip you into shreds of molecular matter."

Theo starts cackling, sounding even more insane than he had a moment ago. "You cannot stop me. Wait and see, oh great god of time. Oh, yes, you will see."

The cackling weirdo vanishes.

Janus stumbles backward a step or two. He holds a hand to his brow, and his eyes glaze over even while he shakes his head slowly.

I hurry to his side, grasping his arm gently. "Are you okay?"

He squeezes his eyes shut, then blinks quickly several times as if he's shaking off a strange dream. He gives me a tight smile. "I am unharmed."

"Maybe he didn't beat you up, but you are not fine."

"Perhaps I am...slightly disturbed. That is all."

"That's all?" I grip his arm more firmly, staring into his eerily beautiful eyes. "Your talent for understatement is incredible, but you need to stop downplaying everything."

He shrugs one shoulder. "I am a god. Theo is... I don't know what he is, but he cannot be like me."

"Why not? He seems pretty damn powerful."

"But I know the name of every higher being in the Unseen. The Four Winds would have told all of us about Theo if he were some sort of nascent god." Janus rubs his brow, bowing his head. "The goddess Hathor gave up her godhood and now is known as Larissa, a mortal. But I felt the ripples in the multiverse when her change occurred. I've experienced nothing like that with Theo."

"Can't you talk to those wind people again?"

"I must wait until they choose to contact me. It's the most prudent option."

"What's the less prudent choice? I think it's about time to ditch the niceties and make your windy friends explain."

He bristles, lifting his chin and aiming his patented cool gaze at me. "I am a god. I do not resort to such infantile means."

"In other words, you're afraid to talk to them."

His nostrils flare. "A god fears nothing."

I can't help snorting out a laugh. "I call bullshit, your godliness."

"This being called Bullshit that you wish to call for cannot offer any useful guidance. You are not acquainted with any beings other than myself who would know anything about this situation."

I like sweet, disarming Janus the best. But strangely, I kind of like the uptight, haughty version of him too. Badass Janus makes me horny as hell, though I don't think I'll tell him that. "Maybe I'm not up on all the lingo of your world, but you clearly aren't up on mine either. 'Bullshit' means you're lying."

He gaze narrows to slits. "You accuse me of speaking falsehoods."

"You're damn straight I do. Why won't you tell me the real reason you're afraid to ask those wind people for help?"

Janus clasps my hand to lead me over to a park bench. We're still shrouded by the fog, but I don't hear any evidence of other people walking the paths. It's almost as if the fog itself cloaks them from us, or maybe it's the other way around. He gestures for me to sit down, then takes a seat himself.

The god exhales a long sigh that seems to deflate him in every way. "To speak to the Four Winds, I must scale their mountain fortress and knock on the door to the temple. But only those deemed worthy may enter the Temple of The Four Winds."

"Okay. You're definitely worthy."

"No, I am not."

I wriggle around until I'm halfway facing him and tuck my leg under the other knee. "Why do you say that?"

"Because I have failed in too many ways, too many times, for anyone to deem me worthy in any sense of the word."

CHAPTER EIGHT

Janus

THOUGH I CAN TELL SHE WANTS TO ASSURE ME MY statement is nonsense, that I haven't erred egregiously, she seems to have concluded that doing so would be pointless. What I have been struggling with for a while is something personal, something I prefer never to discuss with anyone. I doubt she will wait until I'm ready to discuss the situation with her since I never will do that. We are virtual strangers, after all, though it doesn't feel that way anymore.

Felicia seems oddly secure standing in the presence of a god of the Unseen. She shouldn't get comfortable with me. I am a cosmic wrecking ball. I've heard Lindsey use that phrase, though she wasn't referring to me. Not at the time. If she had witnessed my behavior today...

Felicia clears her throat deliberately. "Are you coming back from your vacation in la-la land anytime soon?"

"I have not left this location, therefore I can't return from anywhere."

"You take everything so literally. It's kind of cute. But I need to explain a few things about myself, so you'll understand why I'm skittish about running away to another realm with you."

"But I have not suggested you do any such thing."

"Not yet. But I can see the signs. They're shining bright neon colors at me." When I open my mouth, she holds up a staying hand. "Let me talk first, okay?"

I nod.

"Here's the gist of it." Felicia sucks in a large breath and blows it out. "I've spent most of my life behaving the way others tell me I should. When I finally broke out of that mold, I swore to myself I'd never let anyone boss me around ever again. At work, nobody harasses me. I'm friendly with my coworkers, but they can clearly sense I'm the sort of woman who speaks her mind even if it means getting fired. Oh, yeah, I've been through that too. Instead of whining about the unfairness of my pink-slip departure, I picked myself up and found a new job. A better one. Something I love."

I open my mouth again, wanting to ask a question, but clench my jaw instead.

She pats my cheek. "It's okay, sweetie, you're allowed to speak now."

"In that case, what is the job you love?"

Felicia shoves her hands into the pockets of her coat and hunches her shoulders. "I'm a tour guide at a regional museum in Wisconsin."

I have no idea what a museum is, but I don't care to ask for clarification. I feel foolish whenever a mortal tries to explain their world to me.

Felicia smiles at me sweetly. "Relax. There won't be a quiz at the end of my confession. You see, I used to be a stockbroker on Wall Street. That's the hub of all stock trading." She makes a face that Lindsey refers to as scrunching. "But none of that means anything to you either. Stock trading is a financial thing. People make money off gambling on which stocks will go up or down on any given day."

"I assume you're giving me the child's version, but I still cannot understand what the stock market is."

"Never mind. It's a den of thieves and wolves and downright villains. That's why I left my highfalutin Wall Street job and moved to rural Wisconsin."

I have learned the names of many states in this country called America, but my knowledge of the mortal world remains woefully inadequate. Gods are not supposed to take vacations or visit museums. I'm still unclear about what either of those terms mean.

Felicia curls her arm around my biceps. "This might be a dumb question, but I'll ask anyway. Do you love your job? I mean, being a god is essentially your career, hey?"

49

I've been staring straight ahead, moving only my eyes to scan the vicinity. But Felicia's question surprises me, and I swivel my attention to her as my brows lift. "Career? I do not understand."

"Being the god of time and those other things you mentioned, that seems like a job to me. That means it's something you work hard at, and others rely on your skills."

I relax somewhat, now that I comprehend her terminology. "I suppose that is a strangely accurate description of my life. I operate the portals to the Unseen and determine whether beings who wish to enter that realm should be permitted to do so. Some do slip past me, but that has been a rare occurrence." I wince. "And a recent one."

"You screwed up your job a few times recently?"

I nod solemnly. "Perhaps Theo is one of the creatures I accidentally allowed to leave the Unseen."

"Why would you suddenly start making mistakes like that? I'm no expert on the Unseen, or you, but I have trouble believing you screwed up for no reason."

Her faith in my skills is touching, but the information she has learned about me is but a few grains of sand amidst a massive desert.

Felicia bumps her elbow into my arm. "Fess up, Janus. Why have you made mistakes lately? Sounds like you've never done that before."

"My recent lapses have been disturbing, but…" I bow my head, staring down at my feet. "My worst mistake occurred more than two thousand years ago, and the price of my arrogance was unfathomable torture."

"You were tortured?"

I swallow hard, though my throat has tightened so much that it almost hurts. My mouth has gone dry too. Memories flood through me, reminders of people and places and events that I have tried to forget. But no, I never will forget. Never. "You should walk away from me now, Felicia. Leave and never look back. Forget you ever saw me."

"What could be so awful that you think chasing me away is the best response? It won't work, anyway. The more of your pain I see, the more determined I am to stay with you." She settles her palm on my cheek, gazing up at me with a tenderness I do not deserve. "Please, don't push me away."

Her use of the word please makes me wince again. In this world, speaking that word holds no danger. But if I were to take her into the Unseen... No, I should never do that.

I spring off the bench and stalk a few paces away.

Felicia jogs up beside me, then moves in front of me to grasp my face with both hands. That requires her to stand up on the tips of her toes. "Who was tortured, Janus? You? Someone you cared about? Please tell me."

"Stop using that word. If I take you into the Unseen, speaking that one syllable will have dire consequences."

"What word?" She bites her upper lip, releasing it slowly as realization dawns in her eyes. "You're talking about 'please.' That's the dangerous word."

"Yes. 'Thank you' is also verboten, as is expressing any sort of gratitude, no matter how tepid."

She groans and shuts her eyes briefly. Her hands fall away from my face. "This is getting ridiculous. Does your world actually have all these cockamamie rules? Or are you still trying to scare me away?"

"I have told the truth. The Unseen is a treacherous place for mortals. Most of the rules do not apply to gods, only to the elementals—and humans." I grasp her upper arms and bend forward to meet her gaze. "If you say 'please' in my world, you will become enslaved to the being to whom you spoke that word. Thanking someone will have the same effect. But the worst threat of all is if you allow yourself to become indebted to an elemental—or worst of all, a god."

She shows nothing on her face, which means I can't interpret her response. Is she truly considering my warnings? Or is she about to insult me? Or perhaps tease me?

Deodamnatus. I'm thinking like a woman, or at best, a child.

Felicia smiles with her lips closed. For a moment, she simply gazes at me that way. Then she hoists herself up onto the tips of her toes and plants a quick, firm kiss on my lips. "Thank you for worrying about me. And I can say that because we aren't in your world yet. But I'm ready to go whenever you are."

"I do not know why I want to take you there. Doing so could imperil you, and there's no reason for me to do it."

"Oh, no, you can't back out now. After what I've been through the past two days, you owe me some answers. I want to see your world." She winks. "And your bachelor pad."

"That sounds like something Max would say. I do not have a 'pad' of any sort."

"But you know what a bachelor pad is, hmm?" She tips her head to the side. "Who is Max?"

"A very irritating salamander who insists upon making asinine jokes at my expense."

"He sounds like fun. But what the heck is a salamander?"

I've explained this to other mortals, and even elementals, more times than I care to recall. But for Felicia, I will do it again. "Salamanders are elementals. Their forte is the seduction of other beings. They gain energy to survive by giving elementals and mortals incredible sexual pleasure. Some of them prefer the term incubus while others have no preference."

"So, Max is a superpowered hottie. Interesting."

I clench my fists and my teeth, grinding words out on a snarl. "You will never meet Max."

Felicia grins. "You're cute when you get jealous. And I can't deny I like having a man go thermonuclear over the very thought of another man seducing me. I suppose that makes me a bad person, but I don't care. Being good never got me anywhere."

"Aren't you rather old, in mortal terms, to be employing term such as 'hottie' and similar phrases?"

She straps her arms over her chest, lifting those voluptuous breasts. "You're a bazillion years older than I am, so I don't think you should be criticizing the way I speak." She tilts her head to the side again, squinting at me. "When was the last time you got laid?"

"I often lie down to rest. Don't you do the same?"

Felicia struggles not to laugh at me, though she fails. "For mortals, 'getting laid' means having sex."

"Oh. I see." My face has grown warm. But I cannot be…embarrassed. No one unsettles me. By Jupiter, I am a god, the most powerful in the Unseen. Yet this woman drives me to distraction with her utter lack of concern for angering me.

"Well, Janus? When did you last get some? Sex, that's what I mean."

"I, ah…cannot recall."

"Yeah, right. Men say that when it's been a long, long time. Don't worry. I won't tease you about your celibacy, especially since I've been experiencing a drought of my own."

Talking about sex is the last thing I want to do in her presence. My attraction to this woman is disconcerting. We are still standing in the park, after all, where any mortal might stumble onto us. Though we aren't fucking now, every word she speaks arouses me so deeply that I don't know if I can control my passions. I have done that for thousands of years. I should have no trouble continuing to rein in my desires.

Yet I want to drag Felicia into my arms and kiss her so deeply that she will moan and melt for me.

Felicia glances down at my loins, and her brows rise. She bites down on the corner of her mouth as if she struggles not to smirk. Then her eyes widen. She clears her throat and looks at me. "Your toga doesn't hide that."

"I don't understand."

She points at my loins. "That. Your toga is rising."

My gaze flicks downward. *"Deodamnatus."*

Her eyes widen even more. "Wow. That's one impressive erection."

My chest begins to heave, heat rushes through me, and I can no longer hold back. My carnal instincts take over.

Dragging her into my arms, I grasp her bottom with both hands. Then I grind my erection into her belly. "You've goaded me once too often, *dulcissima*, and now I am going to fuck you."

CHAPTER NINE

Felicia

MY BODY IS PLASTERED TO A GOD. A GENUINE, TOGA-wearing deity from another realm of existence who just declared that he is going to fuck me. About damn time. I can't believe I want this, but I do. More than I've ever wanted anything. I don't care what he does to me as long as I come. A god must have sexual superpowers, right? *Oh, please, yes, make it true.*

I have never been this hot for any man. If I've turned into a slut, so be it. Something about Janus makes me feel as hot as an erupting volcano, and I would gladly let him melt me into a puddle of lava. Sex with Blake had never gotten me this excited, despite his wild appetite for orgasms.

No more thinking about that bastard.

"Do you want this, Felicia?"

"Hell yeah." I experience a brief moment of panic. "You aren't, um, entrancing me or something, are you?"

"No."

And for some crazy reason, I believe him. My long sexual drought might have something to do with why I'm raring to go with a being from another world who I barely know. Screw being careful. That's never worked for me.

Janus is gazing at me with a combination of lust and concern.

"I want this," I tell him. "I want you inside me, and I demand that you give me the best sex in the history of the universe. Plee—"

He slaps a hand over my mouth. "Never use that word or the others I warned you of. I am about to take you into the Unseen. You must never express those sentiments or beg for anything or bargain with anyone."

"Got it. I forgot for a minute, but it's engraved in my brain now."

"Then it is time to leave the mortal world behind, for now. You are sure you want this with me?"

"Yes, dammit. How many times do I have to say it? I want you, I want orgasms, I want all of it."

He wraps his arms around me again, and the world vanishes.

Suddenly, we're standing inside a cavern with a waterfall behind us. The sound of the water pummeling the cliff oddly gets me even more aroused. But the racket of the falls seems muted. I can feel the vibrations, though. And damn, that makes me even hotter for him. I'm so wet that my cream has already soaked my panties.

Janus holds one hand out, then makes a flourishing gesture.

The rear wall of the cavern…melts into a writhing mass of darkness peppered with purple and gold flecks.

I cling to Janus. "What is that?"

"The portal to the Unseen."

His voice has grown rougher and deeper. Janus lifts me up and into his arms, then strides through the portal. Something nips at my skin, but Janus squints his eyes, and the pricking sensations disappear. I can't speak, but for some reason, that doesn't bother me at all.

We emerge in another world—literally.

I barely have time to notice the weird, iridescent blue color of the sky and the stringy stuff that hangs from the trees. Janus whisks us away before I can explore the surroundings. We don't go through another seething black portal, though. No, this time I don't even notice we've traveled. Suddenly, we're inside a…No, it can't be that.

But yeah, it looks just like a Roman temple.

My sex god finally sets me down on my feet. "We are here."

"And where is here?" I turn in a circle. "Did we travel back in time to ancient Rome?"

"No, but you aren't wrong to believe so. You are inside my temple." He flicks one finger, and my clothes disappear. "It is time, *dulcissima.*"

His clothes have disappeared too.

I stand frozen, unable to think about anything except his body. The word wow doesn't even do justice to his gorgeous physique. I mean…holy shit. His golden skin shimmers in the muted sunlight that burnishes his body, transforming him into the image of a Roman god, just as he claims to be. Damn, I believe it now.

He leads me over to a golden chaise, waving for me to lie down on it.

I do what he wants. Why not? I've never lusted for any man the way I lust for Janus, and I don't care anymore whether that means I've lost my mind. He perches on the edge of the chaise. For a minute or two, he does nothing except study my body from head to toe, as if he could be satisfied with doing nothing else for the rest of eternity. Luckily, that's not his plan.

He raises his gaze to mine and cups my chin. "You are the most exquisite woman I have ever seen, and I need to touch you in every way possible." He strokes my lips with one finger, delicately, sensually. "I have lived for such a long time, yet I've never wanted any woman with this intensity of desire."

"Make love to me, pl—Just do it. Now. I need you inside me." Yeah, I'd almost spoken one of the forbidden words. I caught myself just in time, but I'll need to be very careful not to scream the P-word while we're having sex. "Hurry it up, would you?"

He smiles in a devilishly sensual way that makes my breath catch. "Do not worry, *dulcissima*, this will be worth the wait."

Before I can complain again, he presses his lips to mine firmly. He doesn't force me to open my mouth for him. Instead, he holds his lips there until I exhale a long sigh through my nostrils and relax into the chaise. My lids want to drift shut, but I refuse that request. I need to watch his expression while he makes love to my mouth. And that is exactly what he does. As my jaw relaxes, he delicately slips his tongue between my lips, flicking it over and over, round and round, until my pulse revs up and I let out a soft grunt of pleasure.

He tastes like…no flavor on earth. It's pure Janus.

The god paints a trail down my throat with feather-light kisses. I grip the chaise's arms and watch him slide lower and lower, all while keeping his gaze nailed to mine. When he brushes his nose against my breast, I bite down on my bottom lip hard enough to make it turn white. But when he clasps my tit gently in one hand and begins to massage it, my breaths grow shallower and quicker.

"I'm going to devour this beautiful globe," he murmurs. "Lick and suckle and tease the tip until you are writhing beneath me."

Can't speak. All I can do is watch him.

My body responds to his every move by growing slicker deep inside my core. He hasn't even touched my clit yet, or my folds. But I want him so badly that my cream begins to drizzle out in anticipation of a powerful climax.

Janus wraps his hand around my tit again, leaving the nipple and the areola exposed. My eyes insist on following every little movement as he dips his head to lave the peak with his tongue in one rough swipe.

I jerk and gasp.

He covers my nipple and areola with his mouth and begins to suckle.

"Oh, God, yes." I writhe, just like he said I would. "Don't stop, don't stop."

While Janus worships my breast, I grow even more aroused, to the point that I'm arching my back and my ears have started to ring because I've forgotten how to breathe. He shifts position slightly, now straddling my thighs even while he goes on suckling my nipple. The tension inside me builds so rapidly that my heartbeat pounds in my ears.

Then it happens. I come.

Just as I cry out, he pushes my thighs apart and thrusts into me deeply. While he holds that position, my orgasm goes on and on, clenching his impossibly thick erection, making me come even harder. I want to scream, but I have no voice. I want to fling my arms around him, but my body is frozen in ecstasy even as my inner muscles clench his cock fiercely.

He shoves an arm beneath me, hauling me into his body, and starts to fuck me in earnest. The velvety firmness of his cock fills me up, and I swear I can feel the tip of his erection swiping side to side, up and down, teasing my every nerve. The sensation of his length driving into me makes my heart pound even harder, thrashing in my chest like it wants to burst free. I can't believe how big he is, bigger than any human man I've ever been with except maybe Blake. Yet somehow, he fits inside me like a glove.

I take back that thought. Blake was never this good.

The chaise cracks.

And we keep fucking.

Even when the chaise crumples to the ground, he doesn't pause for even a second. Janus whisks us into the outdoor pool and continues hammering into me, grunting and gasping while sweat dribbles down his temples. I've always needed a little break before I can come again, but that rule just evaporated. I sense a climax rising inside me, hotter and harder than before, threatening to devastate me with the power of this orgasm.

The god currently pleasuring me grasps the rim of the marble pool and pummels my body even more deeply. I throw my arms around him and give in to the devastating power of his lust.

His cock begins to pulsate inside me.

Janus grits his teeth, grunting with every inward lunge.

A long cry rushes out of me, heralding an orgasm that I can't even describe. The strength of it overwhelms me, like a tidal wave barreling onto the shore, destroying everything in its wake. When he finally comes, the jet of his release floods through me, hot and unstoppable, generating another devastating wave of pleasure for me.

He throws his head back and roars. The shout echoes through the temple and makes the trees outside shudder.

For a moment, neither of us moves. We're both gasping for breath. The intensity of my pleasure has left me drained in the best way, and I let my head fall back against the pool's rim and shut my eyes.

Janus lays the back of his hand on my cheek. "Are you all right, Felicia?"

"Mm, yes, fantastic." I force my lids to open and smile lazily. "That was…beyond amazing. I have no words that adequately describe what sex with you is like. A god really does do it better."

"I appreciate the compliment, but it's unnecessary."

My brows lift. "Didn't you just make a big no-no? Saying the A-word, I mean."

"Appreciation is acceptable. The rules of the Unseen allow for the occasional loophole."

"I see. Sounds like this world is one big puzzle I'll need to figure out if I'm going to stay with you."

He goes perfectly still, not even batting an eyelash. "You wish to remain with me?"

I kiss him softly and trace a fingertip over his lips. "I want to get to know you better and find out what might happen."

"That is acceptable and indeed prudent."

I can't stop myself from laughing—with affection. "You honestly are the cutest. No man on earth could compete with you for that title." I glance down at his lower region and smirk as I lift my gaze to his face. "Nobody in any world could ever give me the kind of pleasure you do. You rock the sex, Janus."

He averts his gaze and swallows hard, the movement visible in his throat. "This was, ah, the first time in more than two thousand years that I have…enjoyed a woman's body."

"No sex for thousands of years? No wonder you were so uptight."

He bends his knees and leaps out of the pool to land on the marble tiles that surround it. With a brief burst of air, he dries us both off. But the god isn't done yet. He sweeps me up in his arms and saunters into the temple itself, as opposed to the temple atrium where we had just enjoyed incredible sex.

Janus's temple is not what I expected.

He halts in the center of the enclosed space. "Welcome to my home, Felicia."

"You can call me Fliss. It's my nickname, but I only let people I really like use it."

He bows slightly. "I am honored to be among the lucky few who may call you Fliss. It is a lovely nickname."

"My full name is Felicia Marie Vincent."

"I have only one name. Rarely does anyone in the Unseen realm bother with a surname."

I wrap my arms around his neck and give him a quick kiss. "You don't need any other name."

"Would you like to explore this temple now? I would be happy to serve as your guide, but I suspect you're the sort of woman who explores on her own."

He is unusually perceptive for a man—or any kind of person. I barely know him, yet he understands me with a perceptiveness that's uncanny. I should be unnerved by that, but I've become completely comfortable with this man who happens to be a god.

Chapter Ten

Janus

Still naked, Felicia wanders around the temple, starting at the periphery, clearly curious about this place. My temple doesn't look like the Roman ones in the human world. But that fact doesn't seem to surprise her at all. Fliss has landed in a different world, quite literally. Although the portal that brought us into this realm obeys my commands, the Unseen itself controls everything else.

But I control the time stream.

I follow Fliss as she explores my temple, and I find myself appreciating it in a new light. The structure has no doors or windows, though open arches here at ground level provide air and a beautiful view of the scenery outside. Scarlet curtains provide some privacy, and they shiver faintly in the gentle breeze. As she tips her head back to study the upper reaches of the temple, she seems awed by not just the arches at ground level, but also by the similar ones that surround the six levels of the temple. More scarlet curtains flutter inside those arches.

She halts, and her lips curl into a soft smile. "Once, I visited modern Rome and explored the historic places there. The Colosseum intrigued me the most. Now, I'm standing inside the house of a god surrounded by architecture reminiscent of the Roman Colosseum. It's…awe-inspiring."

"I'm glad you appreciate my temple."

"Did you build it?"

"Essentially. I cast a spell to create the temple and the surrounding precinct."

"Nice. Wish I could wave a magic wand and get anything I want." She moves closer to the center of the temple and turns in a circle once again. "This is the most beautiful building I've ever seen. I suppose that shouldn't surprise me. You are a Roman god, after all. I doubt any structure ever built on Earth could compete with the architecture of the Unseen."

"Not all of it is beautiful. The dragon kingdoms are spectacular in their own way but not attractive to the eye."

She shakes her head. "I know almost nothing about this world, yet it already intrigues me."

Now that she has examined the perimeter, she ambles across the space to the center of the temple and stops there. Her gaze wanders over the furniture as well as the sculptures that encircle the precise center of the temple. Lush scarlet rugs cover certain areas, most prominently the space around the large bed. I am considerably larger than most mortal men. The bed is not simply longer than average but also wider too.

Felicia settles her bottom on the bed, letting her feet dangle over the edge. They do not touch the floor. She skims a hand over the crimson silk sheets and aims a teasing smile at me. "How many orgies have you had in this temple? I mean, you must invite hordes of people into your sanctuary. Why else would it be so wide? You could have six people, at least, in this bed."

"Only I have ever slept here."

"I was kidding. You already told me you've been celibate for a long time." She lies back, spreading her arms. "Let's christen this bed. Sort of like a ship christening, but with orgasms instead of a bottle of champagne."

The scarlet sheets compliment her skin tone and the amber and gold shades of her hair. Fliss is the most beautiful creature I've ever seen in all my existence, discounting the years when I was in limbo. I couldn't fuck anyone then. But now, I need to make love to Fliss again. I've brought her to my sanctuary, where no one else dares to even try to enter without my permission. This is the safest place I know.

She shimmies backward across the bed until her entire body lies sprawled on the silk sheets. Then she crooks a finger toward me. "Come here, Janus. I want you inside me again."

"And I desire that as well."

Felicia slithers around on the bed to lie sprawled across its length this time. Her head rests on a plush pillow.

I cannot move. Her beauty and sensuality transfix me even as my cock begins to swell again. She does this to me. No other mortal could entrance me so thoroughly without employing any sort of magic.

Suddenly, her brows furrow. She raises herself onto her elbows and stares at something behind me. Her gaze flicks back and forth between my face and whatever she has noticed behind me. "You have a harp? Do you play?"

"Yes. I enjoy strumming the harp whenever I am... It doesn't matter."

"Tell me. I'd really like to know." She grins. "And I'm so proud of myself for not accidentally using the P-word. I never realized how difficult it is to restrain yourself like that. But I really do hope you'll finish that sentence."

Sighing, I climb onto the bed and lie down beside her. Holding myself up on one elbow, I gaze into her eyes and confess something I have never shared with anyone before. "Whenever I am lonely, playing the harp relaxes me and eases my worries."

"Being lonely is nothing to be ashamed of. I've been lonesome too, especially since my divorce. Even before that, actually."

"I have heard of divorce, but I know nothing about it."

"Don't gods or elementals part ways if their relationships don't work out?"

My brows tighten with confusion. "I suppose they must. But I have little knowledge of relationships."

"Come on, you must have dated now and then, even if you weren't having sex with anyone."

"No, I have not 'dated.' That is a foreign concept to me." I bow my head. "Once, I did..."

No, I cannot finish that sentence. The memories assail me, and I need to squeeze my eyes shut to ward off the pain. That never works. The grief always worms its way into me, infiltrating the deepest reaches of my psyche.

Felicia rolls onto her side, facing me, and lays her palm on my cheek. "I didn't mean to upset you."

Considering how wildly I took her body in the pool, I owe her some measure of explanation. But I still can't gaze into her eyes. "Once, I loved a mortal. But I lost her—and our child."

"Oh, God, that's horrible. How did they die?"

"Vita and Laelia did not die. When I was destroyed, neither I nor Vita knew that she was with child. Our daughter, Laelia, was born nine months later. While I was trapped in limbo, I was subjected to visions of the woman I loved and our child, though I could not speak to them. The Four Winds forced me to endure the worst version of torture—the emotional sort. I could handle physical pain, but watching my child grow up and not being able to know her…"

Felicia wraps her arms around me, burying her face against my neck. "You poor thing. The Four Winds don't sound like good guys to me."

"They are neither good nor evil. They are the balancing power in the Unseen." When she nuzzles my neck, I lose track of what I'd been saying. The scent of her and the softness of her skin both soothe and arouse me. "I want you again, Fliss. Now."

"Mm-hm." She pulls my lobe into her mouth and suckles it. "I want what you want, sweetie." Her head pops up, and her eyes have gone wide. "Oh, shit. I forgot all about birth control. What happens if a god gets a human knocked up?"

"You cannot become with child unless I choose to let it happen." I kiss her forehead. "Relax, *dulcissima*. I should have told you about that earlier, but it slipped my mind. Elementals must be careful of impregnating mortal women due to the perils of a hybrid pregnancy. However, that doesn't apply to a mortal who enjoys carnal relations with a god."

She flops onto her back, sighing heavily. "Whew, that's a relief. You can go ahead and screw me again, Janus." She taps her bottom lip. "You really need a cute nickname."

"Do not invent one for me. I dislike 'cute' things."

"Hmm. I guess you're just like human men in that respect." She eyes me sideways. "You must have purposely gotten Vita knocked up."

"Yes. We both agreed that we wanted children."

"But you never got to meet your daughter or her children or any of the ones who came along later."

I coil a lock of her hair around my finger, over and over, to distract myself from what I must tell her next. "I have watched all my descendants, but it's true I never knew any of them—until I met Lindsey."

"Lindsey from the rock shop?"

"Yes. She is descended from a long line of women, one in each generation, any of whom might have become the Janusite. But The

Four Winds chose Lindsey. A hundred years ago, the oracle Boban-zhistilanovitz, issued the Janusite prophecy."

Fliss is clearly struggling not to laugh.

"Go on," I tell her. "There is no need to hide your humor. The oracle's name is a ridiculous mouthful. That's why everyone prefers to call him Bob."

"I can see why." Her brows wrinkle. "Lindsey is really the only child in her family?"

"No, the birth of Lindsey Astrid Porter shifted the balance of magics in the Unseen." My gaze goes distant as I recall the events that transpired when I was resurrected, but I won't delve into that right now. Instead, I focus on Felicia. "Lindsey has a brother, Ash. His birth changed everything and directly led to The Four Winds freeing me."

"That's interesting. But can we get it on again? Right now?" She rolls on top of me, sliding one hand down to clasp my cock. "It's your fault that I'm addicted to sex with you."

"Perhaps I should ease your burden."

She throws her head back in dramatic, and comical, fashion. Then she thrashes it side to side. "Oh, yes, yes, yes. Give me more of your colossal cock."

Her ridiculous humor affects me in a strange way. I suddenly find myself doing something I haven't done since the day my newest descendant, the babe Liam, was born a few years ago. I grin and laugh. "You win, *dulcissima*. We can fuck now."

"You are even more gorgeous when you laugh."

I roll on top of her, careful not to crush Fliss. My arms hold me slightly above her body. As I begin to kiss her, she releases a soft moan and fastens her hands behind my neck. Her back arches. Her tits brush my chest. The aroma of her desire wafts around us as my cock grows engorged.

Slow clapping erupts inside the temple, echoing off the walls.

I jerk my head up—and grind my teeth. "Theo, you sniveling toad. How did you pierce my temple precinct?"

He saunters halfway across the space, then halts. "You are not as all-knowing or all-powerful as you believe. The great god Janus didn't even sense me approaching." He peers around me and smiles with lascivious intent. "There she is. Come, darling, you belong in my world, not his."

I spring off the bed to land directly in front of Theo. Hands fisted, I glower at him. "No one enters my precinct without permission from me. Leave, before I destroy you."

He clucks his tongue. "You can't do that."

"A god may destroy an elemental. If you don't know that—"

"Who said I'm an elemental? You make too many assumptions, Janus."

I open my mouth, intending to berate him, but I hesitate. Should I reject every word he speaks? His arrogance annoys me, and I have never heard of an elemental called Theo. If I accept his statement that he is not an elemental, that leaves few options for what he actually is. A creature from another realm of reality? No, crossing realms is impossible—except between Earth and the Unseen. Might he be a human who acquired an inordinate amount of magics? That isn't unheard of, though it is rare.

Theo tilts his head to the side and studies me with a cocky smile playing on his lips. "Ahhh, I understand now. You refuse to accept the obvious thing that dangles right in front of your face like a cat toy."

What in the worlds is a cat toy?

I strap my arms over my chest, lifting my chin. "I have no interest in playing games with you, Theo. Tell me what you are or leave this place."

He wags a finger at me. "Uh-uh-uh, Janus the Not-Almighty. I've been sent to make sure you suffer."

My fingers begin to ache, and I abruptly realize why. I've been clenching my fists again.

Theo leans to the side, gazing at something behind me, and smirks. Then he looks at me again. "It's a shame to waste a beautiful naked woman. Why don't we all climb onto the bed and fuck? I enjoy a good threesome now and then. I could invite a few nymphs and salamanders to join us and make it a real orgy fit for a Roman god."

"You will never touch this woman."

"Won't I?"

Theo's casual suggestion of an orgy has me virtually gnashing my teeth. I want to rip him limb from limb and throw the pieces into the deepest fire pit in the Unseen simply for suggesting such a vile thing. I conjure my sword and thrust it toward him. "This is an endued sword, Theo. Leave this place now or I shall destroy you."

He laughs. "Isn't that sweet. You conjured clothing for Felicia. Is that for modesty's sake? Or are you afraid that seeing her naked makes you desperately horny and you might agree to an orgy after all? I know a succubus who would love to suck you off."

"Silence!" My roared exclamation reverberates through the temple. I whisk Felicia to my side, the magical way, and keep my arm firmly around her. "No more talking, Theo."

I thrust my sword into his chest.

Or, I try to do that. The sword splits apart, and the pieces fly in all directions. I shield Felicia with my body until no more shards rain down.

And Theo laughs. "Foolish god. You still cannot comprehend what is about to happen to you. As for your lover..." He grins like a ravenous hyena. "She is to be mine."

Felicia vanishes, then reappears beside Theo. He has his arm locked around her so firmly that she seems incapable of moving, despite struggling to get free.

Theo's amiable, if arrogant, facade crumbles away. His voice changes too, growing rougher and deeper. "Soon, you will realize who and what I am. Then, I will return to show you what I have done to your lover."

I roar and rush at him.

And I bounce off the wards that surround him.

Theo and Felicia disappear.

The roar that erupts out of me this time shakes the entire Unseen.

CHAPTER ELEVEN

Felicia

THE MOMENT THEO WHISKS ME AWAY, WE'RE CATAPULT-
ed into the dark tunnel. But unlike when Janus teleported
us, this time I feel like I've been thrown into a washing ma-
chine that's off balance. Inconstant pounding accompanies our
journey, and screeching noises deafen me. Where is this creature taking me? Why is he doing this? And who the hell is he,
really?

Theo is not his real name. I'm certain of that.

When it comes to the Unseen, is anyone's name their real
one?

Thump. I think we've just landed…somewhere. I see strange
trees, different from the ones that have stringy stuff instead of
leaves. These trees look like amped up versions of normal plant life,
with high-def intense color and soft-looking trunks. I won't touch
one of those trees to find out if it is velvety, though. For all I know,
the bark is laced with cyanide.

Theo keeps one arm lashed around me, and I still can't break
free. Maybe he uses magic to make sure I stay put. His feral grin
gives me the shivers.

"Here we are, darling," he purrs. "Now you are mine, and I plan
on ruining you with debauchery the likes of which a mere mortal
like you has never seen, much less experienced."

"No debauchery for me, jackass. If you try to assault me, I'll claw and bite and kick until even an elemental like you will bleed. You'll beg me for mercy too."

He chuckles. "Aren't you adorable. Threats of bodily harm turn me on, Felicia."

Oh, fabulous. I've been abducted by a sadistic freak. I doubt whatever he has in mind would be anything like the kinds of sex games humans play around with. He did just tell me that bodily harm turns him on, but I can't figure out if he meant that he wants to get beaten bloody, or if he wants to do that to other people.

Theo is a monster, so he probably likes to do both.

And I suspect I'm the one he wants to shackle and assault.

Theo sighs and smiles with deep satisfaction. "Ah, the things I will do to you. But it's the man in charge you should worry about."

"And who might that be?" I'm positive I don't want to know, but...what the hell.

Theo bends his head toward mine and smiles with so much wicked slyness that it makes me shiver again. "You'll find out soon enough. What a pity Janus couldn't figure out who I am. I thought he was smarter than that. His ignorance made it so much easier for me to abduct you, and I doubt he will ever find you."

Yes, he will, you slimy bastard. Janus is a god.

I might have met Janus today, but I've already gotten to know him enough to realize I want to be with him. How that might work—the mortal and the god having a romance—I don't know. But I need to give it a shot. No man of any species has ever made me feel the way Janus does.

"Uh-uh-uh, darling," Theo coos. "I can tell you're thinking about Janus, but it's futile. He cannot save you."

"Bullshit."

"I do love your spunk, but you are wasting energy on fighting me. You'll need it once the...shall we say 'party' begins in earnest. Everyone is waiting to meet you."

"You and your scummy friends can go jump in a lake of lava."

His lips kink up at one corner. "You may wish for that once my master sees you."

The world goes black. Then light returns, and I realize we've moved to another location. "Why didn't we go through that creepy tunnel this time?"

"Shorter jaunts are almost imperceptible." He lays a finger on my cheek and encourages me to turn my head. "Here we are, darling."

I really wish I could whack him with a sledgehammer. I despise being called "darling" by an evil prick. Of course, he is not human, so he would probably laugh if I tried to ram an ax into his skull. But I forget all about that once my mind adjusts to the new surroundings, and I finally absorb the panorama. The huge room features white marble floors and walls, plus columns of the same stone. Barely perceptible red lines zigzag through the marble. I tip my head back to study the dome above me, which includes a circular opening at its apex.

And through that hole, I see the sky. The Unseen realm sky.

I got glimpses of it earlier, but now…I'm awestruck by the deep sapphire shade and the glistening, diamond-like sparkles throughout the sky. I'm not in Wisconsin anymore, that's for sure.

That's not the most shocking thing, though.

As I study the creatures arrayed throughout the building—a temple, I assume—my throat tightens, and my mouth goes dry.

Theo grasps my chin, forcing me to turn my head toward him. "I believe you're finally beginning to grasp the truth. Aren't you, darling?"

I nod as a chill rushes through me. Oh, yeah, I understand what he is. The proof of it surrounds me. Everywhere I look, I see chaises and settees as well as stools and lush velvet rugs. The scarlet theme is occasionally accented with deep purple. But it isn't the decor that leaves me speechless.

Creatures of varying types lounge on the furniture or amble around, chatting and laughing, drinking and eating. They are all naked. Some resemble humans while others have goat horns on their heads or hooves on their feet. The ones with hooves also have long, sleek tails. One woman seems relatively normal—until she snakes her forked tongue out to lick a man's lips. Even I'm not so dense that I don't understand where I am. I've been a student of history for most of my life, and I earned a degree in that discipline.

I'm among satyrs, nymphs, centaurs, and other beings I can't name.

While I watch, the male beast who has a tail—a satyr, I assume—sets his hands on his hips and leans backward while his phallus grows erect in a matter of seconds. Damn, that is the longest dick I've ever seen. His erection might be impressive, but it doesn't turn me on at all. I get slightly nauseous just observing this bacchanalia. But if I remember my mythology right, I'm not witnessing a bacchanalia. It's a Dionysia.

And this is the temple of the god Dionysus, the Unseen version.

Theo pats my cheek. "Are you ready to meet your god?"

"Dionysus is not my god."

"He is now, lover. You belong to the wickedest, most powerful being in the Unseen realm." He chucks my chin. "Don't worry. Dio will give you so much pleasure that you'll forget all about that weakling Janus."

Yeah, sure, you go on believing that, psycho. Whatever this creep thinks, I will never have sex with any of the monsters in this temple. "Where's your big, bad god-boss, Theo? If he wants to screw me, he'll have to show his face."

"Excited already, eh? Relax, darling. Dio will be here any moment. Then the ecstasy will begin."

A female creature emerges from a crowd on the other side of the temple and sashays up to us. Her serpent-like tail moves in a slithery fashion, and her hair does the same. The coppery sheen of her skin glistens in the flickering glow inside the temple, though I can't figure out the source of the flames.

The female sidles up to Theo, who still has me clutched to his side. She lashes her tail around his dick. "Hello, my pet. It's been too long since we enjoyed a good Dionysia. While we wait for Dio to appear, let's have a threesome with your new friend."

Yech. I'd rather kiss a diamond rattler, but I keep that sentiment to myself.

Theo smiles at the slithery female. "How rude of me. I haven't introduced you to Dio's latest conquest. Echidna, this is Felicia. I took her from Janus on the Great One's command. She's mortal. Won't it be delicious to corrupt her, body and soul?"

"Mm, yes, that does sound delicious." Echidna's forked tongue flicked out briefly when she spoke the last word, giving it a hissing tone. "Shall we get started without the Great One?"

"I'm sure Dio would want that." Theo smirks. "As long as we don't wear her out before the Dionysia officially begins."

Wear me out? I need to get out of this place right now. But I don't have magic powers like Janus and these monsters. Maybe I could somehow contact him and scream for help without anyone hearing. He has magic, after all. We developed a kind of bond earlier in his temple, so I might as well give it a try and see if he'll hear my mental cries. I maintain the best neutral expression I can muster and do my damnedest to send out a silent SOS.

Janus, I need you. Trapped in the temple of Dionysus. Theo brought me here. Hurry, they want to do evil things to me.

Theo and his buddies are laughing at a joke some other fiend made, and they aren't paying attention to me.

No response from Janus. Maybe my plea was too wordy. Think I'll try again.

Help! Dionysus temple. Orgy. Ick!

Maybe that sounded a bit like a twelve-year-old girl asking for help, but I don't give a damn. The satyrs are sauntering toward us with their engorged members waving in front of them like signposts.

Theo turns his head toward me, and his grin evaporates. He narrows his gaze on me, flattening his lips.

Oh, shit. He must've somehow figured out my plan. *Hurry it up, Janus.*

"What's wrong, Theo, my lovely?" Echidna asks. "You look positively livid. Personally, I get turned on big time by an angry man. Why don't we screw right here on the floor?"

Theo pays no attention to her. He bares his teeth at me and fists his hands, seeming just as livid as the snake woman proclaimed.

Please, Janus, hurry the hell up.

Since Theo has clearly caught me in the act of contacting Janus, I have no reason to pretend any longer. Time to run.

A satyr pushes between me and Theo, smiling with feral hunger, and begins to pet Echidna's tail. Theo can't see me. The satyr is too tall.

I sprint for the temple doorway.

A hulking figure appears out of nowhere, blocking my way.

I trip over my own feet while trying to halt and avoid running into the massive male creature. My stumble gives him the edge. He seizes my upper arms and drags me into his huge body. He smells like…caramel and spices. His enormous rod is pressed to my belly.

His mouth slides into a smile of pure carnal hunger. He drags his tongue over his lips as he stares down at my cleavage. "Who are you, my luscious beauty?"

Theo materializes beside me. "This is Felicia. I brought her to you, Great One, because Janus covets her."

"You have done well, my child. To ravish a mortal female is always good fun. But to ravish the one Janus covets…" He licks his lips again. "This will be the most exciting Dionysia in many eons. I will enjoy her body first, then you and I will take her together. If she survives that, perhaps I'll allow everyone to take a turn."

His accent…Is that Greek? Not sure.

The huge male who has me in his hold grins at me. "I've been so rude. Allow me to introduce myself. I am Dionysus."

Perfect. I'm trapped with an actual sex god.

Outside the temple entrance, wind erupts in swirling currents that are gentle at first but swiftly become a gale. A deeper sound within the tempest sounds almost like a voice. Theo and Dionysus are busy discussing how best to ravish me into oblivion and don't seem to notice the atmosphere outside. As the gale mutates into a hurricane, complete with swirling clouds and pelting rain, I swear I hear something else. Something living. It sounds like…

The roar of an enraged voice.

Janus. Somehow, I know it's him. My pulse accelerates. A tingle of excitement races over my skin.

The other creatures inside the temple grow restless and wary, now aware of the tempest outside. Even Theo stops chatting with Dionysus and veers his gaze past the hulking god. Only then does Dionysus glance over his shoulder.

He glowers at the sky. "What is this? I did not invite the harpies to my party."

A burst of wind slams into the temple.

The floor shudders. The walls do too. And the earth itself follows suit.

Dionysus releases me and swivels around to glare at the storm outside.

Out of the tempest rises a tall figure, marching resolutely toward the temple. The wind blows leaves and large limbs off the trees in a swirling mass that parts around the figure.

My heart skips a beat. Janus is marching toward us.

He lets out an enraged bellow as he breaks into the fastest sprint I've ever seen, lashing his hands around the neck of Dionysus before the sex god has a chance to react. Janus hoists him into the air and flings Dionysus clear across the temple to the opposite wall. When the sex god slams into the temple pillars, they shatter, leaving a giant hole in the facade.

Oh, yeah, my honey is here.

Chapter Twelve

Janus

I GLANCE AT FELICIA AS I STALK PAST HER, HEADING for the area where Dionysus landed. She gives me the thumbs-up sign, which I know is a form of encouragement. That's what Lindsey had told me once. I still don't understand the significance of a thumb, however. The purpose of a hand signal isn't my priority right now. Dionysus will never touch Felicia again. I will make certain of that.

Even a god can be dissuaded by physical might.

Dionysus shoves the remnants of the pillars off himself and scrambles to his feet. He seems rather dazed, though I doubt the confusion will last long.

I seize him by the throat and hoist him into the air where he dangles an arm's length above me. "Do not ever touch Felicia again or speak to her or even look at her. You might be the god of revelry and seduction, but I control forces you cannot even comprehend in your tiny mind."

"My mind is nimbler than yours, Janus."

"All you think about is making sexual conquests."

He tries to chuckle but winds up hacking instead. A thin line of blood trickles from his lips and spatters onto my face. "You're in a foul mood, eh, Janus? When was the last time you fornicated with anyone? The Protozoic Era, I assume."

I dump him on the floor, where he lands on a pile of rubble. "You speak of the eras in the mortal world, a place you have never visited. Like so many of the petty lesser gods, you are jealous of the primordial deities who fashioned the Unseen into a vast domain filled with myriad creatures."

Dionysus gets to his feet and brushes off the marble dust. "You are essentially a virgin. That poor little Roman girl you fucked thousands of years ago doesn't count. She must have been under the influence of a spell. There's no other reason why the lovely Vita would prefer you over me."

I want to murder him. Want it so badly that my fingernails are digging into my palms. The pain means nothing to me. Yet to kill a god, even a lesser one, is far more difficult than destroying an elemental. What he said about Vita...That is unimportant for the moment. I must focus on what does matter—taking Felicia away from this place.

Dionysus grins at someone past my shoulder, and I know it's Felicia. Then he returns his attention to me. "Let's go outside and finish this argument where we won't ruin my temple in the process."

"Your ludicrous temple should have been demolished long ago. But I will gladly pound you into the earth."

As I leap at him, I begin pummeling the cretin even as we teleport ourselves outside. I summon my endued sword, though it can't destroy him. If only he were an elemental, I'd be done with this bastard in a few seconds. Instead, I will reduce him to a bloody pulp in the shape of a man.

I glance back at the crowd that has moved out onto the lawn and see Felicia there. She has her arms wrapped around herself but doesn't seem frightened. She gives the thumbs-up sign once again, then blows me a kiss. That seems like a strange reaction to a battle between two powerful beings who mean to rip each other apart.

As we wrestle, Dionysus manages to gain just enough leverage to push me off his body. He kicks me and reaches for my groin. I seize him by the throat again and slam him down onto the ground before I resume beating him with my fists. I hit him so hard that he begins to sink into the earth, creating a Dionysus-shaped hole.

His own blood trickles down his face and chest.

And it glistens on my hands too.

Dionysus lies limp at the bottom of the trench I excavated with his body. His head lolls. He moans faintly.

I teleport the excavated earth into the trench, covering the sex god completely. Not that being buried will stop him. But it will slow him down considerably so that he might realize he should give up his quest to annoy me. I whisk Felicia to my side, cradling her with one arm, and gaze down at her. "Did he harm you in any way, *dulcissima*?"

"No. The creep didn't even get the chance to use his smarmy charms on me." She peers down at the freshly filled trench. "I'm guessing you didn't kill him since you said a god can't be neutralized that easily."

"Unfortunately, that is true." I grit my teeth and hiss a breath out through my nostrils. "But I would relish the chance to destroy Dionysus."

The sex god's retinue is beginning to trickle out of the temple. I don't wish to converse with those miscreants, but more than that, I want to keep Felicia as far away from them as possible. So, I whisk us away from the Temple of Dionysus. We touch down at the entrance to the portal we had come through earlier, the one that leads into the mortal world and to the rock shop. I flourish my hand. The portal telescopes open.

An odd sensation ripples through me, and I glance behind me to survey the area. No one else is here, yet I sense a presence.

"Something wrong?" Felicia asks.

"I am…not sure. We must go now."

I take us through the portal and straight into the cavern behind the waterfall. As the portal begins to close, a frisson of magical energy slithers through me, raising every hair on my body. It passes so swiftly that I can't be certain it was anything at all.

We exit the cavern and materialize on the trail beside the falls. I keep my arm around Felicia.

She gazes up at me. "Are you going to tell me what's going on? I get kidnapped by Theo who hands me off to Dionysus, then you dig a god-size hole and bury him in it. To top it off, you're disturbed by something in that cavern."

"The summary of events was unnecessary."

"But you haven't explained any of it." She grasps the leather strap that prevents my cape from falling off my body. "I need to understand what the flying fuck just happened. It sounded like Dionysus knew your girlfriend, the one you met thousands of years ago."

I must explain. I know this, but I feel oddly uncertain about sharing more of my past with her. Still, she needs to know the truth. "Dionysus was acquainted with Vita. He has always enjoyed prowling the Unseen realm to find converts by whatever means necessary. His preferred modus operandi has always been to seduce and then ensorcell elementals and sometimes mortals too. That is how he keeps his temple alive and rich with the powerful energies he needs to remain virile."

"What a slimy snake." She wrinkles her nose. "I met an actual slimy snake in the temple. She called herself Echidna. I assume she's a god of the Unseen too, since I remember the stories of Echidna in Greek mythology."

"The being you met was the inspiration for those tales, but she is not a god. She is an elemental, albeit a very powerful one."

Felicia lifts her brows. "Elemental? I'd love to hear more about that, but first, tell me what happened between you and Dionysus. You mentioned that word, 'ensorcell,' once before. But I still don't quite understand what it means."

At least I can begin with an easy answer. "To ensorcell someone means to use magics to warp their mind so deeply that they become completely enthralled by their master."

"You mean it's brainwashing."

"Lindsey once explained that word to me, but I still think it is ridiculous. One's mind cannot be 'washed' or 'rinsed' or 'put on a spin cycle.'" I twist my mouth into a rueful slant. "Lindsey used those phrases while explaining what 'brainwashing' means. Her clarification failed to clear up the issue. I had to ask Bobanzhistilanovitz about it before I understood."

Felicia sighs. "Tell me the rest about your Roman girlfriend."

"Vita and I met while I was incognito, pretending to be a mortal so I could observe human behavior. At the time, I was quite fascinated by mortals. Ancient Rome was of particular interest to me since I am a Roman god, though I preferred not to invoke my status." The memories play out in my mind, and I can't stop myself from taking my thoughts back in time to that fateful day. "I was wandering through a market to observe the food habits of mortals in Rome. Then I spotted Vita. She was the most enchanting creature I had ever seen. I approached her and initiated a rather awkward conversation. She didn't seem to care that I am 'ruddy awful' at conversing, as Max would say."

"Was it love at first sight?"

"Yes, I believe it was. Vita and I spent the rest of that day together, simply talking while we ambled aimlessly. By nightfall, I knew I did not want to say goodbye to her, so I invited Vita to my home. I had acquired a villa on the edge of the city."

Felicia leads me over to a fallen tree trunk and sits down on it, gesturing for me to do the same. I settle onto the log, remaining close to her without touching her.

I stare down at the ground as I speak. "Vita accompanied me to my villa, and I invited her to come in and join me for a glass of wine. The short version is that I kissed her and then asked her to spend the night with me. She agreed. Before we lay together, however, I revealed my true identity and nature to her. She accepted me, and we became inseparable thereafter."

"When did Dionysus come into the story?"

"Six weeks later. The Unseen grapevine moves with remarkable speed. Someone must have seen me with Vita, and the news spread until it reached Dionysus. He grew jealous and quickly sought out my new companion." I shut my eyes as the rest of the memories take hold. "He has always been jealous of my powers. His attempt to seduce Vita was nothing more than envy. She rebuffed him, and that enraged the sex god. He tried to abduct Vita, but I stopped him."

"And he just gave up?"

I sigh heavily and rub my eyes. "No, he would not abandon his goal. I employed my powers to ensure Dionysus could never take Vita or violate her in any manner. I did that by transporting her into the mortal world and refusing to permit Dionysus to pass through any portal. He could never leave the Unseen again."

Felicia stops blinking, her gaze nailed to mine. "But he got Theo to do it for him. Dionysus ordered his minion to find and capture me since the god himself couldn't do it."

"Yes. I had assumed that after all these millennia, he would have given up his quest, especially after Vita passed away. He must have sensed her death." I pull her to my breast and fold my arms around her, afflicted by a sudden need to keep her as close as possible. "I will protect you, Fliss. At the cost of my own existence, if necessary."

"I don't want you to be destroyed again."

"And I do not want to leave you." I press her cheek to my chest and kiss the top of her head. "That is why I must take you to a place where no being of any world can find you."

"Where might that be?"

"I do not know yet. Perhaps my friends can help us. I must return to the rock shop to find out."

Felicia lifts her head. "I'm sticking with you, wherever you go."

"Even if doing so might lead to your own death?"

"Absolutely. I'm no twenty-year-old coed, after all. If I could handle being in the temple of Dionysus with only a bunch of sexual deviants who have horns and tails and who knows what else, I can survive anything." She brushes her lips over mine. "You aren't getting rid of me, sweetie."

"I never wanted to be rid of you. But your safety matters more to me than my own existence."

She rises and ambles away from me just enough that she can take in the panorama around us one more time. "This is a beautiful spot. I'd love to skinny dip with you, but our situation is too volatile at the moment."

"What does the term skinny dip mean? I have no desire to become emaciated."

Fliss laughs. "Don't worry, sweetie. When people skinny dip, it means they strip naked and go for a swim."

"Oh. I see." Why are my cheeks growing warm? I am a god, and deities like me never experience embarrassment. But that sensation gradually shifts into something much more pleasurable. Yes, I'm growing aroused at the very thought of this woman swimming naked with me. "Perhaps later we can enjoy a skinny dip in the pool."

Felicia grins.

CHAPTER THIRTEEN

Felicia

WE STROLL DOWN THE TRAIL THROUGH THE GARDEN of statues hand in hand, like any normal couple might do. But we aren't normal. A sex-obsessed god is determined to capture me, simply to steal something from Janus and win a bizarre game of chess. He wants to make me, the mere mortal, his pawn.

I've never liked chess. Now I know why.

Janus and I walk into the rock shop, still holding hands. He leads me over to the sales counter where I'd met Lindsey yesterday. Jeez, was that really just one day ago? It feels like forever.

Hey, when did yesterday become today?

When I ask Janus about that, he gives me a patient smile. "Time can behave differently in the Unseen, especially when there is turmoil within the magics the form the fabric of that world."

Turmoil in the magics? Fabric of the world? I wish I hadn't asked that question because now I'm getting a headache. I rub my temples, but that doesn't help.

Janus moves behind me to gently place his fingers over my temples. He begins to move his fingertips in a slow, relaxing rhythm that does more than erase my headache. It relaxes my whole body, and my lids drift shut.

A contented sigh whispers out of me. "You should be a masseur, sweetie."

"I do know what that word means, and I would gladly massage any portion of your body."

The deeper tone of his voice is making me horny.

"Oh! You guys are back!"

Lindsey's cry demolishes the sweet relaxation Janus had given me. Since she sounds thrilled to see us, I can't be mad at her.

Janus removes his hands from my temples and comes up beside me. "Yes, Lindsey, we have returned."

She rests her forearms on the counter, grinning as she glances back and forth between me and Janus. "Well, how did it go? First dates can be stressful, but you guys must have hit it off big time. I mean, we haven't seen either of you for several days."

"It cannot have been that long."

Lindsey rolls her eyes. "You're the god of time. How can you not know it's been three freaking days?"

"There is nothing 'freaky' about days passing."

"Don't get snooty with me. I want details. Right now. Have you found your fated mate at last?"

Janus fists his hands and flattens his lips. "Lindsey—"

"Don't 'Lindsey' me. You sound just like Nevan when you do that."

I decide to step in before Janus blows his top. He's clearly embarrassed by Lindsey's questions. "I guess time must have moved on without us while we were in the Unseen. It only felt like one day to me. The sun didn't set during our little vacation in another world."

"That can happen. I have personal experience with the phenomenon." She gives Janus a motherly smile. "So, what's the apocalypse this time?"

Janus unleashes a gusty sigh, and his shoulders flag. "Dionysus is determined to abduct Felicia and take her as his concubine. And that is the least vile interpretation of his actions."

"Dionysus? You mean the god?"

"Yes. He has a long-standing grudge against me. It is a long story."

"But you need help." Her lips tighten into a closed-mouth smile for several seconds, then she bursts into a full-on grin. "And you came to your family for help. That's so sweet. Of course we'll lend a hand. Better call in Max and Travis and the rest of the gang."

Janus had told me that Lindsey was his descendant, and that she had held his powers inside her without knowing about it until a few years ago. He also said she doesn't have powers anymore. But "the gang" she mentioned must be elementals. Maybe I shouldn't get excited about meeting more of Janus's friends, but I can't help it. I wonder if any of "the gang" will include other gods.

"Have you closed the portals?" Lindsey asks Janus. "Wouldn't want Dionysus or his toadies to slip through."

"No one enters or exits a portal without my permission. You know this, Lindsey."

"Yeah. But you're kind of on edge about Dionysus, and you're worried about Felicia too. A mother can tell. Plus, you did say Theo managed to get through a portal." She raises her brows. "You didn't accidentally do that, did you?"

"Of course not."

Janus's sharp tone clearly takes Lindsey aback. But she seems more confused and concerned than angry. She twists her head around and shouts toward the back of the shop, "Nevan! Call Mom and Dad, would you? I think we're going to need a babysitter. Janus is in deep doo-doo."

The god balks. "I am in no such state."

"Whoops. I slip into kiddie talk sometimes without realizing I've done it. That's one of the hazards of parenthood. Maybe soon you'll give us a few new descendants of your own, huh?" When Janus's eyes bulge, Lindsey winks at me, then shouts to her husband again. "Hurry it up, Nevan! My ancestor is getting antsy."

Those are words I never expected to hear anyone say in public. There are tourists rambling through the shop, but none seem to have noticed what Lindsey said. Maybe they assume she's using funky new slang to describe her parents. Considering the bizarre nature of this place—from the shop itself to the falls and the portal—I would've expected more secrecy.

Nevan emerges from a back room and slings an arm around his wife's waist. "No need to shout, darlin'. Your parents are on the way, and they'll take Liam to their house." He glances at me. "Her family lives nearby, but outside any magical boundaries."

"But that guy Theo found me. He got through a portal without Janus knowing about it."

"Yes, that is a problem." Nevan turns his attention to Janus. "How did you not notice that interloper crossing the veil?"

Janus winces and averts his gaze toward the far wall. "I do not know how it transpired. But Theo is only the vessel for Dionysus. The god is the one orchestrating all of this." Janus freezes briefly, then tips his head back and groans. "We should continue this conversation outside. The others will arrive at any moment. Triskaideka is leading the way, and he wishes to cross the veil at the alternate location."

I can't disguise my surprise. "You know all that with…telepathy or something?"

"Or something, yes."

Lindsey rushes around the counter to hug Janus and kiss his cheek, which requires her to stand on the tips of her toes. "Don't worry. The gang will do everything possible to help you guys. Nevan will go with you, but I need to stay here."

Janus nods, and of course, he seems a touch embarrassed. Any sort of affection knocks him off kilter. And yet, he grasps my hand as we exit the shop with Nevan leading the way. I know Nevan doesn't have powers, but I'm assuming he's coming with us because he has knowledge that might be useful.

We halt at the natural stone benches I'd read about on the shop's website. They encircle a supposed healing vortex. Janus clamps his free hand around Nevan's muscular upper arm while still holding my hand.

And suddenly, we're standing alongside a small waterfall. I can't see any trail that leads to this place, just grass and dirt, as if no one ever comes here. Behind me, I see a makeshift wooden railing that seems to be composed of driftwood. I can't read the sign on the other side of the railing. It's facing the other way. The waterfall itself looks to be no more than ten feet high, but it features a flat area at its base that appears to serve as a natural landing.

Nevan glances at the falls, and his features tighten. He doesn't seem fond of this secluded little spot in the woods. I wonder why, but we have bigger issues right now.

I scan the vicinity. "Are you sure your friends are coming? I don't see anybody yet."

As if on cue, a passel of humanlike beings appears behind Nevan. He steps aside to reveal the newcomers who are are strangers to me.

Nevan gestures toward his friends as he looks at me. "Felicia, allow me to introduce the rest of the 'gang.' You've met Max, but the woman beside him is his wife, Harper, who is something between an elemental and a human. Her status is a bit murky."

Thanks for the crystal-clear introduction, Nevan. I think that but I don't say it aloud. I imagine supernatural creatures are difficult to pin down in terms of what they actually are.

But Nevan isn't done yet. "Beside Harper, you see Travis and Larissa. Travis is a salamander or incubus, though he's no longer immortal. His wife Larissa, who stands beside him, used to be the goddess Hathor, but these days, she's a mere mortal. And the couple beside her are Triskaideka, who prefers to be called Tris, and his wife, Riley. She was a mortal until recently, when she was transformed into a fae, which is the elemental species he hails from as well."

My head is starting to hurt. Gods, fae, salamanders, sylphs, and who knows what next.

Another being materializes on the other side of Nevan. He has dark hair and strikingly pale blue eyes that swirl faintly. When he runs his tongue over one of his two fangs, I fight the urge to back away.

"Don't be alarmed," Nevan assures me. "Cyneric is a vampire, but he has metamorphosed from a villain to a hero."

How comforting. I really don't think Nevan understands the value of keeping his trap shut about certain topics.

Nevan glances around. "Amanda didn't come with you, Cyneric?"

"She has other things on her mind, and I do not want her anywhere near whatever apocalypse might emerge next." The British vampire smirks. "Apparently, I am the only male in this group who cares about the safety of his woman. You lot have brought your fated mates with you to be slaughtered by whatever being means to attack Janus."

"That's not his fault," I announce, for no reason other than because the vamp is annoying me. "Janus cares a lot about all of you. And he blasted his way into the temple of Dionysus just to give that jerk a wicked smackdown. He was protecting me—his woman."

Everyone is staring at me with wide eyes, even Janus.

Riley raises her hand. "Um, who is Dionysus? And why does he want to destroy Janus?"

Travis shrugs. "Who knows why evil god-wankers do anything? They're insane. Except for Janus, of course. He's just arrogant and annoying."

84

Tris slaps Travis's arm. "Everybody knows the J-Man is your bestie."

"Silence!" Nevan hollers. "We are here to discuss a serious issue. Jokes are not appropriate."

A muscle ticks in Janus's jaw. "I concur wholeheartedly with that statement. Will you all cease behaving like children?" When the others fall silent and veer their attention to him, he clears his throat. "Dionysus is a god. We cannot destroy him without a great deal more beings involved. None of the other gods would be likely to assist in such an effort."

I raise my hand. "Doesn't anybody want to talk about how Theo got into the mortal world? I assume that means Janus has, um, performance issues with his powers."

Janus huffs. "I have no such issues."

"Not talking about sex, honey. But you can't deny your powers must be a little off since you didn't allow Theo into this world. He let himself in."

Nevan opens his mouth but doesn't get the chance to speak. All the beings gathered around us have frozen—except for me and Janus—like a tableau in a shadow box. Even the leaves on the trees don't rustle. The birds have stopped singing, and I see an oriole hovering in midair.

Every hair on my arms and at my nape stiffens. Oh, this is not good.

I sidle closer to Janus. "What's going on?"

He shakes his head slowly. "I do not know."

Four figures appear in front of us.

Janus tenses up visibly.

The beings wear flowing white robes that touch the ground, though their heads and arms are exposed. Two of them seem female while the other two must be male. They all share the same pale skin tones and white hair, but their eyes are a fathomless shade of glossy black.

Janus holds me tighter to his side while he flicks his gaze between each of the four beings. "Why have you come?"

One of the females glides closer, halting an arm's length from us. "You should already understand why we are here. This moment was inevitable."

Her feathery light voice has a note of power in it that I can't describe. But it convinces me this female is not as ethereal as she seems. I bet she could give Janus a serious smackdown while barely lifting a finger.

When I glance up at Janus, he doesn't look at me. His focus is bound to the female being. He swallows hard enough that I see the movement in his throat. "Perhaps this was inevitable for me, Miriella, but not for Felicia. Allow her to return to her home. She need not be involved in whatever I must do."

Now at least I know the creature's name is Miriella. "I'm staying with you, Janus. No one, not even these eerie beings, can chase me away."

CHAPTER FOURTEEN

Janus

WHENEVER THE FOUR WINDS MAKE AN APPEARANCE, IT rarely heralds good news. Later, I will need to explain to Felicia what these beings are and why they have interfered in our plans. But even when Lindsey and the others decided to assist me, I realized that could never be the case. The problem I created, however accidentally, must be mine to correct.

Miriella smiles faintly as she turns her attention to Felicia. "Yes, I can see that you are indeed determined to remain with Janus. In fact, we knew this would be your decision well before you met him."

Felicia's eyes widen. "You can see the future? If that's true, then you should tell us what the problem is and how to fix it. I don't understand why we have to waste time on some sort of quest."

"You must do as we prescribe. Nothing we decree is a waste of time." Miriella smiles again, her lips curling up more than a moment ago. "You, Felicia, are an extraordinary mortal. With you by his side, Janus can and will endure the trials that lie ahead."

I try not to clench my jaw, forcing myself to relax. It seems an impossible task under the circumstances. "What trials? I grow weary of waiting for you to tell me."

She shakes her head slowly. "Patience has never been your forte, has it? The quest would not be worthwhile if answers came easily. Whatever comes, you must remember one thing. Never again will we allow you to be destroyed or locked in limbo."

Am I supposed to thank her for that? I can't speak such words even if I wanted to do so. When The Four Winds enter the mortal realm, they bring with them a touch of the Unseen. To express gratitude right now would be dangerous.

Besides, I don't feel grateful. I am, in fact, deeply annoyed.

Felicia ducks under my arm, encouraging me to slide mine around her shoulders. That simple act causes me to relax. How odd. But ever since I met her, she's had this effect on me.

"How will this quest begin?" I ask. "Will my friends play any role in it?"

"Not yet," Miriella says. "But if all goes as predicted, they will take part in the final phase. Now, we must send you on your way. May the Oversoul guide and protect you."

The Four Winds bow their heads in unison, then vanish.

Just as our friends become unfrozen, Felicia and I are whisked away.

I grip her tightly while we hurtle through the abyssal tunnel and the clawing energies attempt to halt our journey prematurely. But my powers are stronger than the portal. The trip lasts longer than any jaunt into the Unseen would ever take. I know what that means. But I will need to help Felicia understand.

At last, we land on grassy earth. The sun burns in the sky. The birdsong and vegetation reveal our general location—the mortal world—but not our exact time and place.

Felicia studies our surroundings. "Where are we?"

"In the mortal world. Where, precisely, I have yet to determine."

"Don't you have supernatural GPS? You are a god, after all."

I must employ all my self-control not to speak in a "snippy" tone. Now I'm using a modern mortal word, one that Lindsey often uses. *Futuo.* Females of any species drive me out of my mind. "Whatever GPS is, I have no knowledge of what it does or how it works."

Felicia nuzzles my arm. "Take a breather, sweetie. You're getting tense again, and I doubt that will help us figure out what you're supposed to do. I was only asking if you have some way of detecting our precise location. That's what GPS can do on Earth. The global positioning system is a network of satellites that encircle the globe, sending signals back to the ground."

"I have no such devices. Magic guides me, though I am hardly omniscient."

"But you are a god. Can't you figure out where we are with all those powerful magics you have inside you?"

For a moment, I consider the specific ramifications of what she said. Perhaps I have discounted my own powers for reasons that have nothing to do with my innate magics, but instead originate from the changes I have experienced recently. "You are correct, Fliss. I've been avoiding the use of my own magics for some time, which is not like me at all. I've often touted my 'vast powers,' which used to amuse elementals like Max and Tris. Now, I avoid even speaking of my abilities. That must end now."

"You have a plan, then."

"Indeed, I do. The Four Winds wouldn't send me on a quest without providing clues."

She bites one side of her lower lip, a gesture that makes me want to kiss her. "Can I ask a dumb question?"

"None of your questions are fatuous, Fliss. You're a clever woman." I brush my thumb over her lip, gently releasing her hold on it. "Ask away."

"What exactly are The Four Winds?"

I hesitate, but only so I may gather my thoughts. The answer to her query is not simple. "Despite their title, The Four Winds are not composed of air, and they don't live in the sky. The best description is that they are both avatars and guardians of power."

"So, they don't reveal what they really look like."

"Only The Four Winds know their true nature. The oracle Bob must know what Miriella looks like in her native form, since he has been engaged in an on-again, off-again romance with her. But he would never disclose her secrets."

"I'm still confused about The Four Winds."

Of course she is. Even I grow somewhat confused at times when discussing other living things. But I will try to clear up the matter. "The Four Winds are the highest beings in the Unseen. Only the Oversoul ranks higher, but no one in the multiverse understands the true nature of that being—if indeed the Oversoul is a living presence and not simply the essence of all power in this world."

"What function do The Four Winds have in the Unseen?"

"They respond when any elemental or god crosses a line they must not breach. That usually means someone is abusing their innate powers or trying to steal magical energies from other creatures. For The Four Winds to send me on a quest means they must believe I am in peril or that I need to seek out answers, perhaps both."

Felicia huffs. "It's damn obvious that you need answers. The peril thing…Well, isn't that where I come in? Theo abducted me to get to you."

"And now we must deduce why he and Dionysus have suddenly decided to harass me." I rub my chin, a longtime habit of mine. Lindsey enjoys teasing me about it. "If I could expand my powers to create a web of magics…"

"You think you could use that to find out what our next move should be."

"Give me a moment to test my theory."

"Sure thing."

I close my eyes and focus all my magical energies on condensing them into an invisible ball centered within my chest. The pressure of the magics weigh heavily on me, but even if I couldn't breathe, I could survive indefinitely, unlike a mortal. Felicia's presence grounds me in a way I cannot describe, keeping me focused on the task at hand. The magics wend through me as if they're testing me, pinching now and then, even burning briefly. They may do whatever they like to me. I have experienced far worse discomfort.

This is nothing like the soul-rending agony of destruction.

My eyes fly open. Realization sweeps through me, and I swivel my gaze to Felicia. "We must enter the time stream."

"What? That sounds…dangerous."

"It is. But I control time which means I also hold dominion over the time stream itself." I grasp her shoulders, turning her toward me. "If you can trust me to keep you safe, I would like you to go into the time stream with me. I'm convinced this is what The Four Winds intend for me to do. My answers will be found only in the past."

"Okay. Let's jump into the time stream."

"You aren't the least bit frightened?"

She rolls her eyes. "Of course I'm terrified. But I've never let fear stop me from doing what needs to be done."

"Yes, I've learned that about you. Despite my vast powers, I can't predict how the time stream will react to our presence. I must keep hold of you at all times."

She nods. "I'm ready."

I lash my arms around Felicia, hugging her to my breast. "Close your eyes. This will not be a pleasant experience."

Felicia buries her face against my chest and wraps her arms around me tightly.

We are as ready as we will ever be. I summon the time stream with a single thought.

As one, we slip into the ethereal energies, though we have not yet entered the time stream. I must move carefully now, else even I might be ejected from the flow of time. The stream knows to protect itself from intrusion, and I sense that I can't simply coax the time stream into submission. This will be a brute force entrance.

I punch my fist into the stream.

A shrieking cacophony reverberates around and through me—through us. I can feel Felicia's fear and pain. She will survive, provided I don't miscalculate our trajectory. As I push deeper into the time stream, the force of its attempts to eject us weaken little by little until, at last, I find a handhold within the writhing whips of energy. As I rein them in gently, I whisper to them in my mind.

No harm will come to you. I am your guardian. Trust me. The snakelike energies begin to slow their movements incrementally. *Yes, good, calm yourselves. You know me. The time stream is my domain.*

The energies wind down even more, and their whiplike movements settle into a serene sideways wave, such as what one might see in a pool of water. I can feel Felicia relaxing and hear her sigh of relief. Neither of us has any physical form at the moment. Thanks to the supernatural nature of the Unseen, I can conjure a visible approximation of our bodies. Felicia will be more comfortable that way. The softly shifting current of the time stream flows on either side of us like sandbars in a river, splitting around the obstacle.

"Open your eyes, *dulcissima*. We have reached the time stream, and it has accepted us."

"Thank goodness." She peels her face away from my chest and glances around. "Holy cow. This is incredible—and beautiful, in an alien way."

"For me, this is not alien. It's a part of me."

"I get that. At first, I didn't. But now that I'm standing inside the time stream, I think I understand you better and understand what your powers mean to you. The two things are inextricably linked."

She truly does understand. Never have I met another being, mortal or magical, who grasped what I am so fully.

Perhaps she is my fated mate after all.

All around us, the whiplike streams of temporal energy slide this way and that, sniffing us as they try to determine who and what Felicia is. Once the time stream has calmed down, becoming a tranquil river with many tributaries, I know I have complete control now. The streams hover around us, awaiting my instructions.

Show me where I need to go.

One tributary begins to glisten with golden energy, beckoning me to follow that path. Felicia and I rush down the time stream, faster and faster, until we pop out into the real world. For a moment, I'm uncertain of what is going on around us. We stand outside a small, thatched domicile in the middle of the countryside. A few cattle forage in a field behind the house, while chickens wander about on the other side of the domicile.

"Do you recognize this place?" Felicia asks. "Kind of seems like you do. You've been staring at the little house. Who lives there?"

I open my mouth but cannot produce words. Felicia is correct. I do recognize this house. The sight of it alone stirs up emotions I've kept buried deep inside me for longer than I could measure. My throat constricts. My mouth goes dry. I cannot breathe. But I am not mortal, and regular breathing is not a necessity for me.

Felicia lays a hand on my cheek and turns my face toward her. "Who lives here, Janus?"

"Vita." It's the only word I can speak, and the two syllables emerged as a soft, almost reverent breath. "The woman I loved once lived here."

"You wanted to come to this place."

"I had no conscious thought to go anywhere. I let the time stream guide me, according to the wishes of The Four Winds." I glance at the house and swallow hard, then swerve my attention back to Felicia. "I never wanted to see this place again. It carries with it too many terrible memories. But I must confront my past. That is what The Four Winds intended."

"Then we'll confront it together. That's also what The Four Winds wanted, right? They sent us here together."

"Indeed, they did." I straighten and lift my chin. "And we begin now."

CHAPTER FIFTEEN

Felicia

THE CLOPPING OF HOOVES IN THE DISTANCE MAKES US both veer our gazes toward the narrow dirt path that wends its way up to the little house with the thatched roof. I hadn't noticed the path before since it's narrow and doesn't seem to be used often. The trail goes through a field of wheat that stands at least four feet high.

I can't believe we're in the past, about to meet Janus's lover and see how he interacted with her. I assume we're invisible, since this is a time in the past rather than our present day. Yeah, I'm suddenly an expert on time streams and time travel.

The rider comes into view at last as his horse canters across the wheat field. He sits up straight, chin lifted just a touch, seeming so confident and yet relaxed too. The closer he comes, the more details I can see.

And I freeze briefly. Then I swerve my head toward Janus. "That rider is you."

"Yes. This is my past. You know this already."

"Sure. But…can you from the past see us?"

"No. We currently exist outside of time, and we will be observers rather than participants."

I return my attention to the rider, admiring the way Janus proudly sits astride his mount with a crimson cloak billowing behind him. His chest is bare, revealing every line of muscle. A gold and silver sword rests in a scabbard at his hip. The closer he comes, the more details I can see. His horse's leather bridle features a silver disk at the center of the leather browband that has some kind of pattern on it, though I can't make out enough details yet to be sure.

Janus of the past slows his horse to a walk as he approaches the little house, finally halting a few yards away. Then he deftly dismounts, readjusting his scabbard and petting his horse while whispering what sounds like Latin phrases. The horse nuzzles his cheek. Janus pats the animal's neck, then saunters up to the door of the house.

He knocks three times.

The door swings open—and a beautiful dark-haired woman flings her arms around Janus's neck. Her toes barely touch the ground. They both grin and converse in what must be Latin. She laughs at something he said. Janus sweeps her up in his arms and carries her inside the house, kicking the door shut behind him.

"Are we going in there?" I ask Janus, the version of him that's with me. "I might not understand ancient Latin, but their tone of voice and how happy they were makes it pretty clear. They're about to have sex."

"Yes, they are." He sighs, and his shoulders slump. His head bows too. "This was the day our daughter was conceived."

"Oh. That's nothing to be ashamed of."

"But it is shameful." He rubs a hand over his cheek. "This was not the first time that Vita and I enjoyed carnal relations. But on those previous occasions, I always ensured that she would not become with child. For any being created in the Unseen, pregnancy can only occur if that being consciously chooses to allow it to happen."

"Are you saying that you wanted to get Vita knocked up?"

He bows his head even more, turning it to the side as if he can't make himself look at me. "I wanted a family. After eons of being alone, I had finally found a woman to love who loved me in return, and I desperately wanted to raise a child with Vita. It was a selfish impulse."

"You loved her. That's not selfish." I bite my lip as I consider what he told me. "Did you secretly get her pregnant? I mean, did you ask her if she wanted to have a child with you?"

He nods weakly.

I grasp his face and force him to look at me. "Then you didn't do anything wrong. Both of you wanted to have a baby. She consented, and so did you. It's time to stop beating yourself up for wanting to have a family of your own."

"Perhaps you are correct. But I still feel…guilty."

"No shit." I tried to squelch my laughter, but it came out as a snort instead. I'm laughing at him because he's so adorably confused. Now, I pat his chest. "It's about time you let go of all that guilt, sweetie. But I assume we've got more jaunts into the past coming our way, and those are all meant to help you."

He lifts his brows. "Why do you assume this journey is only for my benefit? After all, The Four Winds sent you here too."

Noises emerge from the little house, and we both stop to listen and try to figure out what that racket is. Thumping. Creaking. Moaning. Masculine shouts. Feminine cries of…ecstasy.

I grin and punch Janus's chest. "Damn, sweetie, you're one hot lover. Vita's going off like a rocket ship."

His brows wrinkle. "I do not understand."

"The old you is rocking the bedroom." I try not to smirk, but I can't help it. "I know exactly how Vita feels right now. You are the most incredible lover any woman could have."

"You and Vita are the only females I have ever bedded who meant more to me than simply a sexual partner."

"And that makes your prowess even more extraordinary."

His face pinches up, and he clears his throat while avoiding my gaze. "I am the only god or elemental with whom you have enjoyed sexual congress. You can't make such a pronouncement."

"I can, and I do."

Vita's final high-pitched scream of ecstasy winds down. The thumping and creaking noises fade away too. Vita says something, loud enough I can hear it, though I can't translate her words.

I give Janus a light punch in the gut. "You sly dog. What did Vita just say?"

"That she, ah, wishes to…" He winces. "She's begging me to fuck her again."

"And you're going to do it, right? The old you will do it, that is."

He aims a sidelong glance at me while desperately trying not to smirk. He fails, of course. "On this day, we would fuck several more times. Vita would beg me to take her body over and over, but I insisted we must stop at four orgasms."

"What a gentleman you are."

I'm not being sarcastic, and I think he knows that based on his deepening smirk. Maybe this is why we were sent here. Janus needed to remember what a phenomenal sex god he truly is. Vita certainly didn't have any complaints. I can vouch for Janus's bedroom skills too.

Two beings appear just outside the window of the little house.

Every hair on my body goes rigid. A chill slithers over my skin. Why? Because I recognize those two creatures, though I don't know the name of the one that has a tail and hooves. I recognize the type of being he is—a satyr—because I saw those beasts in the Dionysus temple.

Janus pulls me into his arms. "Do not fear, *dulcissima*. These beings cannot harm us. They are in their present—which is our past. We don't exist for them."

"Do you know who they are? The bigger one looks like Dionysus."

"Indeed, it is the god."

"Who is that with him?"

Janus squints as if he's trying to see better. Understandable, since the other creature is facing away from us. "That must be Silenus, the chief satyr. He has always followed Dionysus wherever he goes. As the commander of the satyr army, he is the highest-ranking officer."

"What are he and Dionysus doing at Vita's house?"

Janus gives me a long-suffering look. "What do you think they are doing? Something nefarious, naturally." He puckers his lips. "But I do not recall either Silenus or Dionysus visiting Vita on this day. We must be meant to glean additional information from this moment."

"Then let's move closer, huh? Can't see or hear much from way over here."

He clasps my hand as we skulk nearer to the house and the two slimeballs who are peering through the window. They speak another language, so I don't know what they're saying. Janus mutters something in Latin.

Suddenly, I can understand what Dionysus and Silenus are talking about because it's being translated into English for me. Janus is so thoughtful that way. How many other guys would do that for a woman? Okay, none. Not in the mortal world, anyway, since human men don't have magical powers.

I still can't see the satyr's face, but I get a good look at Dionysus when he whirls around to glower at Silenus. "You will never touch Vita. She is mine and only mine. Keep your filthy hooves off her. You may have any other female in the multiverse to do with as you desire."

"Any other?" Silenus makes a sound that's halfway between a chuckle and a cackle. "Ooh, I will have my way with all the females in your temple."

"Just don't leave them bloodied and mindless afterward. I dislike having my temple tarnished in such a way." Dionysus waves a hand vaguely. "Take them elsewhere if you want to ravage them."

Silenus clacks his teeth as if he's hungry for innocent women to rip apart. "You are an excellent master. I cherish your trust in me."

What sweethearts these two are. If I had the power to annihilate them, I'd do it. When I glance at Janus, he's grinding his teeth. I lay a hand on his arm, and he relaxes visibly. He even gives me a tight smile.

Silenus shuffles closer to the window, using his hand like a visor as he peers into the house. "How shall we take her, my lord? Kidnapping? Ensorcellment? Ooh, I do love the vacant look in a woman's eyes when powerful magics have taken hold of her mind. It makes me so fucking hard."

"Easy, Silenus. We need to tread carefully when Janus is involved."

The satyr grunts. "Don't see why. He's nothing special."

"I agree. But the Oversoul saw fit to grant him vast powers, and we must tread lightly." Dionysus glances over his shoulder at Silenus and smirks. "For now, at least."

"Are these guys actually speaking Latin?" I ask Janus.

"No. They are creatures from Greek mythology and therefore speak that language."

Laughter fills the house, though I still can't see inside. Janus of this time must be having fun with the woman he loves. I haven't heard him laugh that way, but then, the modern version of him has been through hell in more ways than I can count. I admire his tenacity, even in the worst conditions. He's amazing, and not just because he's a god.

Janus the man impresses me most of all.

"Should we go inside?" I ask. "If we're supposed to learn something from this moment, we need more information. Don't you think? Dionysus and Silenus aren't giving us much. I want to know why they're spying."

"Because they want to abduct Vita. They stated their goal explicitly."

"Hmm, I'm not so sure. Come on, let's go in there."

Janus blows out a sigh. "Yes, all right. We shall enter the house, but you must remain by my side at all times."

"I prom—"

He slaps his hand over my mouth. "Never make a vow in any world."

"Right. I forgot. I'll be more careful from now on."

"I would appreciate that." He cups my cheek, and his lips form a melancholy little smile. "If I lost you…"

"Never going to happen."

He takes my hand as we approach the house, passing by the creepy duo who are spying on the frisky couple inside the dwelling. I still can't see Silenus's face. It's turned toward Dionysus. I ignore that for the moment, more concerned with the fact that we're walking through the door. Literally. Stepping through solid wood is bizarre, though I don't actually feel anything. My mind insists on telling me "no, no, no, stop." But I trust Janus one hundred percent. If he says we can walk through walls, I trust that it's true.

The house consists of one large room with a few pieces of furniture and sacks of what I assume is food. In the far corner, I see Janus and Vita lying in bed together, naked but with a sheet covering their bodies from the hips down. He assumes a casual stance with one knee bent and his hand resting on it. Vita lies on her back, gently brushing her fingertips over his chest. They speak in Latin, but I can tell from their tone of voice alone that they're still in the mood.

Janus, the one standing beside me, waves his hand in a negligent gesture. And suddenly, I can understand what Janus from this time period is saying to his lover. "I never wish to leave you again, my love. But I have sensed a dark force out there, seeking you, full of lust for your body and for the chance to humiliate me. Never fear, Vita. I will always protect you."

"I am glad we decided it was time for us to have a child. And I hope we have done that this day."

He lays a hand over her belly. "You are with child. I'm certain of that." Janus leans over, peeling the sheet away from her body, and presses his lips to her belly. Then he smiles. "Yes, I am certain we accomplished our goal. But perhaps we should mate a few more times to be sure."

I can hardly believe the playful, confident man lying in bed with Vita is the same Janus I know. More than anything, I want to help him get back to that version of himself. He must want that too.

And I need to help him get there.

Chapter Sixteen

Janus

AS WE OBSERVE MY FORMER SELF AND VITA PLAYFULLY discussing in what manner they would like to fuck, I feel as if I've stepped into an alternate universe. How could I have forgotten what I used to be like? No one dared anger me. Anyone who attempted to do so would regret it deeply a moment later. I was the preeminent god in the Unseen. All other deities courted my favor so that I might help them achieve their goals. When I rejected a request, the party in question knew I would offer no appeal.

Everyone lusted for my vast and incorruptible power.

That must be the lesson The Four Winds wanted me to learn on this excursion into the past. But I doubt they're done yet.

Someone appears behind us. I haven't looked at them or acknowledged their presence yet, but I sense them and know who they are. Dionysus and Silenus have teleported themselves into the house, though they cannot detect me or Felicia.

I clasp her hand more firmly. "They are behind us. Let's move over to the window so we can see what they're doing."

"Good idea."

We shuffle sideways toward the window, then turn toward the bed.

And a sensation like ice freezing in my veins rushes through me. A soft exclamation hisses out of me. *"Deodamnatus."*

Felicia's jaw has gone slack. "I recognize Dionysus. But is that satyr…"

"It is Theo. I realized he must have been using a pseudonym when I first met him, yet I never imagined he was the chief satyr, the right hand of Dionysus."

"What does this mean? Very bad things, I assume."

I shake my head slowly as I stare at the duo. "Very bad things indeed. Yet I cannot understand Theo's purpose in trying to seduce, then abduct you."

"He wants to take me away from you. That's his plan."

"Silenus obeys Dionysus. He would not have concocted a plan on his own. But there's something about this revelation that I can't yet fathom."

Dionysus whispers something to Silenus, and the two begin to snicker like little boys. What am I missing? I must uncover the full extent of the plot, but I doubt I'll learn the solution to the riddle here in this moment. I sense that the answer will only become clear once we've completed our entire journey through the past.

I pull Felicia against me. "We must go now. I'm certain we've learned all we were meant to in this moment."

"Yeah, I agree. Let's follow the next clue."

This time, I don't need to coax the time stream to accept my commands. It opens up for us willingly, and we slide into the temporal river as if we've always belonged here. I do belong in the time stream, and I hope that Felicia might belong here too. I'd begun to treat my powers as a burden. Somewhere in the past, long after I lost Vita, I had forgotten that manipulating time had once been easy for me—so easy, in fact, that I had no need to even think about it. A single thought would accomplish my task. I haven't quite achieved that level of ease again, not yet. But now I understand that I can once again become the god I used to be—the man I used to be.

Eventually. Not today.

We glide out of the time stream as gracefully as we had entered it, landing in a vastly different place than we had just left. The cozy house with the thatched roof has been replaced by the bustle of Rome, the city I had once called my home. I had abandoned my temple when I met Vita and never wanted to return once our casual acquaintance transformed into a love affair. I despised Rome—until Vita walked into my life.

"Where are we?" Felicia asks. "Is this the city of Rome?"

"Yes. I met Vita here, but I conjured a home for her outside of the city. That was the structure we just visited."

"Got any idea why we're here?"

"Not yet. Let's wander about and see what we find. No one can see us, just as before, so we need not worry about being surreptitious."

Felicia smiles. "I love it when you trot out the big words."

"I use normal-size words, just as you do."

"Don't think I've ever used the word surreptitious in a sentence." She slings an arm around my waist. "Your big vocabulary is hot."

I cup her bottom, giving it a light squeeze. "Are you certain it's my vocabulary that makes you feel that way?"

"Oh, sweetie, it's every inch of you, inside and out."

As much as I love to hear her say that and would love to reciprocate, we must keep searching for the clue that must lie ahead of us. I'd forgotten precisely how much I dislike the city. Our incorporeal nature means we can literally walk through the crowd, though Felicia balks at that suggestion. I assure her we will obey the mortal laws of nature and bypass every individual we see. I gather Felicia still hasn't fully acclimated to the realities of the multiverse or of my powers.

After a slow promenade through the shopping district, during which I needed to drag Felicia away from various stalls that sell various merchandise, we finally move into a less populated area. Felicia marvels at the towering structures like the Colosseum, which we can see in the distance. I expect her to be stunned by the colorful way many buildings are decorated. Most mortals believe Rome had nothing but white structures. But when I mention this to her, she shrugs.

"Nothing I didn't already know."

I raise my brows. "You aren't surprised at all?"

"Museum tour guide, remember? I also have a degree in Classical Studies."

"Ah, of course. I should have guessed. You are quite clever and well-versed in history, a fact that shouldn't surprise me."

We amble past the aqueduct that soars high above our heads, and Felicia pauses to tip her head back and admire the architecture. Her lips curl into a sweet expression, as if she can't believe we're in Rome—the ancient city. I have not visited Rome in three thousand years. I shut my eyes, unable to appreciate the beauty of this city, abruptly overcome by emotions I had tried to suppress for such a long time.

Felicia grasps my hand. "You're thinking about Vita, aren't you? Does this aqueduct have special meaning for you?"

"No. It is only a means of transporting water. The city itself does harbor…ghosts, I suppose."

"Why don't we move on? Not sure when we'll know we've reached our destination, since nobody told us where that is."

"Signposts would be helpful. But I sense that I must feel my way to where we should go."

"That's not natural for you. I might not have known you long, but I can tell you're the kind of man who needs a road map."

I blow out a sigh. "I've begun to realize my rigidity is part of my problem. And I suspect that's one of the lessons The Four Winds intended to teach me. I cannot go on hiding from my past."

We continue past the aqueduct into the section of the city where the Colosseum lies, but we don't stop there. Instead, we leave that district and walk more swiftly as I do what I now understand I must do—let my instincts guide me. The warmth of Felicia's hand in mine anchors me. I ignore the buildings, the people, everything, as we press onward. A mystical call beckons me to the outskirts of Rome where the average citizens live. We wind our way down narrow alleys and out again, emerging directly in front of one specific structure.

I halt, and every muscle in my body seems to turn to stone. My hand falls away from Felicia's. My vision dims, telescoping down until only the house in front of us is visible to me.

"Janus? What's wrong?" Felicia's voice barely penetrates my mind. Even when she snaps her fingers in my face, I cannot respond. "Wake up, sweetie. Don't go catatonic on me now."

I close my eyes, take a deep breath, and exhale it gradually. Then I face Felicia. "I regret upsetting you. But this house…"

"Vita lived here. Right?"

I nod. "But I cannot understand why I was meant to come here."

"Tell me what this place means to you. Then maybe we can figure out the reason."

"The incident with Dionysus and Silenus, which you and I both witnessed, was something I hadn't known about at the time. But soon after that day when Vita and I had conceived a child, she summoned me to our little house. I had given her an amulet that would bring me to her whenever she needed or wanted me." I rub my eyes, though I can't explain why. I suppose I'm simply trying to delay the inevitable, delay reliving the pain. "Vita wanted to move into Rome. She felt isolated and uncomfortable in the countryside without me. I was dealing with troublesome elementals who kept trying to invade the time stream. That meant I was quite busy."

"Something happened. Something bad."

I nod again. "I arrived at Vita's domus—her home—to find her hiding inside with the shutters closed and a gladius in her hand, huddling in the corner." My jaw tenses, causing a muscle to tick there, as I recall that moment. "She was terrified because the satyr Silenus had paid her a visit. He told Vita that she had two choices if she wished to live—go with him to the Temple of Dionysus and become his concubine, or watch as the god destroyed me."

"But I thought destruction was a damn hard thing to do."

"Yes, it is. But Vita didn't know that." I glare at the house in front of me. "But I believe we're expected to watch those events, not discuss them. Not yet."

"I can't imagine how gut-wrenching this must be for you. But I'm here, and I won't leave you to watch it alone."

My eyes begin to sting. My throat constricts. Am I...choked up with emotion? Yes, of course I am. But not for the reasons I would have assumed. Felicia's kindness and support have left me speechless. I doubt I deserve this woman's affection, but I will selfishly accept it.

Hand in hand we approach the house and slip through the walls into the domus, emerging inside the vestibulum. The small entryway isn't as spacious as the homes of the elites, but Vita hadn't wanted a grand domus. Born a plebeian, she felt uncomfortable with the trappings of wealth. I had loved her no matter what her status, and she knew that.

As we move deeper into the house, I still can't see or hear any sign of Vita or the satyr. I grip Felicia's hand more tightly without thinking about why, and as we enter the atrium, I grow even more tense. The sun shines down through the open area that forms the centerpiece of the domus.

Then I hear thumping sounds. Barely audible at first. Then a grunt. Scuffling noises. A growl. The sounds grow louder and louder.

"Release me, you fiend!"

Cackling follows that exclamation.

I seize Felicia's hand so firmly that it must hurt, but she doesn't complain or even gasp. I drag her through the triclinium, where dishes are laid out on the table—awaiting my return—and barge into the cubiculum where two individuals are locked in a battle, physically and mentally. The satyr Silenus grips Vita's wrists and shakes her hard.

"Dionysus wants you," the satyr snarls. "And what the god wants, the god gets. You will be his most treasured concubine."

She spits in his face. "I will die before I will ever permit you or your master to defile me."

"Janus can't protect you this time. We've made certain he is too busy to worry about your safety."

"You lie. He will always come to my aid."

"Will he?" Silenus whips his tail, lashing her with it, making Vita stumble backward. "Janus cares more about protecting the time stream than taking care of you."

She snatches up the gladius, which I had given her in case of emergency, and wields it at the satyr. "Leave my house immediately, or else I will cut off your most treasured limb."

Vita glances meaningfully at the satyr's cock.

He chuckles. "Nice try. But I'm far more agile than you are." He licks his lips as he gazes at Vita's breasts. They aren't exposed, but he is nearly salivating at the prospect of defiling her. "Dio won't mind if I perform a taste test. You are delectable, and I'm craving sexual energy."

She thrusts the gladius at him, sinking the blade into the satyr's belly deeply enough that blood pours from the wound.

But Silenus hardly notices. He is an elemental, after all, and far stronger than any human. He teleports her into his arms and begins rubbing his engorged length against her body. "Yes, I need a taste of you, sweet girl."

Felicia squeezes my hand. "This isn't really happening. You already know the outcome, so try not to get too upset about it. Won't do any good."

"I know that. But I had no idea what Silenus did to Vita. He tormented her, that much is clear. But what else..."

"Don't torture yourself. This event is long gone."

Felicia is not being callous. I understand that, and I know she's right. But witnessing this event is a kind of torture I could never have fathomed, so much worse than when I was experiencing it in that moment.

Because I cannot intervene.

CHAPTER SEVENTEEN

Felicia

SILENUS WHISPERS SOMETHING TO VITA, THOUGH I CAN'T make out the words. Whatever he said, it upsets her even more, and her eyes grow so wide that I swear they might pop out of their sockets. Then the satyr smirks and vanishes at the exact moment when the other version of Janus materializes at the foot of the bed. He rushes over to Vita, who huddles in the corner, sobbing and too terrified to speak. When he tries to touch her, she cringes away from him, though only for a moment. Then Vita flings herself at Janus, clinging to him as if she might fly away into the cosmos without the anchor of his body.

I don't blame her. Silenus is one slimy satyr.

The old Janus whispers wordless sounds meant to comfort Vita, and her sobs gradually fade away. He brushes hair away from her face. "Shh, my love, I am here, and whatever you fear is over now. Tell me what has upset you so greatly."

She shakes her head. Tears trickle down her cheeks.

He kisses her forehead. "You can tell me anything, Vita."

Finally, she wipes away the tears and sits up straighter, aiming her gaze directly at him. "Silenus told me that if I did not allow Dionysus to defile me, he would end the life of our child while the babe was still in my womb."

Janus grinds his teeth. "No one will murder our child. Silenus and his master will suffer for the agony they have caused you."

The version of Janus who has his arm around me watches the scene with a tight expression. "When I had experienced this moment long ago, I had no idea that Silenus had tormented her only seconds earlier. I should have sensed the remnants of his presence the moment I materialized in this house. Perhaps I could have prevented—"

"Cut that out. Second-guessing your actions from three thousand years ago is pointless. And it's just what Dionysus would want, I'm sure. Don't give him that kind of power over you."

"Dionysus is not here—in the present or the past."

"I know that. But you're letting him get inside your head, and he didn't even have to cast a spell to achieve his goal."

Janus shuts his eyes, exhaling the longest sigh I've ever heard. Then he looks at me. "These events disturb me more than I expected. I'd assumed my guilt would have lessened over the eons, but that is not the case."

"I'll say it one more time. You are giving the bad guys more power by agonizing over the past."

"The Four Winds must have wanted it this way. They might be attempting to show me that I am unworthy of my powers." He holds up a hand before I can speak up to contradict him. "You misunderstand. I do not believe I'm unworthy. In fact, observing this moment with Vita has convinced me that they don't want to punish me. They're trying to prove a point."

"And what is the point?"

"That I have forgotten precisely how much power I wield. Ever since my resurrection, I have behaved as if I don't own my powers, as if Lindsey allows me to borrow them." He shakes his head, smiling ruefully. "The truth is that Lindsey was the Janusite, which means she held my powers until I could reclaim them. Those magics belong to me."

"You tamed the time stream. Of course those magics are yours."

"More than that, they are a part of me. Myself and my magics are indivisible." He lifts his chin and squares his shoulders. "And it's time I fully embraced my powers."

He flings his arms around me. I realize why when the world around us abruptly shifts, and now we stand inside the Colosseum—the ancient version, the way it looked back in the heyday of the Roman empire. A massive crowd occupies the stands. The emperor sits in a special box, just like bigwigs in the modern world like to do. Servants attend to the emperor's needs, bustling about as if their lives depend on not making their master wait for even one second.

Well, their lives undoubtedly did depend on that.

I assume Janus and I are invisible, since we're once again in the past. "Is this another pivotal moment in your life?"

He nods grimly.

"Are we about to witness that event?"

Janus twists his mouth into a crooked expression of distaste. "Yes, I believe we are about to relive the penultimate event in my downfall."

I know the term penultimate means next to last. He assumes there will be one more thing for us to witness together, and I believe him. Only he knows what's coming. And I can see his whole body tensing up in anticipation—the bad kind.

"We are in the Flavian Amphitheatre," he tells me. "What mortals in the modern world call the Colosseum. A battle is about to commence."

Before I can ask who is going to fight in the arena, a horn blares out a regal call, clearly designed to announce the next event in this day's festivities. The crowd goes quiet. The arena stands empty. The man with the horn shouts loudly enough that it echoes off the stone walls.

"Hear ye, hear ye," he bellows. "The *ludum gladiatorium* is about to begin. We have two venerable guest gladiators who have been granted special privileges." The announcer spreads his arms wide. "The warriors may now enter the arena."

He picks up his horn and blares it three times.

A metal gate is raised at the far end of the arena, allowing the gladiators to jog into the center of the huge space, which has a dirt floor. This looks pretty much the way I'd always imagined it would. I guess the historians weren't far off base.

For some reason, I whisper when I ask Janus a question. Nobody can see or hear us, but I still speak softly. "What is *ludum gladiatorium?*"

"It is a contest between two men who will fight to the death. No reprieve will be granted to the loser."

"You mean the loser dies."

"Did you expect mercy during gladiatorial games? That only happened on exceedingly rare occasions."

Two gladiators are now sauntering across the arena, where they halt in the middle and face each other from about twenty feet apart. Neither man wears any sort of protective gear, not even a helmet. Both combatants do wear leather kilts and boots. They face each other with a similar stance, body tense, staring down their opponent.

The announcer spreads his arms again. "The brave warriors in this battle are…the gods Dionysus and Janus!"

I swerve my head to gape at Janus. "You fought a battle to the death against Dionysus?"

"Yes. But neither of us could win because we are indestructible."

"Who instigated this gladiatorial combat? Must've been Dionysus. He's an arrogant prick."

Janus lifts one brow. "On the contrary, I initiated this battle."

"You did what? Why on earth would you demand to battle that jerk in the Colosseum? You're both gods. Nobody can win this battle, so it's pointless."

"There was indeed a point, which you will see soon enough."

I trust him completely, more than any other being in any world, so I'll give him the benefit of the doubt here. How a battle between indestructible gods could have any satisfactory conclusion still baffles me, though. I had no idea the ancient Romans treated a god's presence as so…normal.

Yeah, I still have a lot to learn.

The announcer declares, "Let the battle commence!"

Janus and Dionysus begin to circle each other, both maintaining a battle stance—knees bent, swords at the ready, gazes locked. The crowd has gone silent with not even a faint whisper echoing through the stands. The only sounds are the shuffling of the combatants' leather boots and the flapping of the flags that fly at the highest level of the stadium.

Janus appears to be sizing up Dionysus as they continue to circle each other. The sex god seems more concerned with preening for the crowd. He flexes his biceps, then flourishes his gladius in a grand gesture.

Are those two ever going to fight? *Sheesh.*

Suddenly, Janus rushes at Dionysus and thrusts his blade deep into the sex god's chest. He yanks it out again, backing away just enough that Dionysus can't strike out at him. The god is distracted by the blood pouring out of his wound. Unfortunately, that distraction lasts for only a moment.

Then Dionysus roars and lunges at Janus.

"How long does this battle last?" I ask. "It's hard to see what's going on when we're so far away from the combatants."

Janus whisks us away, setting us down so close to his younger self and the sex god that I can smell the blood and hear their labored breathing. Now that first blood has been drawn, the two gods let loose on each other. I lose track of who's doing what as the swords fly and whack against each other so fiercely that sparks erupt in the air. The metallic twang of the blades reverberates through the Colosseum, and soon, the cheers of the crowd deafen me. Those aren't happy cheers, though. It's the sound of a ravenous mob that craves death and pain—for the competitors, not for themselves.

The spectacle sickens me. I wish Janus would tell me why he did this, but he wants me to see for myself, probably so I won't be biased. Screw that. I cannot be impartial during this massacre.

Both gods are now covered in blood.

Yet they keep fighting.

The cheers among the crowd shift into chanting. "Kill Janus! Kill Janus!"

"Why do they hate you?" I ask the version of Janus who still has his arm lashed around me in a protective gesture. "I had no idea ancient Romans were so open about the gods being real. But I really don't get why the average people are chanting for your death."

"The blood lust has caught them. As for why they dislike me, that was a sentiment Dionysus and his followers whipped up to turn mortals against me."

"I despise that cretin more every second."

Janus gestures toward the combatants. "You wanted to know why I fought Dionysus. You're about to discover the reason."

The younger version of him kicks Dionysus in the gut so hard that the sex god goes flying backward into the stone wall that encircles the arena. He bounces off it, tumbling head over heels with such speed that it's hard to keep track of how many times he flips over before he finally stops, now sprawled on the ground spread-eagle style. His face is mashed into the dirt.

Janus, chest heaving, staggers over to Dionysus. "This is the consequence when you beat and attempt to rape Vita. If I could destroy you, I would do it right here in front of your devoted, sadistic followers."

Oh, God, so that's why Janus did this. He gave Dionysus the kind of beating the sex god had given Vita. At least he didn't succeed in sexually assaulting her. But the amount of rage Janus is displaying tells me Dionysus got too damn close to violating Vita's body—and I have a suspicion being assaulted by a sex god is the most depraved sort of assault. I don't even want to think about what Dionysus might have done to her if Janus hadn't intervened.

The younger Janus now sets one boot atop Dionysus's head, grinding it into the dirt. "You tried to distract me, so I would be too late to stop you from harming her. But her desperate cries echoed back to me through the multiverse just in time."

Dionysus laughs with all the dark glee of a maniac. "You are such a fool, Janus. But you won't know until it's too late just how wrong you are."

Janus's brows and lips tighten.

But then Dionysus shuts his eyes as if he's too exhausted to speak or move anymore. Then, he rises up from his own body like a ghost and turns toward us. The specter of the sex god's mouth stretches into a gleeful sneer. "I have bested you this time, for you have no conception of what is coming for you now. Janus the almighty will not be able to protect his woman this time. If you believe you can stop me from taking her, then you are delusional. When the Dark One comes, even your vast powers won't protect you."

Dionysus vanishes.

But the version of him from the past lies bloodied and exhausted in front of us.

"We must go," Janus announces. "This was a trick of some sort, and we must return to the Unseen at once."

"But you said you had one more event to relive."

He goes pale underneath the golden sheen on his skin. "I suppose I must relive it. The Four Winds expect me to do so."

I hug him and kiss his cheek. "We'll do it together."

"What comes next is my destruction. It will not be pleasant to watch."

"You should know by now that I can handle almost anything. And I would never make you relive that event on your own." The words Dionysus had spoken replay in my mind, and one statement in particular grabs my attention. "Who is the Dark One?"

"I have no idea."

"But you're a god."

"Of the Unseen. I'm not all-knowing in any realm."

"Right. I still have trouble reconciling the word god with not all-knowing. But it's god with a little G, not a big one."

He throws his arms around me and whisks us away.

CHAPTER EIGHTEEN

Janus

FELICIA CLINGS TO ME FIERCELY, BUT I DOUBT THAT'S BE-
cause she is terrified. No, this woman would never give in to
fear. The time stream behaves much less amenably this time, and
its golden shades have transformed into green laced with onyx. I
feel something tugging at my flesh. It wants to tear me away from
Felicia, that much is obvious, but I will never let go of her.

We burst out of the time stream and both stumble a few steps.

I catch Felicia before she hits the ground. "Are you all right,
Fliss?"

"Yeah, sure, as fine as anybody can be after a ride like that one. Is
the time stream mad at you? Or at me?"

"Neither. Something else has disrupted its natural flow, and the
time stream is struggling to find its equilibrium. But we will deal
with that after our final journey into the past is finished."

"Um, isn't it extremely dangerous to leave the time stream so
messed up?"

"Yes, but I have no choice. And I would prefer to get this ordeal
over with immediately."

She clasps my hand, huddling close to my side, and studies our
surroundings. "What is this place?"

"The Eternal Plane. It is a location only ever visited by gods or The
Four Winds. The Plane exists in a separate reality that sits atop the

highest mountain in the Unseen." I gaze up at the peak with its wide, flat plateau at the summit. We stand on a smaller flat area that encircles the mountain in a spiral fashion until it reaches the apex. "We must ascend the peak now via this trail. Can you manage such a hike?"

"Can't you just poof us there?"

"Afraid not, *dulcissima*." I had almost chuckled at her use of the term poof, but my humor faded quickly. "Powerful magics prevent it. Anyone who wishes to access the immense power of The Eternal Plane must walk up to the summit. I will carry you."

"That's okay. Just pick me up if I pass out from lack of oxygen." She leans to the side, peering down the slope. "We must be high enough up that the air is thinner. Or doesn't the Unseen work that way?"

"It does, and it doesn't." I raise a hand before she can speak. "This is a world of magic. The rules of the mortal world do not apply, and magical rules are fickle."

We ascend the path hand in hand, trudging ever upward until we finally reach The Eternal Plane. Felicia seems a touch winded, but not so much that I need to give her a boost of oxygenated air. Now, we stand at the periphery of the most enigmatic place in the Unseen. Magics energize the air, though even I can't see them. Felicia rubs her arms, and I'm certain that's because of the energies that surround us and investigate us.

Once they've decided we may stay, the magics recede into the background.

Felicia wraps her arms around my waist. "Glad that spooky little welcome is over."

"The magics of The Eternal Plane are neutral. They wouldn't harm you."

"Doesn't make me feel any better. This place gives me the creeps." She glances around. "When does the, um, destruction thingy start?"

"At any moment."

The earth beneath us shivers faintly, like a small earthquake. And then it begins. The sky darkens, a chill wind teases our skin, and seven figures materialize at the center of The Eternal Plane, arrayed in a circle.

Felicia rises onto her toes to study the beings. "Who are those people?"

"They are not people. They are gods of the Unseen." My throat has tightened and gone dry. But I take a deep breath and explain. "These are the seven most powerful gods in the Unseen realm. Only their combined magics can destroy me."

"Which gods are they?"

"Hathor, Artemis, Hachiman, Kamadeva, Surt, Alator, and Tiamat." Since Felicia seems a bit confused, I explain further. "You know Hathor is a goddess of ancient Egypt because you've met her. I'm sure you're familiar with the Greek goddess Artemis as well. Hachiman is the Japanese god of war, while Kamadeva is a Hindu god, Surt is a Norse god, Alator is a Celtic god, and Tiamat is a Mesopotamian goddess."

"Jeez, it's a real multicultural destruction fest, isn't it? Why were they so jealous of you that they wanted to annihilate you from existence?"

I clasp her hand more firmly, in need of the connection. "I've told you before. They coveted my temporal powers and my ability to control the portals."

She bites her upper lip as she studies the gods arrayed around the plateau. "But that seems like such a petty reason."

"Indeed, it was."

Felicia's brows furrow as she gazes up at me. "I still get the feeling you aren't telling me the whole reason for their jealousy. You know you can trust me. I get that it's going to be painful to watch your own destruction, but that's not a good reason to clam up on me. I'll use the P-word if you don't fess up."

A large sigh gusts out of me. "I also hold sway over beginnings, endings, gates, and doorways. My ability to see into the past, the future, and the present simultaneously has also caused much distrust and dislike of me."

Glowing, glittering magics begin to swarm and swirl around the seven gods, filling the air with energies that grow more powerful with every passing second. Felicia and I both experience it as what mortals call static electricity. I know she feels it too because I can see her hair rising above her head. Mine is too short to achieve the same effect.

I grip her hand so tightly that it must hurt, yet she doesn't even flinch.

My past self materializes at the center of the circle. He glances around in confusion. "Why have you summoned me here?"

Kamadeva nods to his fellow gods, and they all lower their arms. He stares directly at my former self, lifting his chin. "You have become so arrogant, Janus, that we had no choice but to take action."

"When did arrogance become a crime? You may give me a verbal reprimand, but that is all you have the power to do."

Kamadeva folds his arms over his chest. "Why do you think we've gathered here? Because the altitude is good for our health?" He shakes his head slowly. "Your arrogance is only one of your crimes. You jealously guard the portals and the time stream, refusing to let us into the mortal world."

My past self huffs. "If I allowed gods to enter the mortal world at their own whims, the multiverse would have exploded long ago." He waves a hand in a gesture even my elemental friends would call imperious, though they don't mean it as a complaint. "No other god may have these powers because no one can be trusted with them. Do you believe the Oversoul made a mistake? If you are that arrogant—"

"Silence!" Kamadeva roars. "We haven't gathered on this Plane to discuss the matter. We are here to destroy you, Janus."

I place a hand over Felicia's eyes. "You do not want to watch this. I realize I must, but you—"

"Will not hide while you relive your own destruction." She peels my hand away. "We do this together. No arguments."

She is an incredible woman.

My former self fists his hands at his sides and grinds his teeth. "Dionysus talked you into this folly, yet he doesn't have the courage to face me himself. Why do you abide by his wishes? He was humiliated when I bested him in a gladiatorial match." He glances at one god in particular. "Hathor, what have I done to aggrieve you? Nothing. I cannot believe you volunteered to participate in my destruction."

She hunches her shoulders. "Eros wished me to take his place here."

Yes, she had been ensorcelled by the god Eros and forced to do his bidding. I understood this at the time, and I cast no blame on her then or now. Eros and Dionysus had been what my mortal friends would call "besties." They often assisted each other and even engaged in orgies together. Eros no longer has the powers of a god. But I'm still unclear on whether The Four Winds turned him into a mortal or if his magics lie dormant inside him, ready to be activated if he is given another chance. Kamadeva was granted such an opportunity, and now he lives in the mortal world as a human with no memory of his past.

Why was I never given the chance that those miscreants received?

"No more talk," Kamadeva declares. "The destruction ceremony will begin right now."

I watch as the light and dark energies of the destruction ritual swirl round and round the seven gods with my former self trapped at the center of the melee. Wind borne of the magics themselves whirl and wail and whip up anything that gets pulled into its path. The noise of the combined energies makes conversation impossible. I hold Felicia tightly, fearing she might be swept up in the annihilation of my former self. I know that's a ridiculous worry, but I cannot shake it.

The old me screams, his agony palpable.

Felicia's face has gone pale. Mine has too, I'm sure. Coldness has flooded through me, and all I can do is watch my former body being ripped apart molecule by molecule. The man I see now is, quite literally, a different being. Every atom has been torn to bits and scattered.

When his scream finally fades, the magics vanish too.

But now, I witness something I never could have when this event actually occurred because I was gone. Destroyed. No more. What happens next confounds me. The seven gods shuffle around on the platform of The Eternal Plane, seeming dazed and uncertain of what to do. They glance at each other but do not speak. Their confusion might have confounded me, but it isn't the most shocking aspect of their behavior.

Hathor scuffles over to the center of the platform and halts on the exact spot where the old me had been standing. She bows her head, then straps her arms around herself. Her shoulders begin to shudder. A soft sob bursts out of her, and then...

She falls to her knees and begins to weep.

My eyes have gone dry, but only because I cannot blink. Cannot move even the smallest muscle. Hathor assisted in my destruction, yet she seems heartbroken by what she's done.

The goddess sets her hands on the cold stone, huddled on all fours. "What have we done? Oversoul, forgive us, forgive me. I did not want this, but Eros—"

She freezes for a moment, then rises and straightens her clothing.

Kamadeva grabs her arm. "Time to go, Hathor. Eros will be wanting his plaything back. And besides, we've gotten rid of that arrogant boor once and for all. I say a celebration is in order."

Artemis claps and grins. "An orgy, Kamadeva? I do adore those, especially if we invite unsuspecting mortals. I love corrupting them."

Artemis has been in love with Dionysus for as long as anyone can recall, and Dionysus believes orgies are an essential part of life in the Unseen.

The gods vanish.

Felicia and I stand alone on the platform of The Eternal Plane. I know I should whisk us away from here, but something inside me pushes me to approach the spot on which I had ceased to exist. I release Felicia from my arms and march over to the center of the platform, standing directly on the location where…the remnants of my molecular form were scattered into the aether.

Felicia comes up beside me, curling her arm around mine. "Don't punish yourself this way, sweetie. What they did to you was horrific, but you can't dwell on the past anymore. Let's get out of here."

"Do you have any conception of how long I languished in limbo? I had no choice but to watch Vita move on with her life and bear our child. Then I watched as our daughter Laelia married and bore her own babe." I shut my eyes briefly, then stare into Felicia's eyes. "*Perpetuum et unum diem.*"

"What does that mean?"

"Forever and a day. That's precisely how long I was trapped in the Temple of The Four Winds, languishing as a spirit, formless, alone, forced to watch as the generations of my lineage went on and on and on."

She steps in front of me, grasping my face with both hands. "It's time to leave this place. Right now. We have problems that are way more immediate. Or have you forgotten about Theo, Dionysus, and the Dark One?"

I snap my spine straight, lift my chin, and drag her into me. "You always know how to stop me from wallowing in self-pity. I would speak the T-word, but I have no wish to indebt either of us. Let's go, Fliss."

"One second. I'd like to know more about your time in limbo."

"Why?"

"Because it still causes you a lot of anxiety. That's obvious."

She will insist on receiving a response. I owe her that much after everything she's done for me and with me. "I told you that I spent many thousands of years in limbo, not alive but not dead, unable to communicate with the ones I loved. Watching their lives go on but not being able to touch or speak to them, that was the worst torment of all. But seeing Hathor's reaction to my destruction…"

"What? You can't leave me hanging like that."

"Hathor was ensorcelled by Eros, but the magics of the destruction spell freed her momentarily. She regretted what she'd done."

Felicia studies me for a moment. "Are you saying you forgive her?"

"Yes. Larissa is the mortal incarnation of Hathor, but she had no choice in the matter. She was compelled to participate in my demise. I forgive her. And I need to tell Larissa that."

Felicia opens her mouth but has no chance to speak. We are both spirited away by an outside force, and we hit the ground so hard that I'm briefly stunned motionless. Forest surrounds us. The darkness of night blankets the sky. Felicia has been dropped on top of me. And I suddenly realize my powers have been circumvented. I cannot whisk us away or crush whomever is doing this.

A familiar figure approaches us.

Silenus bends over to stare at me and Felicia. His lips curl into a vicious smile. "Enough horsing around, Janus. It's time for the real fun to begin." He shouts over his shoulder at someone behind him. "Come out, oh Dark One, and reveal yourself to these pitiful creatures. The end of everything is coming."

CHAPTER NINETEEN

Felicia

I AM SO DAMN SICK OF THESE WEIRDOS FROM ANOTH-er world issuing vague, apocalyptic threats. Silenus flicks his tail and smiles at me with a hunger that I don't care to analyze. Maybe he wants to screw me. Maybe he wants to eat my flesh. Who knows what a creepy creature like him craves? All I care about is not getting murdered or assaulted by a satyr.

Should I worry more about Dionysus than Silenus?

No, I assume the Dark One is the big baddie here.

The satyr rises and stretches with more satisfaction than seems necessary. Then he moves aside to reveal another being.

It's not Dionysus.

The name "Dark One" had sounded like pure hype meant to cow us. But I'm not ashamed to admit that this being terrifies me. As the creature saunters toward us, at first, I think it has no arms. But then the being spreads its wide black wings, revealing that its entire body is composed of black scales. The head seems humanoid. With only a partial moon to light the area, I can't say for sure. The beast has humanlike feet, except for the long claws attached to them—and to the creature's fingers.

The monster is definitely female. Her perky boobs prove that. She also doesn't have a dick.

Janus leaps to his feet with me in his arms and shuffles backward. He can't move very far, though. I assume Silenus and his buddy cast some type of spell to prevent us from escaping.

Two more creatures materialize. *Oh, great.* The monkey-men who had assaulted me on the day I met Janus have just arrived. The party is in full swing now. If I remember right, these winged baboons call themselves Freknel and Stiodel.

I pretend nothing I've seen bothers me because I for damn sure won't let them know I'm scared shitless right now. So instead, I wave and smile. "Nice to see you guys again. Help me out here. Which one of you is Freknel and which is Stiodel?"

Janus throws me a baffled look. He'll figure out my strategy soon enough.

Not that I actually have a strategy. Well, maybe half a strategy. So, I aim a polite smile at the kerkopes. "My name is Felicia, by the way. I don't want to get your names wrong, but nobody told me who's who."

One of the monkey creatures puffs up his chest and smirks. "My name is Freknel the Clever. I am the good-looking one that all the other kerkopes are jealous of. Women love me."

Sure, pal, whatever, you delusional freak.

The other monkey creature shoves his buddy out of the way, sending Freknel flying, and he smacks into a tree. Stiodel lifts his chin as he gazes at me, laying his palms on his upper chest. "Freknel is a liar. I'm the one every female in the Unseen wishes to mate with. I am called Stiodel the Strong."

"Nice to meet you boys, officially." When I glance up at Janus's face, I see a muscle ticking in his jaw. Out of the corner of my mouth, I murmur, "Calm down, sweetie. Let's not start the apocalypse accidentally."

He relaxes, though I suspect it took a lot of willpower to do that.

Silenus hustles over to the big, winged female. "May I have Felicia? You said there would be a reward for me."

"And there will be," the dragon lady assures him. "Eventually. You haven't fulfilled your entire obligation to me."

"May I at least destroy Dionysus? I grow tired of waiting my turn."

She pats the top of his head. "Patience, my pet. I've allowed you great leeway in how you handle the tasks I assign to you. Don't get greedy, Theo."

I know I shouldn't speak up, not with these evil creatures surrounding me and Janus, but I can't stop myself. I need some answers to make sense of what in the world is going on here. So, I look at the satyr. "I thought Theo was just the fake name you used when you were trying to seduce me away from Janus. Silenus is your real name."

The satyr puckers his lips and huffs. "That was the moniker given to me by Dionysus. I have always preferred Theo. It was the name chosen by my mother and father before Dionysus abducted me and forged me into a satyr against my will." One corner of his mouth kinks upward. "But I've made the best of my lot in life. Satyrs are the horniest creatures in the Unseen, and I get plenty of action."

A guy with a tail and hooves really shouldn't brag about his sexual prowess. I huddle a little closer to Janus and whisper, "What does 'forged' mean?"

Janus whispers too. "He claims he was born a mortal. The forging process turns a human into an elemental."

"Do you believe his claim?"

"I'm not sure. But it certainly could be true. My friend Max was a soldier in the Roman army until an incubus forged him into the salamander he is today."

The terms incubus and salamander mean the same thing. I remember Janus explained that to me. Feels like years ago since that moment, but it couldn't have been more than a few days. Probably. This is all too damn confusing.

The winged female pushes Theo away from her and saunters up to me and Janus. She tilts her head side to side, seeming to study us. "How rude of me not to introduce myself. I already know who you two are, Janus the god and Felicia Vincent the mortal." She lifts her chin. "I am The Dark One, Dasheramal the Ravager."

Well, she does have the raspy, husky voice I'd expect from someone who calls herself the Ravager. And I can't deny that being this close to this creature gives me a case of the shivers. Her eyes are a dark shade of emerald, her black skin glistens with an eerie sheen of cobalt blue, and short fangs are visible whenever she speaks.

Janus keeps his arm strapped around me like he worries I might fly away into the sky. He looks directly at the winged woman. "I have never heard of a god or an elemental known by that name. I am a primordial god. That means if I don't know you, no one does."

She chuckles, and it sounds like beads clacking against each other. "I am not primordial, though I did devour many beings who were almost that ancient."

"Tell me what you want. I grow weary of your boasts. Having never heard of any creature called Dasheramal the Ravager, I'm less than impressed by your ostentatious display." Janus waves a hand negligently, lifting his chin. "But if you insist on flaunting yourself, go on. I'll take a nap in the meantime."

Dasheramal puckers her lips tightly and glowers at him. Her nostrils flare.

I squint at the self-described Ravager as if I'm confused, which is not an act. This creature must be insane. "Are you a dragon? Those are the only creatures from mythology I can think of that have wings. Well, other than gargoyles."

"You would compare *me* to a gargoyle?" Dasheramal bares her teeth at me and hisses, "I am the Ravager of worlds, of beings, of anything that stands in my way. You, puny mortal, should watch your mouth—unless you want me to command Theo to ravage your body. I'm certain he would relish the chance to make you with child. A hybrid pregnancy would lead to your demise, you foolish mortal."

Janus looks like he's about to blow his top.

But neither of us knows what sort of powers Dasheramal has in her arsenal, so I think I'd better try to calm him down. I don't get the chance, though. Janus does it himself. He pulls in a deep breath and releases it slowly while his demeanor becomes calmer. I can still see the magical fire in his eyes, but he isn't dumb enough to let his fury show, not anymore.

Yeah, we are in serious trouble. Even I can sense that. But I'm getting damn sick of waiting for the winged whackjob to tell us what she wants.

Screw waiting.

I set my hands on my hips and stare straight into Dasheramal's eyes. "Come on, Ravager of Worlds, you know you want to spill the beans. Do it now. We can't be impressed by your ingenuity unless you share it with us."

She squeezes words out between her teeth. "Janus cheated me out of the powers that should have been mine."

"That's it? You're miffed, therefore you'll start an apocalypse? Talk about a temper tantrum. I was expecting something grander and more elegant."

Dasheramal stomps her foot, and the ground quakes. "When the seven gods destroyed Janus, his powers should have been scattered into the aether. Instead, The Four Winds held them in stasis."

Janus crosses his arms over his chest. "And you believed...what would happen? That my powers would be in the public domain for any vile creature in the multiverse to commandeer? You are the stupidest creature I have ever met."

This time she stomps both feet so hard that the trees shudder as if a giant shook them. "Your plaything destroyed my soul mate!"

"I have no idea to whom you are referring."

Something about his use of the stuffiest way of speaking, in absolutely perfect grammar, makes me want to rip is toga off and go down on him in front of these evil nutjobs.

Dasheramal growls, and spittle sprays from her lips. "You destroyed Setesh."

Janus rolls his eyes. "No, I did not. The vampire Cyneric destroyed Setesh, and he is not my plaything. He unsettles everyone."

Are there more vampires out there? I'd love to ask him about that, but now is not the time.

"Your grievance is erroneous," Janus tells Dasheramal. "Perhaps you should track down Cyneric and attempt to kill him. You'll find that he's much more difficult to destroy than the average elemental." He waves a dismissive hand. "But go on, try it."

"You murdered my soul mate!" She smacks her hand into his chest so hard that the sound reverberates through the clearing, but Janus doesn't even flinch. "The vampire *is* your plaything. Stop lying!"

I can tell he's getting quite annoyed, but he knows how to rein in his anger. If I were in his shoes, I'd probably have thrown a boulder at the bitch five minutes ago.

Theo sidles up to Dasheramal. "It's time to give me Felicia. You swore I could have what I wanted most if I brought Janus to you."

"You cannot destroy me," Janus tells the crazy dragon lady. "I am a god, and you are...whatever you are. Not a god, that is for certain. Give up your childish vendetta."

"It's true that I'm not a god. But I have amassed more power than any being in the history of the Unseen ever has managed to acquire." She spreads her wings. "That is how I will eradicate you. But not until you have suffered greatly."

Janus glares at her with his eyes narrowed to slits. "You are not a harpy, a gargoyle, or a dragon shifter. But I sense elements of all those things in you. I suspect you have copied the style of the sorcerer who attacked the Janusite once upon a time. He absorbed the powers and knowledge of three beings to create an amalgamation. Doing so required magics of the darkest kind, and that was his weakness."

"I am not weak, but stronger than any being in existence."

Humility is not in her wheelhouse. But if she has done what Janus suggested, then I imagine she'd be one whacked-out creature.

Janus leans in, sniffing the air near Dasheramal's face. "You stink of dark magics. No wonder Theo is the only creature willing to be in your presence. He smells as revolting as you do."

I think he's trying to goad her into admitting what other beings she has devoured or whatever she does to them. This tactic seems risky, but I get that we're in serious trouble.

Theo flies at Janus, his teeth bared and his tail whipping wildly, but Dasheramal smacks him aside. The satyr lands on his ass.

The self-proclaimed Ravager shakes her head at Theo. "And you wonder why I haven't devoured you yet. Morons taste worse than gnomes."

I'll take her word for that.

Theo leaps up and flings himself at Dasheramal, seizing her neck. But Freknel and Stiodel drag him away, punching him so many times in so many places that he goes limp. His eyes are open but glazed.

The two kerkopes glom onto their mistress, purring like kittens and petting her skin. Freknel speaks since his buddy is too busy licking the dragon lady's hand. "We have done well, haven't we, mistress?"

"Very well. Now, keep Theo restrained while I devour Janus."

He snorts. "I am a god, you idiot. Even an endued weapon can't destroy me."

She taps one taloned finger on his nose. "I said I would *devour* you, not destroy you." She sighs. "Since you lack the understanding of my words, allow me to show you how it works. I dislike consuming a lower being, but you simply won't comprehend without a demonstration, will you? All right. I shall give you one."

Dasheramal stalks over to Theo, clamps both hands around his throat, and hoists him up. His feet dangle a foot off the ground. She bends her arms to draw him closer, closer, inch by inch, as she opens her mouth just as gradually. Her jaw separates, but she doesn't care. Theo begins to whine and beg for mercy. Still, she keeps opening her maw wider until she can't open it any further.

Theo stares directly into her maw—and screams.

Dasheramal doesn't literally devour him. As far as I can tell, she's using a haze of magics to melt him little by little. That's grotesque, but I don't get to see much.

Janus pulls me closer and holds a hand over my eyes. "Don't look, Fliss. This is pure evil at work, and even I cannot gaze upon it. To do so would taint us with the vile magics of this creature."

Just when I thought things couldn't get worse, they do.

CHAPTER TWENTY

Janus

$\mathcal{A}$ LOUD BELCH EMITS FROM THE VICINITY OF DASHERA-
mal, though I still cannot open my eyes to see what she's
doing. I sense the vile magics the self-proclaimed Ravager had invoked to consume Theo are still writhing in the air like wicked
serpents. No one should watch one being devouring another. It
must stain a person's soul to witness such a thing.

Soon, the magics dissipate.

I open my eyes just enough to determine if the vile energies
are indeed gone. Though I had felt it when they faded away, I
needed to be certain before I tell Felicia it's safe to open her
eyes. The kerkopes cower near the trees, their eyes wide, and
gape at their mistress. Dasheramal appears quite pleased with
herself, not to mention satiated from the magics and the being
she just consumed. I cannot comprehend how much dark energy
she must have gained from that revolting display.

Did she actually devour Theo? Or was this a hoax to confuse
us? Her magics clouded my view, so I can't be certain.

I whisper to Felicia, "You may look now."

She peels her lids apart gradually. I still hold her close, unwill-
ing to let go yet after the disturbing display we just witnessed. She
clutches a handful of my toga as she murmurs, "Did she really eat
Theo in one gulp?"

"I'm not certain, but Dasheramal wanted us to believe so. I recommend not dwelling on what she appears to have done. It might have been a gruesome hoax."

"At least I didn't see any of it. That would've left me permanently nauseous for the rest of my life."

"And stained with dark magics. To witness an evil act in the Unseen can have that effect, and Dasheramal summoned those magics into the mortal world."

The creature in question stalks closer and jabs a finger into my chest. "Cease your whispering, puny god. Your puny mortal lover must be silent now too, for I have more news to impart to you."

Yes, I so look forward to that. Who will she devour next? The kerkopes? I wouldn't mourn their loss any more than I did Theo's. However, her penchant for claiming to devour other beings is quite disturbing, even if it turns out to be trickery. It's the magics Dasheramal invoked that disturb me. Remnants of the dark energies linger, though only as echoes.

Dasheramal tips her head forward to squint at me. "If you believe your puny elemental friends will save you"—She grins, though it's not a pleasant expression—"then you are even more foolish than I thought."

She suffers from a rather small vocabulary. This creature has used the word puny several times. No one with that sort of limited imagination could have accomplished the feats she brags of having achieved. I wonder if she isn't actually the one in charge of this operation. Her boasting and snarling might be nothing more than a delay tactic until her master arrives.

Felicia glances up at me, and I can tell by her expression that she has reached the same conclusion.

"Your plaything destroyed my soul mate," Dasheramal says, repeating what she told me earlier. The creature truly does have a limited imagination. "Now, you shall suffer for that. Setesh was the greatest god in the multiverse and the most inventive lover. But you allowed the filthy vampire Cyneric to eradicate Setesh. As punishment, I will now take away the thing you love most."

She closes her eyes and sniffs the air, then smiles with feral delight as she looks at me.

No, I don't like that expression, not one iota. It bodes ill, of that I'm certain. Without my powers, I cannot stop her from doing anything she likes. Why can't I? *Deodamnatus*. I am the god all others

127

fear, the one who holds the time stream in his hands. Dasheramal is nothing but an abomination created by someone else. She will reveal the truth to me. Right now.

While the winged abomination continues to drone on and on about the destruction of her lover Setesh, I surreptitiously watch and listen to the atmosphere in this little clearing. I curl my fingers loosely against my palms, an action Dasheramal fails to notice. Felicia seems to understand my plan without me speaking or glancing at her, since she feigns fear. I know it's false anxiety. I feel that truth deep inside me.

The leaves on the trees begin to shiver faintly, creating a sound akin to a light rain shower. But an electrical tingle burrows beneath my skin.

Magics. *My* magics.

I want to smile, but I dare not do that. Instead, I continue drawing in the white magics that magnify my powers. The energies tingle inside me, escalating in strength with every passing second. Suddenly, I am...invigorated and powerful.

Now is my chance to test Dasheramal's power.

In the space of two seconds, I push Felicia behind me and summon my war cloak. Its magics will hide Felicia from the view of anyone other than me. Already, Dasheramal has reacted to the shift, though she is clearly confused—about more than Felicia's apparent disappearance. Dasheramal has felt the power that envelops me, the magics that are far more potent than hers.

The vile creature stumbles backward a step, shaking her head in confusion. I no longer wear a toga. Instead, a leather kilt surrounds my hips and thighs, and my sandals have become leather boots while my red war cloak flutters behind me as if a soft breeze has picked it up.

I also hold a gleaming silver sword in my hand. An endued sword, the only kind that can kill an elemental.

Dasheramal's eyes flare wide.

One side of my mouth kinks upward. "Do you still wish to destroy me? I'm certain that by now you've realized the futility of such an attempt. My powers eclipse those of all other beings in The Unseen, save The Four Winds."

Dasheramal's bravado has evaporated. She attempts to teleport herself away, intending to leave her kerkopes friends behind, but she can't do it. I have thwarted her. She races toward the dirt path but gets knocked backward when she hits the force field I've erected around this clearing. Dasheramal lands on her backside in the most unceremonious manner, spitting and hissing and gnashing her teeth.

The kerkopes try to whisk themselves away, apparently too stupid to realize that their mistress's failure affects them too. They huddle against a large tree, quivering like the cowards they are.

"Rise, Dasheramal," I command. "Come forth and accept your punishment."

She clambers to her feet and scuttles up to me. "Please, do not destroy me. This wasn't my idea."

"You claimed to be the most powerful creature in the Unseen. Now you wish me to believe you're a weakling and a coward?" I huff. "The mighty fall hard, don't they?"

Dasheramal cowers a few feet away from me, shivering—with fear, no doubt. "What will you do with me?"

"I might spare your useless existence—if you tell me everything I want to know."

"Yes, of course, anything."

"Firstly, reveal your true self." I aim my hardest glare at her. "Do it now. No more trickery." She couldn't deceive me even if she wanted to do it. My magics trump hers.

Dasheramal slumps her shoulders, bows her head, and releases the spell that had altered her appearance.

I lift my brows. "You are one of the kerkopes, just like those two wretched creatures over there." I point toward Stiodel and Freknel, then chuckle. "That means you are no more powerful than the average undine."

Fliss pokes her head out from under my cloak and smirks. "She doesn't look threatening at all anymore. The wicked witch of the Unseen is just a scared little monkey-girl."

"With extremely limited powers. But don't discount her physical strength." I tip my chin down and glare into Dasheramal's eyes, making her tremble. "What really happened to Theo?"

"He has returned to our master."

"That grotesque show you put on a few moments ago was sheer fakery."

She nods and winces, bowing her head.

I grasp her chin and force her to lift it. Once our eyes meet, I narrow my gaze again. "Tell me who your master is."

"No, no, don't make me tell. He will run me through with an endued sword if I confess to you."

"And I can do far worse than that. God of time, remember? I could force you to reenact your own destruction over and over until the end of eternity." I lean in until her face is millimeters from mine. "That means your torment will never end."

"No, I beg of you, don't do that to me."

For an elemental to beg means that she finally grasps the severity of her situation. Of course, we're in the mortal world right now. She may plead all she likes without incurring a debt to me. But I have no wish to do that. Having this vile creature following me everywhere, doing my bidding... I'd rather be destroyed again.

I grasp Dasheramal by her upper arms. "Listen carefully. I won't harm you as long as you do precisely as I say. Can you do that?"

She nods vigorously.

"Now, Dasheramal, you will travel into the Unseen to find your master and deliver this message—he will come to me here. On this spot. Immediately. You will accompany him, and the pair of you will have ten minutes to accomplish that task." I release her arms and straighten. "Remember, I control the portals, which means you cannot cross the veil without my permission. If you fail in your task, I will destroy you myself."

"I will not fail."

Dasheramal vanishes.

Stiodel and Freknel still huddle against that large tree.

I sigh and wave a hand at them. "You may sit down. And do try to relax. I have no desire to kill kerkopes today, not unless you annoy me."

The sad little creatures collapse onto the ground, sighing and almost crying with relief. Freknel raises his arms toward me and says, "We are so very grateful for your clemency, oh divine master."

I gaze up at the sky, shaking my head.

Then I sweep the cloak aside so Felicia can come out again. She grasps my hand, now standing beside me, and aims a quizzical look at the kerkopes. "They're strange little creatures, aren't they?"

"Male kerkopes are as large as an average mortal man."

"Yeah, but they seem smaller when they're lying in a puddle on the ground."

"True."

Fliss wraps an arm around my waist. "How will you know when Dasheramal's time is up?"

I smile and wink. "God of time, remember?"

"Right. Sometimes I forget you're a literal god and not just a god in the bedroom."

Stiodel pushes up onto his knees and pretends to gag. "Must we listen to your lovey-dovey talk? It makes me nauseous."

I lift my brows. "Would you prefer to be torn apart into molecular mist?"

Stiodel slumps back down onto the ground and moans.

"Dasheramal and her master are coming," I tell Felicia. "Before I permit them to cross the veil, I need to summon our backup plan."

Before she can ask what I mean by that statement, I flourish my hand.

Several elementals materialize. The gang has arrived.

And I am not ashamed to admit I'm glad to see them. Naturally, I pretend as if I don't care that they've come to assist us. It wouldn't be godly to say so. "Though my vast powers overshadow yours, I appreciate having all of you here." Yes, I purposely placed emphasis on the word vast. Everyone expects me to be slightly arrogant. It's my shtick, as Triskaideka would say. "Prepare yourselves. Dasheramal and her master will arrive in three seconds, twelve milliseconds."

Travis rolls his eyes, shaking his head. "You've just got to include the milli-whatevers, don't you?"

"Of course." I tap my temple. "God of time, salamander."

Dasheramal materializes first. Then the one she claims controls her makes a grand entrance with a swirling black cloud surrounding the being who remains cloaked by the magics. I can see the vague outline of the figure who hides inside the cloud. As the magics dissipate, I finally recognize the figure.

My brows shoot up. "Kali? What are you trying to accomplish with three kerkopes and a satyr working for you?"

Felicia and my elemental friends all gape at the being to whom I had spoken. Their expressions convey shock, disbelief, and confusion. I am confused as well, though for a different reason. My friends have likely never seen Kali, the incarnation of the Hindu goddess, who resembles her namesake only in certain aspects. She is a god of the Unseen, after all.

"Tell me, Kali, why have you done these things?"

"I will explain when I feel like it, Janus."

She strides up to me, nude and with her four arms gently swaying at her sides while her breasts sway. Her skin is a pale blue with golden overtones, not quite the description mortal mythology prefers. She does not wear a necklace of severed heads or have blood dripping from her tongue. Mortals often get the details wrong. Kali does wear a crown of elephant teeth, though no one has ever explained to me why she does that. Her bare feet made hardly a sound when she approached me. But her more fearsome quality is her power over destruction and transformation.

Still, I have never known Kali to do the things her minions have done on her behalf.

I lean forward since the goddess is shorter than I am. "You will tell me now, Kali, or else I will ban you from crossing the veil for the rest of eternity."

She shrugs one shoulder. "That doesn't matter to me, darling. The inevitability of time is on my side."

"No more evasions." I seize her upper arms and shake her violently. "Why have you done all of this? You convinced your minions to lie and obfuscate their true nature, all to convince me that first Theo, then Dasheramal, was the true enemy. But it's you, Kali, who orchestrated this bizarre plan. And I will know why."

Her smile is placid, yet the stormy colors in her eyes belie that expression. "You want the truth? As you wish. I am the goddess of destruction and transformation, but I grow tired of my limitations. I want more."

"Such as…" I sense the answer, but I maintain the vague hope I'm wrong for two point two seconds.

Kali swipes her tongue over her lips and spreads her lips in a nasty grin. "I will appropriate your powers, and there is nothing you can do to stop me."

CHAPTER TWENTY-ONE

Felicia

O H, THIS IS BAD, SO SO BAD. I MIGHT NOT FULLY UNDER-
stand what's going on here, but when a creepy goddess declares
that she will steal Janus's powers and he can't stop her… Well, I just
felt the sharpest, creepiest shiver of my life race up my spine. Kali
can't do that. Can she? No, Janus is about to tell her she's nuts and
kick her blue ass all the way back to wherever she came from.

But instead, he simply stares at her. Motionless. Expressionless. Like
a statue in a Roman temple.

I sidle up to him and whisper, "You okay?"

"No," he says out of the side of his mouth.

Yeah, my hopes of getting some reassurance have disintegrated.

Janus gently pushes me behind him, but he doesn't fold his
cloak around me as he'd done earlier. He does keep one hand on
my hip, though. "You are insane, Kali, though everyone in the
Unseen has known that for a very long time. You made Setesh
seem coherent. Your convoluted plan involving kerkopes and a
satyr is bizarre, at best." He shakes his head slowly. "But to think
you can commandeer the time stream… You are out of your ever-
loving mind, Kali."

I can't believe Janus used that phrase. It's a mortal thing, as far
as I know. And besides, my adorably uptight god of time always
talks like a Victorian. He must be well and truly stymied right

now. His elemental buddies look surprised too, but they quash their shock swiftly.

"Out of my what?" Kali says with a laugh. "I have never heard the almighty Janus use that sort of language. Too much time with mortals and elementals who used to be mortals has clearly lowered your standards. Maybe that explains why you didn't deduce my master plan."

Janus scrunches up his entire face. "No sane being could guess that you would enact such an absurd scheme."

"Absurd?" She wags a finger in his face in clocklike fashion. "It's pure genius. And I'm about to show you just how brilliant the scheme is."

I poke my head out around Janus's massive biceps. "No offense, Kali, but so far your plan sucks."

Kali tosses her head, which makes her waist-length black hair fly up behind her like a slithering cloak. "I'm done explaining. Now I will show you."

She backs up several paces.

When Max and Travis inch around behind her, she waves a hand negligently, and the two salamanders go flying backward into separate trees.

Kali sighs. "Do not try that again."

Janus assumes his dangerously-hot god pose and gazes down at Kali with disdain. "No one here takes your orders. I am in control."

The chick with four arms laughs.

Janus raises his arms in front of him, sending out a massive gust of wind that affects only Kali. She goes flying backward end over end, snarling what sounds like naughty words in another language. Whatever she's saying, I don't think it's "I want to kiss you, Janus." Kali winds up wedged against a tree with her feet in the air in front of her face.

"Give up your ridiculous quest, Kali," Janus declares. "Go home and tend to your followers. You might be a god, but I am the almighty Janus."

Kali shrieks and flies to her feet, racing toward him.

Janus flicks one finger, and Kali is sucked up into the sky. As she flies through the atmosphere, her shrieks and snarls fade away swiftly.

I wrap my arm around his thick biceps and nuzzle it. "That was amazing. You took her down fifty or sixty pegs with a wave of one finger. Bye-bye, Kali."

"She is not gone. I sent her back to her fortress, but I do not have the power to destroy a god on my own."

"You're amazing. Of course you can do it on your own."

He pulls me close and kisses the top of my head. "Your faith in me is touching. But I have not gotten rid of Kali. We must keep searching for the ultimate source of the threat."

I lift my head, gazing up at his beautiful gold eyes. "But I thought Kali was the big bad wolf."

"As did I—until she revealed herself. No, she is not the ultimate source of our travails."

Tris blows a breath out between his lips. "Are you kidding me? We still have more baddies to take down? Sheesh. It never ends."

Max crosses his arms over his chest and puckers his lips as he studies the two pitiful creatures who still huddle on the ground. "What are we meant to do with those two? I'd rather not touch them. They smell bloody awful."

Freknel and Stiodel have their arms wrapped around each other as they sniffle and hiccup. Freknel manages to eke out a few words. "P-please don't kill us."

Janus tips his head to the side, studying the kerkopes. "Perhaps they can be of use."

I look up at him. "You have an idea, sweetie?"

Max bursts out in uproarious laughter. "I never thought I'd see the day when anyone would call Janus the almighty 'sweetie.'" The salamander switches to a baby-talk voice. "Does the wittle god of time need a bwankie?"

Janus grits his teeth and booms, "Shut up, Maximus!"

I slap my hands over my ears, but I can still hear his bellow echoing through the clearing and probably all the woods from here to Wisconsin.

Once the noise fades away, Tris frowns at Janus. "Are you trying to burst my eardrums? Jeez Louise. Talk about a tantrum."

I wouldn't characterize it as a tantrum, but Janus is definitely getting frustrated. So am I. This roundtable discussion might work if we already had a rough outline of what we need to do—but we don't. I've held back during this group chat. No more. Despite the fact I've known Janus for only a short time, I'm positive I know him better than his friends do. I doubt he shares his innermost fears with them.

I seize his hand. "Come on, sweetie, we need to have a private talk."

He swerves his head toward me, his brows furrowing. "We must confer with everyone about—"

"Not yet." I can see the others watching us and glancing back and forth at each other as if none of them can figure out what I'm doing. Let them wonder. My top concern is Janus. I tug his hand. "Come on. We need to talk."

He nods once.

Then he lets me lead him away from the group, out of the clearing into the woods. I don't stop until we can just barely hear the rumble of the waterfall. This feels like a good spot for our heart to heart.

I turn to face him, clasping both his hands.

He lifts one brow. "Why did we need to visit this location? There's nothing here but trees and grass."

"Wildflowers too. But that's irrelevant." I thread my fingers with his. "Listen to me. We're all going about this problem the wrong way. I'm sure you'll agree with me if you stop and think about it."

He studies me intently for a moment. "What is it you believe I've done incorrectly?"

"It's not that you're wrong. It's that we're all allowing the bad guys to lead us around by the nose." I shuffle closer until our bodies almost touch. That means I need to crane my neck to see his face and gaze into those shimmering gold eyes. "First, Theo led us on a merry little chase with that restaurant bullshit, knowing that you would come to my rescue. Then other beings got involved, and I no longer believe any of this was a series of coincidences."

"But the haphazard manner in which they revealed themselves…" His voice trails off while his eyes widen. He shuts his eyes briefly and groans. "You are correct. Nothing about any of this is mere coincidence."

"Let's walk through all the events that led us to this moment."

He nods. "Not here. We need time to discuss everything, and we need a secure location where we can do that."

"Okay. Where should we go?"

Janus puckers his lips, which I've realized means he's thinking hard. "A place beyond time. That is where we must go."

"I don't understand. What place is beyond time?"

He smirks. "I am the god of time, remember? The only place where I may go but no one else can is the time stream itself."

That sounds bizarre, but I trust him with all my heart and soul. "Let's do it."

"You should know that I cannot promise we will be completely safe there. The harpy Aello once breached the time stream. If she could do it—"

"When did that happen? Before or after you got your powers back?"

"Before. But it still means that I might not notice—"

I seal two fingers over his lips. "Shush, sweetie. No more negativity. You are the most powerful god in the Unseen. And you're smokin' hot."

He clears his throat and wraps his arms around me, plastering my body to his with barely a millimeter between us. "Then we will enter the time stream now. No one will realize we've been gone, no matter how long it takes for us to complete our task."

I don't get the chance to say anything else. The sizzling-hot god whisks us both away. The world vanishes, then reappears for a second only to disappear again as we breach the time stream. The rivers of energy slither and swirl, releasing glittery bits of who knows what. Janus holds me so tightly to his body that I have trouble catching my breath.

Our journey into the time stream looks and feels different now.

The slithering serpents of temporal energy part for us and give us little glittery kisses on our skin. I guess they like me now. Janus halts us mid-stream, glancing around, then whooshes us up, up, and away, like Superman or Thor in those movies. Janus doesn't have a magical hammer, though. He doesn't need it. Time itself obeys and worships him.

I worship him too.

When I glance down past my feet, the darkness and the golden slithering of the time stream has become so faint that it might vanish at any second. I tip my head back to gaze upward at the starry sky. Its shimmering pinpoints zip around and pulse as if they're welcoming Janus to...where, I have no idea.

Janus grasps my chin with his thumb and forefinger, urging me to look in a different direction. "We have arrived, *dulcissima*."

We're zooming toward a gleaming white temple that floats in the clouds. Glittering gold specks flitter around in the air as Janus touches down on the first step of the temple's staircase. He sets me on my feet but keeps one arm secured around my waist.

"How do you like my home, Fliss?"

"It's incredible." I sound awed because I frigging am. The temple seems to give off its own golden glow, and veins of gold run through the entire structure. "I've never seen anything like this. You actually live here?"

"Not always. This is my first and truest home, here in the hidden center of time itself."

"Holy shit. I can't believe I'm here with you in this astonishing place."

Janus begins to walk up the steps while keeping hold of me. "You are the first being I have ever brought to my home."

"The first *being*? You don't mean just the first mortal."

"No. Even The Four Winds have never visited my temple."

And he brought me here. I'm awed by more than the building in front of me. The man beside me has gifted me with his most precious gift—his trust. I will never break that bond. Never.

As we mount the last step, the golden doors of the temple swing open for us. Janus takes my hand to lead me into the building. What I see surprises me, though maybe it shouldn't. The temple Janus had shown me in the Unseen was lavishly decorated and furnished with all the sensual comforts I would expect from a god.

I turn in a circle to drink in the grandeur that surrounds me. "Your temple in the Unseen is piddly compared to this one."

"That's because it is my ancillary temple and houses none of the temporal energies." Janus spreads his arms wide. "This is my home."

As he saunters toward me, his clothing vanishes. The god of time now stands nude before me, so close that I could run my hands over all those muscles and clasp that gorgeous cock.

He flicks one finger, and my clothing vanishes too. "I need to make love to you, Fliss. Right now. It won't be like the first time, though. The energies of the time stream suffuse this place, and you will feel that energy while we make love, I'm certain. Having never fucked anyone in this temple, I cannot tell you what it might be like."

"I trust you, sweetie. And I'm getting horny just being inside this building. Maybe that's the temporal energies."

"Yes, I'm certain it is." He sucks in a ragged breath, and when he speaks again, his voice is rougher and deeper. "I am already growing aroused. Intensely so. If you wish for me to send you back to the mortal world—"

"Screw that." I fling my arms around his neck, standing on my tiptoes, and rub myself all over him. "Fuck me, Janus. No holding back. No worrying about what might happen. I need you inside me so badly that I think I might go crazy if you don't take me this instant."

His breaths have grown heavier, making his chest heave. "You will surely become bonded with me after this in a manner neither of us can predict."

"For pity's sake, Janus, fuck me already."

In less than a second, he teleports us onto the huge feather bed with me on top. I'm straddling his hips, held up by my knees. His cock waves between my thighs, engorged and glistening with golden dew on its crown. I scrape my tongue across my lower lip, so aroused that I'm almost panting.

He reaches out to pet my mound with his fingertips.

"Oh, shit, Janus, that feels incredible. I'll come any second if you don't stop."

"Never will I stop." He shoves his hand between my folds and thrusts his longest finger inside me, making me cry out and shudder. "I can ensure that you will come for me over and over and that the pleasure will never end—until I say so." He gives me the sexiest smirk I've ever seen, rife with lust. "Salamanders aren't the only beings who can make a woman climax again and again until she's drenched with sweat and gloriously exhausted."

I believe it. Janus can do anything.

But when he thrusts his whole hand inside me, I come so suddenly and so fiercely that a scream is wrenched out of me. My body convulses around his hand while he strokes my inner walls, milking all the pleasure he can from my orgasm.

Then he removes his hand. As he licks each finger clean in a deliberately slow manner, he keeps his gaze nailed to mine. "You taste so fucking good, Fliss, and I could devour you for the rest of eternity."

His erection is waving between my thighs, and I know that when he's inside me this time, everything will change between us in ways I can't even imagine. Maybe I should worry about that, but I don't give a damn.

And I slam my body down on his cock.

Chapter Twenty-Two

Janus

THE MOMENT FLISS IMPALED HERSELF ON MY COCK, ANY threads of common sense that I'd clung to immediately snapped. A lust like none I have ever experienced in all my existence has taken control of me, and the only thing I can see is her—rocking those hips, biting her lip, slapping her palms down on my chest to get more leverage. The liquid sound of her flesh meeting mine fills the air along with her hungry noises and my grunting growls. I thrust upward every time she slams herself down on me as our pace increases and our cries echo throughout the temple.

Never could I have imagined I would fuck a woman so wildly, but I can't stop. The power of our passion has seized control of us both while the slithering energies of the time stream twist and glide around us, kissing our skin. Neither of us pays any attention to our surroundings. But every time the glittering magics touch us, I grow more aroused. My lust for Felicia has become an unstoppable force.

"Oh, God," Felicia cries out as she throws her head back, exposing the sensual column of her throat. "The magics... They're alive and inside me, just like you."

The bed has begun to leap off the floor with every mutual lunge of our bodies. Her cream dribbles onto my skin, and the scent of her desire intoxicates me more than any drug from any world could do. Her pupils have blown. She seems dazed and ravenous at the same time, and I can't help worrying that I've somehow ensorcelled her without meaning to do so.

But I need to know for certain.

I lash my arms around Fliss to halt her wild movements. The way she abandoned herself to the lust was incredible to watch, but I must make sure. As I brush damp hairs away from her cheek, I keep her hugged to my body. "Fliss, *dulcissima*, are you all right?"

"Oh, yes, fantastic."

The enraptured look on her face doesn't lessen my concerns. I cup her face with both hands, lifting until she finally looks at me. "Fliss, are you certain you're all right?"

She laughs. "You can stop asking me if I'm okay. I'm exhilarated and satisfied and ready for more."

"But you seem almost enthralled. I had no intention of ensorcelling you, and I didn't feel as if I did that, but—"

She pushes up onto her straight arms to aim a squinty stare at me. "You will not worry about anything until after we're done. Got it?" She slaps a hand over my mouth when I try to speak. "You were going to say something guilty, weren't you? That is not allowed. What did I just tell you? Uh-uh, no guilt. So erase that pained look from your face this instant."

Fliss peels her hand away from my mouth.

I can't resist palming her buttocks and smirking at her. "As you wish, *dulcissima*."

"Good." She glides her hands up and down my chest, lightly scraping her nails at the same time. "That was just the appetizer, right? I need more of you, lots more."

"And I need more of you as well, for as long as you can handle it. I can, of course, keep going for days, weeks, perhaps even years." I pretend to consider my claim. "I am immortal, and I rarely grow tired. Our only limitation is what your mortal body can bear."

She drapes herself over me once again. "I'll let you know when I need a break. And I expect you to feed me all sorts of luscious foods to sustain me."

"It will be my pleasure to feed you." I hesitate to ask a question, though only for a moment. Felicia will not strike me, no matter what I ask of her. "How adventurous are you, sexually?"

"Never had a reason to find out the answer to that question. But with you, I'm sure I could be very, very adventurous."

Just to hear her speak those words makes my cock thicken even more and the blood in my veins run as hot as molten metal. The temporal energies begin to gather around us again, clearly sensing that our lust for each other is ramping up.

I conjure a pair of soft leather handcuffs and hold them up. "Do you trust me this much, *dulcissima*?"

"All the way, sweetie." She rolls off me to stretch out on her backside. Then she raises her arms above her head, holding her wrists together as if they were shackled. "Anything you want, I'm game."

"You are wonderful, my sweet."

I wrap my arms around her and teleport us directly to a pillar of the correct size for what I plan to do to and with her. She now stands up against the marble pillar, smiling with sensual sweetness. Her half-closed lids attest to her state of arousal, and the way she catches her bottom lip between her teeth makes it crystal clear. She wants what I want. For the first time in my existence, I have found a woman who will do anything with and for me.

She feels the same way, of that I'm certain.

I gently slide one of the cuffs around her left wrist, then reach behind the slender pillar to attach the other cuff to her right wrist. Now she is at my mercy in the most provocative manner. Her areolas have turned a dusky shade of rose while her nipples protrude, stiff and ready to be tasted.

Fliss wriggles her hips. "Touch me, Janus."

"Soon, *dulcissima*, soon."

She wriggles her entire body this time. "Where in the world did you find such buttery soft leather? It's like nothing I've ever seen on earth."

"You are not in the mortal world. We are inside the temporal pocket realm where my true temple resides." I rake my gaze over her nude body, groaning with a hunger like none I've ever experienced before. "The leather was crafted by magics, the sort only a salamander could conjure."

Her brows wrinkle as she twists her head around to try to see the leather cuffs. "That's bizarre and fascinating at the same time."

"Would you be more comfortable if I said the cuffs were made of the dead flesh of a mortal cow?"

"Oh, no, no, no. These cuffs are amazing, and they make me feel so…'Good' doesn't even cover it."

Now that I have her at my mercy, I move closer until I hover inches away from her body. A flush speckles her chest and cheeks, a sure sign that she wants me to do wicked things to her. I push one knee between her thighs, encouraging her to spread them. Then I glide my hands up her arms to her shoulders, across her collarbone, slowly dragging my fingers down to her breasts, though I avoid her nipples for now.

Fliss has trouble catching her breath. "You're torturing me, and I love it." She bends one knee, exposing her slick pink flesh to me fully. "Lick me, please."

Her plea did not invoke a debt between us. My temple is protected from such things.

She lowers her gaze to my groin and licks her lips.

My mouth gradually slides into a salacious smile. "You enjoy gazing at my *verpa*, don't you? But I have other plans before I let you take it into your mouth. *Futūtiō* is what we both want, but not yet."

"No idea what you're saying, but I don't care."

I chuckle. "You're anxious to have *rigidam* inside you."

"Just do me already."

"As you wish, *dulcissima*." I plaster my body to hers and rub my rigid erection up and down her belly. "Talk to me, Fliss. Tell me what you feel."

"Uhn, so turned on I can't think." She bucks her hips. "Need you inside me right now."

I let my cock drag across her skin as I lower myself into a kneeling position, inch by inch, flicking my tongue out every so often to ensure she stays intensely aroused. Her back arches. I flick my tongue into her navel. She writhes and moans. I bury my face in the hairs on her mound, then snake my tongue out to tease her swollen clitoris. Just to taste her *landīca* makes my cock even stiffer, and a deep groan resonates through my chest.

Fliss throws one leg around my neck to pin my face to her clit.

She needs to come, that much is obvious, especially when she bites down on her lip so hard it turns white. I latch on to her *landīca* once again. This time, I pull her whole clitoris into my mouth to suckle it fiercely. She cries out. Her leg tightens around my neck. Fortunately, I can survive being choked with no ill effects. Wild cries emerge from her while I suckle and lick her nub, rasping my teeth over the head too, until she explodes.

A strangled cry tumbles from her lips while her body tries to fold in on itself but can't quite do that in this position. I thrust two fingers into her sheath. Her inner muscles clench me, but she comes hard enough that she doesn't last long before she collapses against the pillar, struggling to catch her breath.

I hook her other leg around my neck, now shackled by her knees, and surge to my feet. My cock impales itself inside her. Now I am standing upright with her legs locked behind my head while I fuck her, my pace measured at first, then growing wilder with every thrust as her cream dribbles onto my chest and my groans mutate into animalistic grunts and snarls.

The temporal energies gravitate to us. The glittering magics envelop our bodies and the pillar while I fuck her so brutally that her buttocks bounce up and down with every thrust. Then, with a swift flick of my wrist, I vanish the handcuffs and stagger backward while still pummeling Fliss. Her legs remain locked around my neck even while I pull her tightly to my chest.

And then I come.

The pleasure ricochets up and down my spine as my seed erupts inside her womb. A roar erupts out of me, echoing throughout the temple and making the entire structure shudder. When I finally finish, I can't speak. I've lost my breath in the most pleasurable way, and the look on Felicia's face assures me she experienced the same thing. Perhaps making love to her is this intense only because I had remained celibate for more years than any human could count. Perhaps she pretends to enjoy our sensual encounters.

But no, I do not believe that. She has a beautiful soul and would never sully it by lying to me.

I carry Fliss over to the bed and lay her down on the mattress, then conjure a bottle of massage oil and pour a measure onto my palm. She smiles with sweetness and satisfaction, watching as I rub the oil with my palms to warm it up. I begin the massage with her feet. She shivers a touch as I glide my palms up and down her soles.

Felicia links her hands above her head on the pillow. "You sure know how to take care of a woman after mind-blowing sex. I wouldn't have expected that since you told me you'd been celibate for thousands of years."

"Yes, but I had been with females of many species before that—and before Vita—though not often." I slide my hands up her calves, rubbing gently as I go. "Though I was hardly a lothario like Max or Nevan."

Her brows crinkle. "Nevan was a man-whore? He seems like such a straight-up guy."

"And he is—now. But before he met Lindsey, Nevan had been a sylph warrior enslaved by magics, forced to do his king's bidding." I can't help smirking as I explain. "Nevan got his revenge on Notus, the sylph king, by having an affair with his daughter."

"Boy, you supernatural men could star in your own soap opera."

"Lindsey has explained to me what a 'soap opera' is, but it doesn't sound appealing." As I move my palms up her thighs, she shivers with palpable desire. "But I don't wish to discuss anyone else right now. Only you and I."

"You are the best masseur ever."

I pat her hip. "Roll over, *dulcissima*. I want to rub down your backside."

She wriggles about until she's lying on her stomach. "I would love to massage you after this."

"I would like that too."

Fliss glances at me over her shoulder. "But for now, I think we should talk about all the crazy nonsense that's been thrown at us and what it actually means."

"The meaning is clear. Lunatic elementals and gods are trying to drive us both insane."

She shakes her head. "It's more than that, and you know it. Not even the dumbest god in the Unseen would hire incompetent wackos to do their dirty work. Something else is going on here."

"Such as what?" I cup her buttocks and delicately massage them. She moans with pleasure. As I shift my hands to rub her back, I begin to wonder about what she said. "Perhaps you are right. Still, I can't yet fathom what Theo, the kerkopes, and Kali are trying to accomplish. Their actions have begun to seem nonsensical."

"Yes, exactly." She flips onto her back, propping herself up with both elbows. "What if all the nutso things those guys have done were crazy on purpose? To confuse us. To keep us guessing and searching in the wrong direction."

I sit back on my haunches and rub my chin, a habit I've had for longer than Fliss or any of her ancestors have existed. "I suspect your theory is correct. Yet how are we to make sense of the nonsensical?"

"By reevaluating the clues." She sits up and repositions herself cross-legged before me. "Let's go back to the beginning and look at everything with a skeptical eye."

"The beginning? Do you mean the day we met?"

"Yes."

I move into a cross-legged position too, facing Felicia. "On the day we met, I frightened you with my odd behavior and then you drove away in your conveyance. That's how you met Theo."

"Yep." She tries not to smirk but only ends up twisting her lips into a strange expression. "You can call it a car, sweetie. Nobody on earth uses the term 'conveyance.'"

"I realize my terminology is often outdated, but that seems irrelevant at the moment."

"You're right. Sor—Whoops. I almost got myself indebted to you, not that I'd mind being your slave."

"I am already your servant." Mentioning Theo reminds me of the next encounter I had with Felicia. "Theo, whom we now know is a satyr, somehow gathered enough magics to conjure a restaurant, food, and a few patrons. But satyrs, even the highest-ranking ones, don't have that much power."

"And since we now know Theo wasn't working on Dionysus's behalf, that means he got that power from someone else."

"Precisely. He also had the power to glamour and conceal his true nature. But again, a satyr can't summon that much magic on his own."

And that is the most disturbing aspect of what has transpired recently. How am I meant to unravel a Gordian knot that I cannot see or touch or sense? I must do that. I have no choice. *We* have no choice, that is. Only together can Felicia and I solve the Gordian riddle that has become the crux of our dilemma.

Chapter Twenty-Three

Felicia

"Theo claimed he was going to screw me, but he never did anything more threatening than offering me food and saying creepy things." I tap my fingers on my knees for a moment with my head bowed, then lift my gaze to Janus. "On that night in Wisconsin, you said 'something' compelled you to find me, though you didn't know it was me you were looking for. Then you whisked us back to the spot where the restaurant had been earlier, but nothing was there. I remember how you knelt and studied the dirt."

"And I told you I'd sensed dark magics like none I had ever encountered before." Janus compresses his lips as he considers the clues we've amassed so far. I can tell that's what he's doing. Finally, he looks at me. "Theo lied to us at least once. He claimed that he was the dark power that would annihilate me and the entire Unseen, but that is impossible. A satyr has no such power."

"Exactly. And what did he want with me? I bet whoever's in charge of this crazy, evil scheme still hasn't shown their face. The beings we've bumped into so far clearly aren't the bosses of anyone."

Janus folds his arms over his chest. "As I thought back on all the events that led up to this moment, a realization suddenly struck me. Theo can travel through portals—without my permission. He has teleported himself into the mortal world several times. That confirms my suspicion that I have become lax in guarding the portals. I told you once that some creatures from the Unseen have slipped past me. It's rare, yet even if that happened only once, it could have dire consequences."

"Why do you think you've been slipping up? Your job is vital for protecting the Unseen and the mortal world, right?"

He wipes a hand over his mouth, and his lips flatten. "This is all my fault. I should have taken better care of the portals instead of spending time with my descendants. Lindsey and Liam have become important to me, yet that's no excuse for how poorly I've done my job."

"Cut yourself some slack, sweetie. You have the hardest job in the universe."

His lips curl up at one corner. "By what measure have you determined my job is the most difficult?"

"I don't need to measure it. I've seen you in action, and I've listened to everything you told me. That's all the proof I need." But I doubt he will accept my claim. Janus is determined to downplay his importance to the multiverse or even to the Unseen realm. But I still have a few questions. "Theo must have more magics than the average satyr, considering that he breached your temple and kidnapped me."

Janus scrubs a hand over his mouth. "I have failed you in too many ways to count. I should have destroyed Theo then and there, but instead, I hesitated. Theo took you before I moved one inch, and he erected wards around himself and you, the sort I could not break through."

"Ugh, stop that. Not everything is your fault. I wasn't too smart when I walked into a mysterious restaurant alone and didn't leave immediately when I felt how eerie it was." A word he'd used a moment ago resurfaces in my mind, and I need some clarification. "What are 'wards'?"

"Magical barriers. Elementals often use them to deter enemies from breaching their sanctuaries."

"So, it's kind of like a magical burglar alarm."

"I suppose it is." Janus conjures clothing for us both. "We must go now."

"Go where? You must have needed to visit this temple for a reason. I don't believe it was strictly for a round of hot Roman-god sex."

Janus hops off the foot of the bed and starts pacing in front of it. He taps his chin with one finger, humming softly, tunelessly, as if he's thinking. I wish we had time for him to ponder the facts we've laid out together, but we don't. I have no valid explanation for what I feel, but I'm positive time is running out for us. Maybe for the whole multiverse. I know nothing about the multiverse except that, apparently, it holds myriad universes within it, and nobody really understands how it works.

Not helpful at all. I could ask Janus for an in-depth explanation, but I doubt that would clarify anything. I flunked out of science class my junior year of high school and had to redo it the next year. So no, I am not the right woman to expound on the totality of the worlds. I'd probably push the wrong button and detonate the entire multiverse.

Janus halts and turns toward me. "You are correct that I brought you here for more than one reason. When Dasheramal and Kali appeared, I began to wonder about something I'd felt earlier. I brushed it off as nothing at the time, but now I believe I was wrong to do so."

"Are you talking about the spooky sensation you felt in the cavern behind the waterfall?"

His brows shoot up. "How did you know that?"

I crawl across the bed on my hands and knees until my face bumps into his impressive dick and fight the urge to take it into my mouth. Instead, I rise and loop my arms around his neck. "Tell me about that spooky feeling."

He latches his arms around my waist. "A frisson of magical energy had slithered through me, raising every hair on my body. It passed so swiftly that I can't be certain it was anything at all. But not long after, Theo abducted you. At the time, I believed he took you at his master's behest. But I'm not sure of that anymore."

"Yeah, it seems much too coincidental for my taste."

"Coincidences have no flavor."

I'm about to tell him that's not what I meant, but then I notice the slight upward tick of his lips. The formerly uptight god just cracked a joke. I use the word formerly because he is not at all uptight when we're having sex. And he hasn't behaved that way at all since we teleported into this temple of the time stream. The temporal magics chase over my skin every so often, though it's only a faint sensation.

I peck a kiss on his lips. "That was a good one, sweetie. Coincidences might have no flavor, but they do have a smell. One too many of them piling up stinks to high heaven."

"We are in fact much higher than the heavens at the moment. The time stream exists above the multiverse itself."

"That's kind of creepy. But let's get back to your strange feeling in the cavern. What do you think it means?"

"Perhaps the Unseen is sending me a message the only way it can—by giving me an unsettling sensation."

I can't stop my brows from rising or my eyes from widening. "The Unseen is a living thing? That's what you're making it sound like."

"No, the Unseen is not alive. But it is inextricably linked with me in ways that even I do not understand. My powers are derived from the Unseen itself, and in broader terms, the multiverse." He holds up a hand when I'm about to speak. "I cannot give any further explanation of that connection. Though I am well versed in how to use my powers, I have no idea from whence they come."

Damn. I was hoping to get all the juicy details about his powers. Of course, I can't explain how my own brain works. It wouldn't be fair to expect him to know everything about himself.

His use of the word whence makes me want to kiss him. His perfect grammar reminds me of my high school English teacher, Mr. Sampson, who all the girls would swoon over, including me. But Janus is the sexiest man bar none. Not even Mr. Sampson could complete.

Janus scratches his neck while staring past my shoulder—at nothing, I imagine. He often gets that look on his face when he can't figure something out. He's probably trying to work out these conundrums in his mind before he offers up his take on our problems.

I sit down on the bed and let my legs dangle over the edge. "You know, just because Dionysus and Theo don't seem to be the ones in charge of this bizarre operation doesn't mean Theo wasn't acting on the orders of some other powerful being."

"But who could it be? That's the dilemma." He resumes pacing along the length of the bed's foot, clasping his hands behind his back. After the third circuit, he abruptly stops and swivels his head toward me. "There is one way to solve this mystery."

I tip my head back to look into his eyes. They're shimmering with iridescent gold. Gazing into those irises gives me a shiver that's both chilly and hot. That sounds impossible, but here in the time stream, I suppose anything goes. "What's your idea, sweetie?"

"We must gather all the involved parties in one location. That would include Theo, Dionysus, Freknel and Stiodel, Dasheramal, and Kali."

"Okay. How do we manage that? They've been able to traipse in and out of portals without your permission."

His mouth slides into a self-satisfied smile. "I am no longer alone and weary of my duties. You have played a significant role in my transformation. Until we came to this place, I had not visited my temple in ages. But you awakened my soul and inspired me to bring you here. My powers are always the strongest in the time stream and especially in this temple."

"Don't give me all the credit. I was happy to help, but you figuring everything out was a joint effort."

"Indeed it was." He crouches in front of me, setting his hands on my knees. "Felicia, I love you."

My heart swells, and the hairs on my arms and at my nape stiffen. It doesn't disturb me, though. His words have electrified me in the sweetest way. "I love you too, Janus."

"Does it not unsettle you, *dulcissima*? We've known each other for such a short time."

I kiss his forehead. "What I feel for you is the best thing that's ever happened to me, and I've always had a tendency to move fast. I dated my ex-husband for nine days before we got engaged, then we tied the knot in Vegas a week later. Maybe I should've slowed down to save myself from heartache. But I know you will never break my heart."

He kisses my hand. "And you would never break my heart either. We are two halves of a coin." He freezes, as if he just thought of something. "In fact, that is demonstrably what you are to me."

"Not sure what you mean."

Janus closes one hand, then springs it open. In the center of his palm lies a coin. He bows his head to study the coin, flipping it over several times. Then he looks at me and smiles, dimpling his cheeks. "I was right. I am the obverse, and you are the reverse."

"Huh? I'm no coin expert, so you need to explain that."

"Any coin has an obverse, or front side, as well as a reverse, or back side. You must have seen this on coins in the mortal world."

"Sure. But in the modern human world, coins are just currency."

"The Unseen is different." He closes his fingers around the coin again. "Open your hand palm up, if you will, and I shall demonstrate the truth of my assertion."

I still don't get what he's trying to prove, but I'll roll with it. So, I turn my hand over and spread my palm.

Janus lays the coin on my skin. "What you see on the obverse is a depiction of me wearing a toga and a crown of laurels. I'm shown with two faces, one looking left and the other right. This is simply a graphical representation of my powers, which are far-reaching."

"That makes sense."

"As for your connection to the coin...flip it over and you'll see."

I flip the coin—and my mouth falls open. "That almost looks like..."

"You, my love. The other side of the Janus coin depicts you. Only since you came into my life has the reverse of the coin changed. The time stream knows you belong with me."

"It's that smart, huh?"

"Yes. Does that bother you?"

I lift the coin and kiss the side that features his face. "Does that answer your question?"

"Quite well, yes." He rises and offers me his hand. "Come, *dulcissima*, we have much work to do to gather the six beings we need to interrogate."

I get up too and stretch my whole body. "Well, it just figures. One round of hot sex, then you're ready to go play with your friends."

He tugs me into his body. "We will play together alone as soon as possible. Although this is the time stream, and I control it, so I could rewind our fucking to let us relive it as many times as you like."

"That sounds wonderful. But we'd better behave like mature adults and go kidnap six bad guys."

"One of them is female. That means five bad guys and one bad girl."

"Mortals often use the word guy in a more general sense." I pat his chest. "You need to learn more about mortal slang."

"Perhaps you could teach me."

I stand on my toes to kiss him. "You need to teach me dirty Latin. I have no idea what most of those phrases you used mean."

"Another time."

"I'll hold you to that."

He hugs me even more firmly, then whisks us away.

Chapter Twenty-Four

Janus

WE MATERIALIZE IN THE SAME LOCATION FROM whence we had departed, in the exact moment that we had left. Our friends do not realize Felicia and I had experienced at least an hour inside the heart of the time stream. Trying to explain that to them might prove difficult. Perhaps we don't need to explain. I dislike needing to expound on my theories and suspicions. Rarely does anyone appreciate them.

Felicia does. No one else's opinion matters to me.

Returning to the same place and moment means we're standing in the forest again, in a small meadow, with the rumble of the falls faintly audible. I take Felicia's hand. "We will need the assistance of all our friends in this endeavor. Let's go."

She doesn't complain that I've made a decision without asking for her input. Fliss understands the gravity of our situation and the need for alacrity. I could teleport us back to the waterfall path, but I prefer not to waste even one iota of energy unnecessarily. The task ahead of us will be arduous.

We jog to the clearing, and all our friends are still here.

Of course they are. For them, only a few milliseconds have passed.

Tris eyes us both while smirking. "Back already? I've heard of quickies, but not that quick."

Max smirks. "Couldn't get it up, eh, Janus?"

"Janus is a god," Felicia tells him. "And he *is* the time stream, so stop harassing him. We have important things to talk about."

"No teasing the god, then? How boring."

I conjure my sword, turning it this way and that to make the metal gleam and glint off the edges. "This is an endued sword that could destroy any of you. Be silent and listen for a change."

Max raises his hands. "All right, all right."

"Felicia and I have developed a plan. This is step one." I hoist my chin and gaze imperiously at the elementals gathered here. They expect me to be imperious, after all. I can't disappoint them. "We must gather the six beings who have been complicit in whatever plot their master has devised."

Travis raises his hand.

"Yes, what is it?"

"Why did you say 'six beings' are complicit? Kali is their master. That means only five are conspirators."

I shake my head. "Felicia and I learned much during our sojourn in the temple at the heart of the temporal world. And I realized that we have been looking at everything in the wrong way. Theo, Dionysus, Freknel, Stiodel, Dasheramal, and Kali are all pawns of the Dark One."

"But that bird Kali said she was the Dark One."

I can't stop myself from rolling my eyes at Travis. "Before Kali declared she was the Dark One, Theo also proclaimed that of himself. Don't you see the pattern? They are all pawns whose sole purpose is to confuse and distract us."

Tris folds his arms over his chest and puckers his lips. "What's the big plan, then? We're still screwed, we still know nothing, and we still have no clue who the Big Bad is."

"I told you the plan, Triskaideka. Do you have wax in your ears? That is the only explanation for you ignorance. Once more, the plan is that we must gather all six of the aforementioned beings and interrogate them."

"Wax in my ears?" Tris repeats with a chuckle. "Felicia must be teaching you how to have a sense of humor. Needs work, though."

I have no time for his moronic jokes, and so I behave as if I didn't hear what he said. "Max, Travis, Tris, Felicia, and I must capture the beings in question." I glance around the clearing. "What happened to Cyneric? I summoned him here as well."

155

Travis huffs. "You know the vamp. He does what he wants and screw everyone else."

I suck in a deep breath and bellow, "Cyneric!"

The vampire appears instantly, scanning the clearing in a casual manner. He brushes off his leather coat and aims his pale blue eyes at me. "I was about to shag Amanda. I hope you summoned me away from her for a valid reason. I'm getting thirsty."

"You will be able to feed soon, don't worry. But right now, we need all of our gang here."

"Why?" Cyneric never seems perplexed or angry unless a villain arouses his blood lust. That single syllable—why—sounded almost placid.

I approach him, staring down at the vampire who is somewhat shorter than I am. "The reason is simple. I summoned you. The rest I shall explain shortly."

Max trots over to us and slaps the vampire's arm. "Janus ticked off a horde of gods and elementals, and now he wants us to help capture them. Piece of cake, eh?"

Cyneric gazes coolly at the salamander. "I don't eat cake."

His emphasis on the word cake makes his meaning clear. He survives on blood, not food.

I push Max away.

He taps my shoulder. "Ah, just out of curiosity, how the bloody hell are we meant to capture these wankers? They're slippery buggers."

"Yeah, Max is right," Travis interjects. "You've been sort of forgetful about maintaining the portals. No offense, mate."

I do take offense, but saying so will not help. Instead, I tell the others, "I am going to shore up the portals with the additional magics I acquired in the time stream."

"You mean when you shagged Felicia in the time stream, right?" He holds up his hands. "Not trying to annoy you. It's dead obvious, that's all."

I suppose it is. Making love to Felicia in the time stream temple injected me with enough magics that I'm certain I could do anything, even lift the entire universe with my bare hands. But I'll keep that information to myself. The others wouldn't understand.

And they would tease me. It's quite annoying.

Cyneric aims his cool gaze at me once more. "We can't retrieve six powerful beings with only four of us."

I consider his assertion, and my shoulders flag. "You're correct. We need more beings on our side, especially if we're going to capture Dionysus and Kali. We must gather as many allies as possible."

"Tell us who we should abduct, and we'll do it."

I sigh. "Cyneric, how many times have I told you that we don't do such things? We are the heroes, not the villains."

Max tries to repress a laugh, but he winds up spluttering. "I don't think Cyneric got that memo. But maybe he just doesn't understand what 'abduct' actually means."

"He knows, and he is deliberately trying to annoy me." I take another, deeper breath, and exhale it gradually. "We have more allies, though I have resisted calling upon the females. Harper has powers. So do Riley, Ennea, and Pendi. Quindecim may also be useful. I hesitate to call on Larissa, since she has no magics, though she possesses a great deal of knowledge about the Unseen thanks to being a former goddess."

Felicia has remained in the background, but now she moves up beside me. "Is ten enough? I mean, we're hunting down powerful beings including two gods."

Cyneric lifts one brow. "I hope Janus isn't going to let you participate in this mass abduction of evil beings. You have no powers."

That isn't entirely true, but I don't care to discuss it with anyone other than Felicia.

Max's eyes go wide. "The bloodsucking fiend cares about someone other than Amanda? It's a miracle."

Two beings materialize behind us. I sense their presence and instantly know who they are, so I turn toward them. "Why are you two here? I can't believe you intend to participate in my plan."

The oracles Bob and Ken both give me harried looks, but only Bob speaks. "You wanted our help, and so we came."

"I didn't summon you."

"Not consciously. But you've been worrying about how much backup you might need on this quest to hunt down those rotten imbeciles." He spreads his arms. "And here is your answer. Ken and I have powers beyond anyone but yours. But if you don't want our help…"

"We will accept your assistance."

Ken clears his throat. "We have a few gifts for you, including the ones you've chosen, and we hope you'll accept the others at face value. They are here to help, after all."

Bob snorts. "Ken should have warned you. Don't look these gift elementals in the mouth."

The oracle waves his hand.

Harper, Larissa, and Riley appear first and approach their husbands. Then Pendi, Ennea, and Quin materialize. They are all copper fae, just like Riley and Tris.

I nod to each of the newcomers. "Now we may begin—"

"Ah-ah-ah," Bob says while wagging his finger at me. "You don't want to insult the others by beginning your speech without them."

"What others?"

"Do bear in mind that they have volunteered to take part."

Before I can even open my mouth to protest, two more beings appear.

And I swerve my squinted gaze to the oracles. "Have you two lost your minds? I cannot allow a Valkyrie and a succubus on the team. At least Sigrun is a warrior. But Anthea...All she can bring to the table is lust."

Bob sighs heavily, giving me a long-suffering look. "Was I misinformed by my own foresight? The answer is no. I would never have invited Anthea without a bloody good reason."

"And that would be…"

He lifts his chin, gazing at me down the bridge of his nose. "Two of the beings you intend to abduct are a satyr and a sex god. Don't you think Anthea might be useful in capturing Dionysus and Theo?"

"All right, yes, I do see their value now." I glance at Max and lift my brows. "Are you capable of playing nice with Anthea?"

Before Max can speak, Riley shoves him aside. "Better ask me that question. I was kidnapped by the succubus, and I got to know her a little during that time. Then Cyneric freed me." She winks at the vampire. "He had the most intimate experience with Anthea."

"Yes, we are all aware of the fact that Cyneric let Anthea seduce him. Let's move on to the details of my plan."

For the next fifteen minutes, I lay out the specifics and listen to the concerns and suggestions of my friends. Sigrun and Max both have significant battle experience in their pasts, and so I invite them to provide options for fighting our way out of any "sticky situations," as Felicia describes it. Travis was once a mortal sheriff, and that gives him a unique perspective on hunting for fugitive elementals. Harper is quite skilled with various types of knives and swords, not to mention firearms.

158

The fae Quindecim, who prefers to be called Quin, is Tris's brother. They both fought in the battle between Tris and the now-deceased dragon prince Drakon. Ennea is a fae witch who concocts powerful spells, potions, and other sorts of magical mixtures. Tris is the guardian of the healing vortex that lies here on the property of the rock shop. Pendi, like Tris, also guards a vortex—though in a location far distant from this one.

Unfortunately, their healing skills might become necessary. I pray no one will die in this endeavor, but even as we stand here discussing our plans, I can sense darkness rising from the depths of the Unseen. I should tell everyone about that.

And so, I do.

Sigrun eyes me with suspicion. "Darkness rising from the depths of the Unseen? For you to say such a thing means whatever we're facing is like nothing ever encountered in the multiverse. Are you positive this isn't simply anxiety?"

I fist my hands and compress my lips. "Yes, I am certain."

Felicia clasps my hand, erasing all my irritation with that simple act.

Quin balks at my description of his usefulness. "I can do way more than watch Tris fight a dragon, you know. I served in the fae army, unlike my whiny brother. Can't tell you how many times my regiment was dispatched to chop down a gnome who had a grudge against…Well, pretty much anybody. Gnomes aren't famous for their self-control."

"Your army experience will be quite useful. I'm glad you shared it with us."

Another being materializes.

Everyone in this clearing freezes and stares at the creature. He seems to be a vampire, yet I don't recognize him. My ability to see in all directions does not give me the sort of foresight the oracles possess.

The vampire smirks. "None of you recognize me, do you?"

I shuffle closer to him, intently studying this being but having no more luck determining who he is.

The vampire's lips spread into a smug smile. "Shall I introduce myself?"

"Do so before I grow tired of your games and destroy you." I conjure my sword to make that point clear. "Who are you?"

The creature chuckles, then leans around me to grin at someone else. "Tell your friend who I am. Or are you going to pretend we

159

haven't been hanging out together for months here in the mortal world? We're chums."

I glance over my shoulder at Cyneric. "Do you know this creature?"

Max and Harper stomp up beside me. Harper points an accusing finger at the newcomer. "He looks a lot different from the last time we saw him. But yeah, Max and I know this guy. His name is Gundisalvus, and he used to be one of Hathor's flunkies, along with Sigrun."

"Are we meant to trust these two?" Max asks. "Gunny is a villain. Not entirely comfortable with Sigrun either, for the same reason. Maybe we should rethink letting them help us."

Larissa marches up to me on my other side, so that now I am surrounded by angry females. "You shouldn't judge Gundisalvus by how he behaved back then." She bites her upper lip and hunches her shoulders. "I used to, um, ensorcell everyone I brought into my temple. Sigrun and Gundisalvus weren't in control of their own actions."

I consider Larissa's statements. "We shall accept him into our group with Cyneric's approval. And he will be responsible for any bad behavior from"—I wave my hand toward Gundisalvus—"this one. Are you prepared for that, Cyneric?"

He nods.

"Now, we must determine which of us will pursue which of our quarry." My gaze returns to Larissa, and I suddenly realize what I must do. "Only one of us is mortal. However, Larissa possesses a depth of knowledge garnered over thousands of years that may prove essential. She will remain here in the clearing to provide information as needed. Therefore, I will grant her temporary powers to cloak herself and make her immune to any and all sorts of personal harm. Do you agree with this, Larissa?"

She gives me a somewhat grim smile. "Yes, I'm ready."

"Now, I will assign the rest of you to your teams."

Chapter Twenty-Five

Felicia

I NEVER COULD HAVE IMAGINED I'D WIND UP PARTICI-pating in a hunt for supernatural villains with a bunch of su-pernatural beings as the bounty hunters. Well, there's no payment involved. I probably shouldn't call them bounty hunters, but I can't think of another word for it. Janus and I give our fourteen hunters their marching orders, splitting them off in pairs. We took a moment to discuss how to form the best matchups.

Nobody balked at our choices. We chose complementary pairs. For now, this will be reconnaissance only to figure out where our six baddies are hiding out and how much backup they'll have from their followers.

We've given out the assignments—Max and Riley, Travis and Sigrun, Tris and Cyneric, Harper and Anthea, Bob and Pendi, Ken and Quin, Ennea and Gundisalvus. Aside from Travis and Sigrun, who are both warriors of a sort, the other pairs contrast each other. Janus and I hope this will bring bet-ter, faster results. The last thing any of us wants to do is spend days or weeks hunting for ways to subdue the six powerful beings.

Janus has that covered, though. And he announces the final step of his plan before dispatching our hunters. "While you are hunting, I will grant you the temporary power to freeze time. Use this power judiciously. I will be watching over all of you through-out this mission at all times."

Larissa seems shocked. "You can watch all of us at the same time?"

"Yes." He conjures the Janus coin and sets it on the tip of his finger. The coin slowly rotates. "Just as this coin has two sides, I also have two faces that allow me to see ahead and behind. I will always know where you are during this mission." He poofs the coin away. "Be vigilant and take care of each other. Now, be on your way."

Our fourteen hunters pair up and vanish. That leaves me, Janus, and Larissa in the clearing.

Janus approaches Larissa and waves his palm in front of her face. "You are now invested with all the magics you'll need for this mission. I recommend you obscure yourself as a safety mea-sure."

I squint at Larissa. "She looks the same. I guess the obscuring thing didn't work."

"Of course it worked. My powers are infallible. You and I can still see her, and she can see us, because we are immune to the mag-ics I gifted to her." He gives me a long-suffering look. "If I made her invisible to our eyes and her voice inaudible, how would we find her or hear anything she has to say?"

"Good point."

He looks at Larissa. "Felicia and I will retreat into the cavern behind the falls. That's where I sensed a strange, slithering type of energy unlike anything I've experienced before. It must be related to our current problems. Remain vigilant, and do not hesitate to scream if you need us."

"Scream?" Larissa says, clearly confused. "Won't you sense if I'm in trouble?"

"Yes, that should be the case. But nothing has been as it should be of late." He clasps her hands, softening his voice. "Don't worry, child, I won't let anyone or anything harm you."

With that final reassurance for Larissa, he whisks us away to the cavern.

The falls tumble down the cliff mere feet away from us, but the magics inside the cavern dull the roar of the water. The pock-marked floor is slightly treacherous for walking, but Janus keeps his arm around my waist, hugging me to him for support—physically and emotionally. Yeah, I can't deny this place gives me the willies. Janus had told me once that the cavern isn't supposed to affect anyone that way. What I sense now is dark magics, apparently.

Janus didn't create that garbage. Someone else left the remnants of those dark energies in this place.

I can't believe we're kidnapping two gods and four powerful elementals.

"What if our teams fail?" I ask. "If they can't find their quarry, this whole plan will fall apart."

"Do you have so little faith in me? I have a backup plan."

"Why didn't you tell me that?"

He shrugs one shoulder. "I forgot. We have been rather busy of late."

"Okay, I forgive you for not sharing your backup plan with me." I gaze up at him. "Will you tell me now?"

"Yes, *mea lux*, I will." He turns toward me to wrap both arms around my waist. "I will invoke the time stream itself to lead us to our quarry."

"Is that dangerous?"

He kisses my forehead. "Don't worry."

"That doesn't answer my question."

"I can't promise you that nothing adverse will occur. However, I won't permit anyone or anything to harm you as long as I exist."

This man knows how to craft a solid magic-free vow, that's for sure. I feel better even though he didn't really answer my question. Whatever happens, we'll handle it together.

Janus crouches to examine the damp rock floor of the cavern. The pockmarked surface makes it harder to walk without slipping, though that doesn't bother him at all. I have to navigate around the holes. Though he seems to be laser focused on studying the floor, I can tell he's also keeping an eye on me out of the corner of his eye. His power to see forward and backward gives him an unerring ability to do that.

I wander around the cavern since I have nothing else to do.

Janus pinches his lips, then scuttles across the floor to examine another spot.

This cavern gives me the creeps, but I also feel something else. It's hard to describe. Is it possible to experience unease and solace simultaneously? A few days ago, I would've adamantly denied it. But now...

How can I dismiss any weird thing as impossible? I'm sleeping with a literal god, for pity's sake. And I'm in love with that god. Yeah, my life is crazy in the best way.

As I approach the rear wall, a faint shiver raises goosebumps on my skin. I halt and analyze the area, then drop to my knees for a closer look. This little patch of rock features water-filled pockmarks just like the rest of the cavern. But the water itself shimmers with a strange purplish hue. It reminds me of an oil slick, except for the odd color.

"Could you come over here, sweetie," I call out to Janus. "Need your expert opinion on this."

"On what?"

"Get over here and you'll find out."

He saunters up to me. "What did you need me to see?"

"The water in these holes is shimmering purple. Is that normal? I realize this is a supernatural cavern, but still—"

He squats beside me. "This is not normal, not even in the context of the Unseen realm. You are correct to be suspicious."

"Glad I wasn't just imagining it."

Janus dips his fingers into the closest hole and swishes them around. When he lifts his hand, the purplish color clings to his flesh. Clearly perplexed, he raises his fingers to his nose and sniffs a few times. His brows hike up briefly. Then they knit together. He sniffs his fingers again, and this time, his head pops up and his eyes widen.

I scuffle closer to him. "What did you sense?"

"Something that should not be." Janus raises his wet, purplish finger to his lips and…thrusts it into his mouth. His nose crinkles. He removes his finger from his mouth and spits out the purplish gunk. "I would recognize the vile taste of the darkest magics even if I'd lost all my senses. The being who traveled through this portal recently is a purveyor of black spells on a scale none but the most ancient beings would even attempt."

"I don't suppose you have any idea who that being is."

He rises and offers me his hand to help me up. "I believe I do know their identity. But it cannot be."

The shock in his voice convinces me that whoever the bad guy is, that being scares even Janus. Not good. Not good at all.

I grasp his arm, gazing up at him, dismayed by his shock. "Who is the Dark One?"

"Kronos, the Devourer of Time."

"Are you sure?"

He nods gravely. "No other being would leave behind this sort of signature. Elementals never leave visible evidence of their magics, and neither do most gods. Only the most powerful and terrible among them is capable of crafting a deliberate trail to lead us where they want us to go."

"I thought Kronos was a time god like you."

"Technically, yes, in Greek mythology. But Kronos the god of the Unseen is a different creature altogether. In myth, he was king of the Titans who ruled the cosmos. But he was a devouring force, a destructor of time rather than a guardian of it."

My mind is spinning already after what he just told me, but I know he isn't done explaining yet. If my head explodes, I hope he can cobble it back together.

Janus pulls me close, turning us both toward the portal—or where it would be if someone activated it. "The Kronos of the Unseen is a devouring force, consuming time like a drug, never bothering to amass followers because beings in the Unseen fear his awesome power. And I mean 'awesome' in its most literal sense."

"You mean 'awesome' as in 'terrible,' right?"

He nods gravely. "Kronos has remained in hiding for eons, ever since I refused to let him into the time stream. You see, my powers are vaster than that of any other being in the Unseen realm. Kronos has always coveted the time stream, coveted my powers. Now, it seems, he has at last found a means of trying to appropriate them— or he believes he has done so."

"Why would he call himself the Dark One? Is it because he's so evil?"

Janus shakes his head. "The term dark also means 'ambiguous.' He and his minions have been intentionally vague. They use that ambiguity as a tool to confuse us."

"No kidding. They've been acting like nutjobs. But I'm sure you're right. They behaved that way on purpose."

"We still have many mysteries to unravel, but at least one has been solved." I glance down at the eerie purple oil slick, and the hairs at my nape stiffen. "If Kronos devours time, doesn't that mean he could defeat you?"

"No. He lost that power eons ago when The Four Winds stripped him of it, though he continued calling himself the Devourer of Time."

"Isn't it possible that he found a way to regain his lost powers?"
Janus shrugs.

For a god to seem helpless does not bode well for the health and longevity of the mortal world or the Unseen.

I grip his arm so tightly that my fingers dig into his flesh, though he doesn't seem to notice. "What about our friends who are out there hunting for half a dozen evil jerks? If Kronos has regained his powers…"

Janus jerks his head to look at me, his eyes wide again. "We must warn them."

A flash of lightning blinds us, then a crack of thunder reverberates through the cavern from outside. The blast makes the ground shudder so violently that we almost fall down. Only Janus's extraordinary calmness and fortitude prevents that. Chunks of the cliff tumble down from the head of the falls to crash into the water so hard that small geysers burst upward. I can just see them through the cascade.

Janus whisks us out of the cavern, straight into the clearing where Larissa waits for us. She seems alarmed, for sure, but keeps her cool far better than I would have expected under the circumstances. Janus gives her a quick hug that seems to stun her more than the explosion had, but she recovers from the surprise quickly.

I slip an arm around Larissa. "Are you okay? That was the loudest sound I've ever heard."

"Oh, I've heard much louder things. When Eros and Setesh fought over me, the noise of their battle ricocheted through the Unseen."

"Never had men fight over me that strenuously."

"Be grateful you haven't. Those two weren't battling for my love. They were trying to determine who would get to ensorcell me."

"I see your point."

While I was chatting with Larissa, Janus had started circling the clearing with his head tipped back as if he were studying the sky. The rumbling and the landslide ended as soon as we exited the cavern. But Janus hasn't stopped searching the area visually, as if he expects worse trouble to fall out of the sky at any moment.

Kronos-shaped trouble? I hope not.

Janus veers his attention to me and Larissa, then tackles us both to the ground with himself on top. He's shielding us. But from what? I can't see anything with Janus's big body covering me like a muscular curtain.

A high-pitched sound, like a missile heading straight down from the sky, whistles through the air, growing louder and closer every second. Tree branches crack as the object crashes through the woods. The whistling becomes a prolonged, angry cry as the object slams into the ground with a loud *whump*.

Janus jumps up with me and Larissa in his arms, then sets us down as he approaches the man-shaped missile lying prone on the ground. "Tris? What in the worlds are you playing at? You were to stay with Cyneric."

Tris scrambles to his feet. His hair and clothes are a mess, and he looks completely frazzled, not to mention ticked off. He glowers at Janus. "You didn't warn us about the big, bad monster who likes to chuck elementals into the Unseen with his bare hands."

"What did this 'monster' look like?"

Another man-shaped missile sails downward from the sky, though he doesn't shout. Cyneric smacks into the earth on his back. For a few seconds, he just lies there as if he's dead. But then the vampire hops up and brushes himself off as if getting slammed into the ground from the upper atmosphere is just another day at work for him.

Janus folds his arms over his chest as he glares at the vampire. "I assume you were also ejected from the Unseen in the same manner as Tris."

"Yes." Cyneric's mouth tightens, and his eyes narrow. "I do not appreciate being treated in this manner. I want to hunt down that enormous wanker and use his body to drill down to the earth's core."

So far, our plan has gone sideways in spectacular fashion. Maybe the other teams will have better luck. I mean, things can't possibly get any worse. Right?

Then more noise erupts overhead, and my hopes are dashed.

CHAPTER TWENTY-SIX

Janus

IWANT TO ASK CYNERIC WHAT "ENORMOUS WANKER" he was referring to, but I have much more pressing issues to deal with right now. Our teams are being systematically tossed out of the Unseen like meteors aimed at the mortal world. However, those objects are living beings, not missiles. I did not permit anyone to enter the Unseen, not even my friends who had been diligently working on their missions.

They could have been severely injured. It's my fault.

If Kronos is the cause of this tumult, then we have a much larger problem than I anticipated.

"How could anyone but you eject us from the Unseen?" Cyneric asks. "Maybe your powers aren't as vast as you claim, Janus."

"Of course they are." I rake my gaze over the vampire. "Perhaps you will describe your attacker to me, Cyneric."

More high-pitched whistling erupts in the sky as multiple voices howl and shout. They crash down in a pile of six jumbled bodies. They aren't dead. They don't even seem to be injured. They have simply become entangled. For a moment, I can't tell who's who because they're all sniping at each other and struggling to extricate their bodies. Once they've accomplished that feat, they face the rest of us.

Bob and Ken gravitate to each other, despite the fact they had been on different teams for the hunting expedition. The oracles both scowl at Pendi and Quin, who seem quite annoyed by Bob and Ken's reaction.

Ken brushes off his clothes and conjures a comb to fix his hair. "What the hell just happened? I don't like being flung through the air like a cannonball."

Bob huffs. "Neither do I. You leprechauns need more flying lessons."

"We aren't birds or planes," Quin snaps. "When you fly Air Fae, you get what you get."

Quin holds one arm around Pendi, who seems less affronted by what happened than either of her brothers or the oracles do.

Tris frowns at Bob and Ken. "Why didn't you boneheads warn us about the big, bad monster who has a serious hard-on for flinging elementals out of the Unseen? So much for the all-seeing oracles. You guys suck."

That ear-piercing whistling starts up again, this time accompanied by a woman's ear-splitting scream. When Max and Riley hit the ground, the salamander lies beneath her on his back as if he intended to cushion her fall with his own body. How chivalrous, and unexpected. Max springs off the ground, setting Riley on her feet.

Before anyone has a chance to speak to the newcomers, that blasted whistling recommences. Trees crack. Branches tumble to the earth. Oddly, this time there seems to be no screaming or shouting. Travis and Sigrun land in a heap on the ground but quickly disentangle.

Sigrun brushes off her clothing while her lips form a smug smile. "That was invigorating."

Travis shakes his head at her. "You're one twisted piece of work. But I can't deny you're a bad-ass warrior."

He hurries over to Larissa and wraps his arms around his wife, kissing her forehead. "You okay, baby?"

"Fine. What about you? That fall might've ground you into dirt."

"Nah."

She punches his chest. "You aren't immortal anymore, remember? Still a salamander, but one hundred percent mortal."

He shoves his hands under her bottom and hoists her up until their mouths align. Then he kisses her as if the multiverse might explode in the next few minutes. Maybe the apocalypse is coming. Who am I to say it isn't? By the time Travis releases Larissa, her cheeks are pink, and her lips are swollen.

Two more living missiles impact the earth. Harper is pinned beneath the succubus Anthea, who seems to be attempting to undress Harper. Max's beloved slugs Anthea in the gut, causing the succubus to stumble sideways and stagger toward me.

I employ a small burst of power to subdue her.

Anthea has no interest in me, though. Her salacious grin is aimed at Harper. "Come, little girl, you know I can give you orgasms the likes of which no male in any world could provide."

Harper rolls her eyes. "How many times do I have to tell you? I will never have sex with you. Never, never, never. You're way too creepy." Harper waves toward Cyneric. "He's more your type."

The vampire bares his fangs and hisses. I assume that indicates a rejection of Harper's idea.

When Anthea moves toward Harper, Max leaps out to drag her away from his wife. "Keep your ruddy paws off Harper. Nobody here wants to shag a filthy slag like you. I bet you don't even take a bath afterward."

The final two living missiles crash down, but not together as the others had done. Ennea hits the ground first, followed a few seconds later by Gundisalvus. The fae witch has just brushed the grime off her clothing when the vampire arrives. He immediately rushes at her, clearly intent on dragging her into his arms.

Ennea throws out a small pulse of magics to stop him in his tracks. Quite literally. He freezes. She sets her hands on her hips and lifts her chin. "That'll teach you to mess with a fae witch."

Bob lifts his chin to gaze with disdain at Gundisalvus. "I told you to play by our rules, vampire. That was the deal when Ken and I summoned you. If you can't accept orders, perhaps we should transmute you into a toad."

The vampire sniggers. "You need me. There's no other reason why two oracles would beg me for help."

Max pushes past Gundisalvus, nearly knocking him down in the process, and jabs a finger in the air near the vampire's face. "No one begged for your help. We let you tag along, and if you touch any of these women—"

"Enough!" I bellow so loudly that the trees shiver and my voice echoes off the waterfall cliff. Now that everyone has ceased talking, I survey the group. "Shouting at each other will not solve our immediate problems. Felicia and I have discovered who our true enemy is, the being calling himself the Dark One."

Everyone watches me and waits.

Until Pendi thrusts her arm into the air and waves it about like a child trying to gain her parents' attention.

I nod to her. "Yes, Pendi, what is your question?"

"How long are you going to stand there looking haughty before you tell us who the Dark One is?"

"Precisely one second. The Dark One is Kronos."

All my friends, and even Gundisalvus and Anthea, wait for me to explain. I give them a moment to absorb the information I've just delivered. I realize this is a shock and completely unexpected.

Finally, Tris clears his throat. "Uh, I thought Kronos got blown to smithereens in the last battle of the Titans."

I resist the impulse to make a curt remark, though I must point out the obvious. "The Titans are gods. They cannot be destroyed in the manner of an elemental. You know this."

"Yeah, okay, I'm still kinda dizzy from getting lobbed into the mortal world like a giant baseball."

I have no idea what the word baseball means, and it hardly matters right now.

Cyneric huffs. "I am not a baseball, whatever that is. You and I were flesh-based missiles."

I snarl through my gritted teeth. "Would you all be silent? I have more to tell you."

Felicia sidles up to me, wrapping her arm around mine. She speaks softly so no one else will hear. "Don't be too hard on them. I'm amazed none of the gang got seriously injured when Kronos ejected them from the Unseen."

Bob sprints up to me, seeming more disturbed than I've ever seen him before. "Kronos ejected us? That is a very distressing sign."

"I am aware of that. Kronos should not have that much power, and yet he seems more potent than ever, despite what his fellow Titans did to him during the last battle."

Pendi raises her arm again, waving it about. This time, she doesn't wait for me to acknowledge her. "What did the Titans do?"

"They, ah…castrated him. But I believe his member grew back."

Max makes a disgusted face. "Why the bloody hell did they do that to the bloke? Kronos isn't a sex god like Dionysus. I doubt the bloke even noticed when they, ah, nipped him in the bud."

"I'm certain he did notice. However, Kronos doesn't seem to have been slowed down by that incident. Somehow, he has amassed dark magics of the vilest nature." I scan the group, making eye contact with each of them. "I cannot ask you to assist me in whatever comes next. All of you, except for the oracles, are elementals who can be destroyed far too easily. I would never have sent you out to hunt for Theo and the others if I'd known who our true enemy was. You should go home."

"Like hell we will," Quin declares. "Everyone here, except for Anthea, has fought in epic battles more times than we can count. You aren't getting rid of us, Janus. Tell us the new plan."

The rest of the gang voices their agreement with various noises and words.

Harper points at Anthea. "Should we send the succubus packing? She isn't much good for fighting, or anything else other than screwing."

"On the contrary," Bob says. "Ken and I suggested bringing Anthea along because we shared the same insight about the pivotal role she will play in the coming battle."

Tris's jaw slackens, and his brows knit together. "What, is she gonna slap her boobs in the enemies' faces to confuse them?"

"You forget that two of the beings we're looking for are sexual creatures—Dionysus and the satyr Silenus, or Theo as he seems to prefer."

I tip my head toward Bob. "The oracle is correct. Anthea will remain with us, if she chooses."

The succubus grins. "Oh, Janus, you stud. I'll go anywhere for you."

"Hands off the god," Felicia pronounces. "He's taken."

I study the succubus. "Anthea, are you certain you want to participate in what might come next? I trust Bob's foresight, but—"

Anthea abruptly drops her temptress persona and speaks in a steady voice. "I fought with the Amazons back in the day, before the Titans eradicated them. Those women taught me a lot about warfare."

I tuck my chin, stunned by her confession. "In that case, we welcome you to our small army." I clear my throat. "But you should, ah, conjure some appropriate clothing. I will dispense the weapons."

Sigrun crosses her arms over her chest. "Are we continuing with the same teams?"

"No. We will all enter the Unseen together this time." I turn to the oracles. "Bob, Ken, I'm relying on you to provide insight. However, Kronos is a time god. Will that cause any issues with your ability to see into the future?"

Bob flicks his gaze toward the sky briefly, then blusters out a sigh. "Who the bloody hell knows? Kronos isn't a normal god. He is the Devourer of Time. That means if you get too close to him, he might consume your powers. Honestly, neither Ken nor I can say for certain what might happen when you meet Kronos."

Ken nods his agreement. "This is a unique situation. Janus has never met Kronos in person. Their conflicting powers might prove extremely volatile."

"I agree," Bob says. "We really must capture those beings before any of us attempts to hunt down Kronos."

While the others begin a rapid-fire discussion of the problem at hand, my thoughts and my focus retreat into the back of my mind. Only deep inside myself can I find the solitude I require to examine the facts and the possibilities. I know my friends are trying to help. They will provide valuable assistance, of that I'm certain, but I need a kind of support only one person can provide.

Her name is Felicia.

But I can't ask Fliss to risk her life, and indeed her mind, simply to assist me. Despite having retreated inside myself, I hear every word the others exchange. They have good ideas. Yet I'm certain that anything they do will be nothing more than a distraction to give me the time I'll need to defeat Kronos. If I can defeat him. Never have I battled a being on the level of Kronos. My gladiatorial combat with Dionysus millennia ago will seem like child's play compared to what is yet to come.

"Don't second-guess yourself, sweetie. You'll go crazy doing that."

I glance at Fliss, but she isn't speaking. I heard her thoughts in my mind. She spoke to me that way. It's impossible.

"No, it isn't. You are the most powerful god in the Unseen. You can do anything."

Though I keep my head and my gaze positioned straight ahead, I can also see her beside me. Not as a sidelong glance. I can actually see her—and everything around us in all directions. *Ecce*, it can't be true. And yet it is. I have seized control of all my powers for the first time in more than thousands of years.

"Yes, you did, sweetie. Good job. I'll give you a scorching reward once this craziness is all over. By the way, what does 'ecce' mean?"

"It's an exclamation of surprise, *dulcissima*. The Janus coin is no longer a simple trinket but a conduit for enhancing my magics." I give her the sort of kiss only I can offer, the magical variety imbued with all my love and lust and pride in Felicia Vincent. "You are a part of me now, and I am a part of you. Nothing can sever us from each other, no matter what happens."

"I don't want to leave you, not ever. And you can call me Felicia Lagorio. That's my maiden name."

"Why did you keep your ex-husband's surname?"

She shrugs. "It was too much of a bother to stand in line at the DMV to make the official change."

"Felicia Lagorio…That is an Italian surname, which means it was derived from the Latin version. I had no idea you were of Italian extraction, but it makes sense that my soul mate would hail from my homeland."

"We're even more perfect for each other than we thought, huh?"

Warmth rushes through me, and I fight my body's wishes. Yes, my cock insists I must drag Fliss into the trees and fuck her. "Stop trying to arouse me, *dulcissima*, it isn't helpful at the moment."

"Can't blame a girl for trying."

A piercing whistle yanks us out of our telepathic discussion.

My focus returns to the world around me, and I give the whistling offender a haughty glance. "What did you want, Maximus?"

"Not to die in a horrifically painful way."

"You will not do so. Probably."

The salamander throws his hands up. "Well, that's bloody brilliant."

"If you're frightened, Max, you're welcome to take your wife home. The rest of us will fight Kronos."

"No, I won't be a ruddy coward. But I'd like to hear whatever telepathic plan you and Felicia came up with."

I glance at Fliss and realize I'm smirking. She wears a similar expression.

My telepathic discussion with Felicia has given me an idea. "Come, we must all enter the Unseen together. Immediately."

Chapter Twenty-Seven

Felicia

Janus wastes no time explaining why everyone must go into the Unseen right this minute. He doesn't even send me a telepathic explanation. He simply grabs my hand, stalks over to the wooden railing, and teleports us directly into the cave. The second we touch down, he flourishes his hand to dry us off. I wish I'd had a magical boyfriend when I was growing up. It would've saved me a lot of embarrassment and annoyance.

When he opens the portal, I don't feel uneasy like I had every other time. Now, I find myself mesmerized by the eerily beautiful colors that coruscate within the open doorway to another world. Maybe my deepening relationship with Janus has given me a new perspective on…everything. He controls the portals. They're a part of him, and he's a part of me.

"Do we go through the portal now?" I ask. "Or should we wait for the others? Not sure we'll all fit inside this cavern."

"Have no fear, *mea lux*. This cavern can hold an unlimited number of beings when I am here to grant them passage."

"You just called me something in Latin, didn't you? I heard you say it once before. Sounded like *mea lux*."

He takes my hand, lifting it to his lips. "The phrase *mea lux* means 'my light.' That is what you are to me, the light that conquered the darkness inside me." He pulls me close but keeps us near the portal. "Careful, Fliss, the others aren't as adept at using the portal as I am. But I'm about to give you a gift." He goes perfectly still, then closes his eyes and opens them again. "There. You now share my extended vision."

"You mean I can see three hundred and sixty degrees?"

"All around you, yes. Without even turning your head."

I can't help feeling a little smug about that. A mere mortal shares the vastly extended vision of a god.

Our friends don't materialize inside the cavern like Janus and I did. Clearly, they don't have the power to do that. Instead, thanks to my new three-sixty vision that Janus gave me, I can see them on the ledge outside, struggling not to fall off before they can jump inside. Most of them are elementals and therefore won't drown. Larissa is the only mortal in our group besides me, and Travis would never allow his wife to fall from a high ledge without catching her.

Am I still just a mortal? Not sure anymore.

Once everyone has jumped through the waterfall into the cavern, Janus turns to face the gang. "Our first plan for capturing the miscreants failed because we split up. That was my mistake. From this point forward, we will remain together, no matter what happens. Agreed?"

Everyone nods their agreement, and some voice their acceptance.

Janus grasps my hand tightly. "Then it is time to cross the veil."

I survey the cavern and all the beings gathered here, then gaze up at Janus. "How do we all fit in here? The cavern isn't that big, though it does seem like it's...expanded."

"It has."

"How is that possible?"

Janus taps a fingertip on my nose. "Magics, *dulcissima*."

"Hey," Max hollers. "That's my pet name for Harper. Get your own."

"I am the almighty Janus, remember? You labeled me as such. That means you must find a different pet name for your wife. Felicia is my *dulcissima*."

Harper rolls her eyes. "Who cares about which immortal hottie called his girl that first. Anybody remember the impending apocalypse?"

"I do," Janus tells her. "And you are correct to remind us of that, Harper. Now, we will cross the veil as one."

I hope that doesn't mean we merge into one being, but I doubt that's what Janus meant. He approaches the portal while threading our fingers, and we halt so he can flourish his hand, the signal for opening the gateway. The portal telescopes open, but I have no time to admire the coruscating colors. Janus traipses through the opening, still grasping my hand.

Is it my imagination, or did he tighten his grip? A touch of anxiety would be normal considering the dire circumstances.

The portal here consists of a small pool beside a large boulder. That vanished the instant we entered the Unseen, however. Janus leads me a short distance away to give the others plenty of room to cross into the Unseen. Once everyone is here, the portal spirals shut.

Janus faces the gang. "First, we must arm ourselves." He conjures a pile of weapons that lie on the ground. "Choose your weapon of choice, but I would prefer it if you don't argue about it like children."

"Do I get a weapon?" I ask.

"Of course. I have chosen some for you, if you don't mind."

"You know more about magical weaponry than I do. I trust your choices."

First, he conjures his own sword into his hand—the gleaming silver blade that glistens with faint, moving stripes of golden hues. His gold torque is always wrapped around his right biceps, but now he also has silver plate armor covering one shoulder as well as a wide belt around his waist. He ditched the toga in favor of a white kilt. The belt has a large buckle that has a shimmering silver disk at its center. His red cape is draped over one shoulder.

I appraise his outfit visually and smile. "Love the new gear, sweetie."

"This is my battle attire."

Next, he whips up gear for me including a smaller but no less deadly sword, leather boots that go up to my knees, and another, smaller blade sheathed in a leather holster. Now that Janus and I are both equipped for whatever lies ahead, he hands out weapons to the others—the magical way, of course. It's so much faster.

The gang gathers to listen to our plan, facing us and waiting to receive their orders.

Janus jams the tip of his sword into the ground and sets both hands atop it as he sweeps his gaze over the group. "What we must do next will be the most treacherous battle of all. Anyone who wishes to leave, should do so now."

No one leaves or even seems to be considering skipping out.

He nods once. "Then we now begin. Our first quarry will be Freknel and Stiodel."

Tris lifts his brows. "We're starting with the low-hanging fruit, eh?"

"Naturally. We need to weaken Kronos by divesting him of his minions one by one. Or in this case, two at a time. After that, we shall capture the others in this precise order—Theo, Dasheramal, Kali, and Dionysus."

Pendi raises her hand.

Janus turns his gaze to her. "You have a question?"

"Yeah. Aren't Dionysus and Kali pretty much on the same level? They're both gods. I'm just wondering why he's last. Kali is much deadlier, right?"

"True. But she is a Hindu god, where Dionysus is Greek. He is undoubtedly working with Kronos, who is one of the Titans and therefore Greek as well, not to mention more powerful than Dionysus or Kali."

"Okay. That does make sense."

He surveys the gang. "If there are no other questions, it's time to hunt down our quarry. We will contain them within my temple here in the Unseen, and two guards shall keep watch over them at all times."

"Which of us gets that crap job?" Quin asks.

"None of you will. I have engaged two beings of superior strength who will die before letting our prisoners escape. We shall meet them at the temple when we deposit Stiodel and Freknel there." He sweeps his gaze over the gang one last time. No one raises a hand or speaks up. "Let's go, then. Felicia and I will lead the way."

He tugs me tightly to his side, and we vanish.

I barely get a glimpse of the creepy tunnel that transports us to our destination. We move through it so swiftly that I almost can't tell we've moved at all, except for the fact that we touch down in a different place. The others appeared at the same time.

"Why are we in this location?" Cyneric asks. "No one lives here anymore. Hathor's temple is nothing but rubble."

Max flattens his lips as he squints at Janus. "I want to know the answer too. I hate this ruddy place. It's rubble like Cyneric said, and the magics have been denuded."

Janus lifts one brow. "Precisely. That's why Freknel and Stiodel have been hiding here. No other elemental would dare to set foot in the cursed hollow where Hathor once had a temple and ensorcelled countless souls." He shifts his gaze to Larissa. "I am not denigrating you, child. It's a simple fact."

"I know, and it's okay. The goddess I was back then isn't the woman I am now. Let's get those creepy kerkopes."

Sigrun raises a hand like a visor as she scans the vicinity. "I see no one here. Are you certain the kerkopes have taken up residence in this area?"

"Are you questioning my powers? Or those of Bob? I brought us here, but he provided the insight."

"But I did not hear you two speaking to each other."

The oracle taps his temple. "Telepathy, my dear, telepathy."

Pendi crosses her arms over her chest. "Then why can't you just tell us where to find Kronos?"

Bob sighs heavily. "Because that's not how an oracle's powers work."

"Enough bickering," Janus barks. "Bob, lead us to the kerkopes."

Riley waves her hand to get his attention. "Can't you just teleport us to the right spot?"

"Unfortunately, no. When a location has been cleansed of all magics, the only way to access it is via perambulation."

I just barely stop myself from laughing. His stuffiness is adorable. "Janus means we have to walk there."

Bob leads the parade across the deserted hollow with me and Janus right beside him. As we pass by the crumbling remnants of the temple, a chill chases over my skin. Whatever went down in that place at the end, it must have been horrific. I swear I can almost hear the agonized cries. A lot of people must have died here.

We continue past the old temple, heading straight for the other side of the valley. I don't see any buildings or tents or anything resembling someplace two winged slimeballs might hide out. Bob is an oracle, so I'm sure he knows where he's going. Within a few minutes, we reach the far side of the valley and halt at its base.

Bob points toward something about ten feet above us. "There. Freknel and Stiodel have been hiding out in a bolt-hole they dug with their bare hands."

I squint at the shadows but can't see anything yet. "Why would they dig an actual hole instead of going back to wherever they live?"

Janus tilts his head back to gaze at the spot Bob had indicated. "The kerkopes are terrified of their master."

"But who is their master? Dionysus or Kronos?"

"They wouldn't fear Dionysus this deeply. The kerkopes must realize that Kronos is the true Dark One, though I suspect they only came to that conclusion after Kali arrived."

I peer down at the bolt-hole. "Who gets the privilege of climbing in there to drag those two out? All you men are too big."

"Hmm, that is a rather small bolt-hole." Janus leans forward, sniffing the air near the entrance to the cavity. "Come out, Freknel. And you as well, Stiodel. We won't do you any harm."

Silence. It drags on for several seconds before a shaky voice replies, "You assaulted us, nearly crushing poor Freknel's chest with your foot while you nearly crushed my throat with your hand. You'll murder us if we leave this hole."

Janus rolls his eyes heavenward and shakes his head. Then he kneels to get closer to the pathetic monsters and speaks in a soothing voice. "I will not harm you unless you threaten an innocent being."

"I don't trust you."

Stiodel's petulant tone won't earn him any brownie points with Janus. And we won't get anywhere by threatening either of the kerkopes.

Gundisalvus steps forward. "Let me retrieve the little monsters. I'll drain just enough of their blood that they won't be strong enough to fight."

The kerkopes in the bolt-hole both shriek at the same time.

Janus slaps a hand on the vampire's chest, shoving him backward. "I don't care to hear any more of your suggestions."

Cyneric snatches up Gundisalvus and tosses him several yards away.

Before anyone else can volunteer to scare the shit out of the slimy monkey-men, I turn toward the group and set my hands on my hips. "Enough of the macho nonsense. I will crawl into the bolt-hole and convince the kerkopes to come out."

"No, you will not," Janus snarls.

"Yes, I will." I slap a hand over his mouth when he opens it, about to speak. "Trust me. I'm no fool."

His insulted expression fades away. "All right, Fliss. But you have precisely three minutes before I blow that hole open to retrieve you."

I pat his chest. "Good boy."

Then I march up to the bolt-hole, drop to my hands and knees, and crawl down the steep incline that leads into the hideout. Halfway down, I stop and shout to the gang, "Could somebody toss me a flashlight or something?"

A glowing ball of light appears in front of me.

"I appreciate that, whichever of you sent me the orb."

"The 'orb' is a fairy light." That's Janus talking. "Be careful, *mea lux*."

"Uh-huh."

I crawl deeper into the hole with an orb guiding me, halting when I finally reach flat ground. This is a dank hideout, and it smells like mildew. Once I get over the stench, I notice two dark figures huddled in the corner.

Freknel and Stiodel are hugging each other. How sweet.

I crook a finger at them. "Come on, boys. I'm your rescue team."

They both gape at me while shivering.

Oh, jeez, this could take a while. "No one is going to kill you, I promise. Let's all climb up out of this clammy rat's nest, okay? You must be freezing."

I hold out my hand.

Freknel cautiously stretches out one shaking hand. The moment I clasp it, he starts to sob. Stiodel rushes over to claim my other hand. Then they both hug me.

"Okay, boys," I say while patting their backs. "It's time to climb out. Do you want me to go first?"

They both nod vigorously while still crying. Their tears dribble down the back of my neck.

I did not sign up for this.

While I climb up the incline, the kerkopes follow and stick very close to me. These creeps attacked me a few days ago, yet now I've become their nanny. Well, at least we've captured two of our quarry.

Janus lifts me out of the bolt-hole as soon as I get close enough and pulls me into his arms.

When the kerkopes emerge, they stand up and stretch, then yawn.

Shackles materialize on their wrists and ankles.

Freknel stomps his foot and whines, "That isn't fair. We cooperated."

Janus glowers at the creature. "Would you like me to recite every evil thing you've ever done? Then we could have a trial and convict you both. You'll receive eternal sentences."

Stiodel tests his wrist shackles and whines. "This is all your fault, Freknel."

"Me? You're the one who—"

"Shut the hell up," I snap. For good measure, I smack them both. "Be quiet, or I'll sic my boyfriend on you."

The kerkopes eye Janus—and shut up.

Janus claps three times to get everyone's attention. "We will transport the kerkopes to my temple, then search for Theo."

Chapter Twenty-Eight

Janus

THANKS TO THE DEPLETED STATE OF THE MAGICS IN THIS region, our journey across the valley floor takes longer than it should. I cannot simply teleport us to our next destination. Freknel and Stiodel whine, whimper, and wail the entire time. They behave like children. Yet both creatures are quite ancient. I could destroy them, but I believe we need all our quarry in one location, alive and conscious, in order to hunt down Kronos.

Once we exit the desolate plain where Hathor's temple once resided, I whisk our group away to my temple.

We land just inside the doorway.

Quin turns in a circle and grins. "Wicked pad, Janus."

"There is no evil within my temple."

"I meant your home is really nice."

"Oh, I see." I do wish everyone would stop assuming I understand their slang. They have all spent years in the mortal world. I have not.

Felicia claims my hand.

I relax. That happens every time she's near me and especially when she touches me.

She folds both her hands around mine. "Where are your guards? I don't see anybody other than our group."

I slide my lips into a smug slant, then shove two fingers into my mouth and blow a piercing whistle.

Two beings materialize.

"Are you having me on?" Max says indignantly. "The raven shifter and a gnome? Those are your prison guards. A ruddy gnome killed Nevan, you know."

"He was resurrected. But this particular gnome has never harmed anyone except in battle—and never without provocation." I wave toward the two beings. "Felicia, the raven shifter is Brennus. He has helped us on a number of occasions. The gnome is Vandren, and I trust him."

I scan my gaze over the group, daring them to complain. None do. "Vandren and Brennus will guard our prisoners while we search for Theo. Let's go."

"No snack?" the oracle Ken asks. "I'm starving."

Bob rolls his eyes. "You are immortal. That means you won't die of starvation. Man up."

I have no idea what "man up" means. Am I the last being in the Unseen to learn modern human slang?

We don't have time to waste on idle complaints. With that in mind, I whisk our group away to where we will hopefully find our next quarry. Theo will undoubtedly be more difficult to capture. But we have numbers on our side.

We land outside a nymph's abode. I know this because nymphs always construct their homes from the natural environment. Most of this house consists of trees that have grown around the structure in a rectangular fashion. Inside the home, I see candles, or perhaps lanterns, burning.

And I hear a woman's sharp, rhythmic exclamations.

"Oh! Yes! More, more, more!"

All the men in our group cover their wives' eyes with their hands. Well, all but me. I don't need to shelter Felicia. She is a mature woman, and I'm not a child.

"Theo! Oh! Gods! Yeeeeeesss!"

A throaty roar echoes through the clearing in which we stand.

"For cripes' sake," Tris complains. "I thought we teleported here to capture the satyr, not listen to his porno exploits."

Anger swells inside me, though not because of what Tris just said. "You will all remain here. I must handle this capture alone."

Before anyone can harass me about my announcement, I kick open the door of the treehouse and stalk into the bedroom. The nymph lies tangled in the sheets, clearly high on magically enhanced endorphins. Theo kneels at the foot of the bed.

And I yank him off his feet, hurling him through the wall.

By the time I stalk out of the house, the rest of our group has moved away from the house and the satyr. Theo lies sprawled on the ground, dazed, mumbling wordlessly.

I clutch his throat in one hand to hoist him off his feet. "I've caught you, satyr, and this time you will not escape."

Theo laughs with a touch of maniacal glee. "You still don't understand, do you? None of your followers do either. What fools you are. When the Dark One reveals himself—"

I squeeze his throat just enough to restrict his breathing and make him splutter. "Don't waste your breath on hollow threats. I no longer believe any of it."

He tries to kick me in the groin, but I slam my knee into his gut, preventing him from doing anything more than gnashing his teeth. I drop him, and he tumbles to the ground in a heap. Then I kick him in the ribs repeatedly until he stops trying to sink his teeth into my shins. Once he has finally given up, I sling him over my shoulder.

The nymph emerges from her partly demolished home, naked, with only a string of leaves draped over her breasts and groin. "Where are you taking Theo? We aren't done yet."

"Yes, you are, Creusa. Theo has committed crimes for which he must be punished."

The nymph shrugs. "I'll call for a salamander. Those boys never say no to me, and they aren't particular about where they hold their orgies."

She wanders back inside her home.

I turn toward my friends. "We must imprison Theo immediately."

Travis pushes through the crowd and studies my prisoner with a curious expression. Then he waves a hand toward me. "You liked beating the shit out of that cretin, didn't you? Not that I blame you, mate, but I've never known you to be so violent."

Felicia comes up beside me and looks directly at Travis. "Janus has his reasons for hating Theo. They're personal, and you shouldn't try to force him to explain."

"Fair enough. Who are we after next?"

Instead of answering his question, I teleport us all back to my temple where Brennus and Vandren await our arrival. The raven shifter and the gnome have kept the kerkopes in shackles—for good reason. Those creatures might be intensely irritating, but they are also more dangerous than they seem.

Vandren has taken control of Freknel and Stiodel, holding one under each of his arms. The winged villains occasionally thrash but cannot break free of the enormous gnome. Mortals associate the word gnome with garden decorations, I've learned. That is far from the reality.

"Who's up next, boss?" Quin asks me. "Dionysus? That jerk needs to be taken down several thousand pegs. I'd love to get in on that action. Never met the douche, but I'm sure he's a real sweetheart."

The leprechaun is being sarcastic. Even I can determine that much. "I'm afraid you will need to wait, Quin. Dionysus is the most powerful being we will need to neutralize. Dasheramal is next on the list."

Cyneric squints his eyes a few millimeters which I have come to know means he is excited about what lies ahead. He is a difficult elemental to pin down, physically or emotionally. The vampire takes one step toward me. "I am ready to sink my fangs into Dasheramal. She will taste like rotting sewage, being a kerkopes, but I can endure the rancid flavor in order to capture her."

"Yes, I'm certain you can." I face the group. "Dasheramal is third highest on our list because she has been imbued with so many dark magics. We must be exceedingly careful when capturing her. She may also be very close, physically, to Dionysus and Kali, perhaps even Kronos. Let's go."

Because of the dark magics Dasheramal has ingested, I cannot simply teleport us to her location. The black energies cloud my vision. As I gaze down at Felicia's face, I wonder if she might be able to assist me with this problem.

"Why aren't we teleporting yet?" Ennea asks. "Something wrong?"

"Give me a moment. I must speak to Felicia alone, then we will spirit ourselves to Dasheramal's location."

I take command of Felicia's hand, leading her to the far end of the temple, behind the bed and its accompanying furniture. Though I doubt anyone will hear our conversation this far away, for good measure I throw out a sound-dampening spell.

Fliss splays a hand on my chest as she gazes up at me with wrinkled brows. "What's wrong, sweetie?"

"I need a power boost, as my friends would say. My ability to see Dasheramal is clouded by a large amount of dark magics."

"Okay. Do you need Bob or Ken to—"

"No, *dulcissima*." I clasp both her hands to my chest. "You are the only one who can give me that boost. Your love empowers me."

She hesitates for only a matter of seconds. "Tell me what to do."

"Kiss me, *mea lux*. Your passion fuels my powers."

Fliss winks. "Well, it's a tough job, but I'll make the sacrifice just for you."

I wink. "I appreciate that."

She twines her arms around my neck, balanced on the tips of her toes, and crushes her mouth to mine. The second her jaw relaxes, I thrust my tongue deep, coiling it round and round hers, as the sexual energy of our kiss rushes through us both. When I slide a hand down to her buttocks, she rubs herself against my thickening cock. The magics have done their job.

Someone whistles loudly. "Oy! Is this a hunt for villains or an orgy? If you two mean to shag in our presence, I should conjure a bucket because I'll definitely vomit."

I peel my lips away from Felicia's mouth and shout over my shoulder, "Shut your mouth, Max."

"Never heard you say that before. The almighty Janus only ever says things like 'cease talking, you irritating salamander.' About bloody time you got more casual."

Max tried to imitate my voice in his attempt to annoy me. The others have begun to snicker, so they apparently thought it was humorous. I won't waste time on telling them why the asinine joke wasn't amusing.

I whisk us all away to our next quarry.

The magics I imbibed thanks to Felicia's kiss have dissipated the fog that prevented me from seeing Dasheramal's location. I set us down cautiously, making certain we aren't seen or heard. Bob casts a quick spell to cloak us from view and from the hearing of our quarry. We huddle just inside the periphery of a small clearing inside of which someone has erected a makeshift home. The tenant used twigs and larger branches as well, not to mention clods of damp earth and grass.

The structure is atrociously constructed, but I would expect no less from a member of the kerkopes clan. They prefer to reside in tall trees. For Dasheramal to choose a ground-based residence would seem to suggest she's afraid of something or someone.

Grunting and scrabbling noises emerge from the makeshift abode.

I inch forward, pausing briefly when I reach the periphery of the clearing. Felicia and the others follow. Fliss wants to stay beside me. I can sense that much. But I wave for her to stay behind me. The fact that Dasheramal has hidden herself away just like Freknel and Stiodel makes me uneasy. Those three kerkopes tried to conceal themselves as if they're terrified. Whether of Kronos or for some other reason, I cannot say.

Theo hadn't crawled into a bolt-hole, yet he did slink away to a nymph's home to weather the storm. Why the devoted lackey of Dionysus would do so baffles me. What storm did he seek refuge from? I haven't figured that out. But I'm certain Kronos is plotting something. And whatever it is, none of his minions thus far care to participate in the plot.

Just as I approach the makeshift hut, something stirs inside it, rustling the leaves and twigs within the structure.

I hold up a hand to stop the others from coming closer.

More rustling noises. Soft grunting.

I call out, "Dasheramal, come out now. You will not be harmed unless you assault one of us."

Hissing emanates from the hut. Then a gravelly voice declares, "You intend to destroy me."

"If you mean us no harm, then no harm will come to you."

A flurry of rustling, scuffling, and grunting ensues briefly, then fades away. "If you vow it, I will come out."

"You know none of us can make a vow, not here in the Unseen." I move closer, mere inches from the hut, and crouch at the opening. "You must know my reputation as one of the few beings in this world who does not deceive others. Place your trust in me, and I will free you from whatever or whomever has frightened you so deeply."

Silence follows. Even the forest seems to have gone quiet and still.

One hand, sprinkled with dark hairs, snakes out of the hut. Dasheramal stretches out her fingers and wriggles them as if waiting for me to clasp her hand. I do so, and she begins to crawl out of her hiding place. The moment her whole body has emerged, she flings herself into my arms and begins to sob.

I cannot believe the Dasheramal I had met near the waterfall in the mortal realm is this same creature. I have no doubts her fear is real. And that realization makes me circle back in my mind to when we rescued Freknel and Stiodel. They hid underground, just like Dasheramal. Theo hid inside a nymph's home, yet also appeared frightened beneath his blustering attitude.

A shiver of awareness rushes over me. Every hair on my body lifts, and gooseflesh pebbles my skin. I am not afraid. No, the sensation I'm experiencing now is a warning from my own powers.

Without alerting the others, I transport us back to my temple.

Dasheramal flies out of my arms, racing toward Stiodel and Freknel. Vandren scoops her up. Shackles and handcuffs materialize around Dasheramal's wrists and ankles. She seems relieved to be in custody.

Felicia walks up beside me. "Am I hallucinating, or are the creepy evil critters behaving like the universe is about to go supernova?"

"You have assessed their mental state accurately. They are terrified beyond measure."

"Because of Kronos?"

"We won't know until we capture Dionysus and Kali." I whirl around to address the group. "Cyneric, Bob, and Ennea will come with me to seek out Dionysus. Once he is safely here in the temple, we will discuss how to handle Kali. She boasts a marginal amount of temporal magics, though nothing as potent as my powers or those of Kronos. The greatest danger with Kali is that she possesses destructive magics that can rise to near-apocalyptic status if she becomes infuriated."

"Oh, great," Quin says. "Just what we need. Another apocalypse."

"I have not asked you to help us capture Kali. Besides, we must first detain Dionysus. And our task begins now."

The others have no idea where I'm taking Cyneric, Bob, or Ennea because I have whisked us away without explaining. Though I haven't voiced my concerns to anyone yet, not even Felicia, I sense a multiverse-wide cataclysm looming ahead of us. This could be worse than anything any of us has ever witnessed. Even I, one of the oldest gods in the Unseen, sense the danger slithering through the air.

Who will trigger the apocalypse? Either Kronos or...me. We are the only mighty time gods left.

Cyneric, Bob, Ennea, and I have reached our destination. But as I survey the area, a knife-sharp chill delves deep under my skin. Where are we? Not the temple of Dionysus.

We are damned now, for we have materialized inside the domain of Kronos. But he hasn't shown himself. Instead, his minion Kali lies dead on the ground, torn to shreds.

A two-word curse tumbles from my lips. "*Heu, deodamnatus.*"

CHAPTER TWENTY-NINE

Felicia

TRAPPED INSIDE THIS TEMPLE WITH THE GANG, I CAN DO nothing except wait and pray that Janus and the others aren't in trouble. But I feel as if they are. Since I don't have genuine powers, only the ones he temporarily gifted me with, I can't zip myself to wherever he and his companions are.

Heu, deodamnatus.

That phrase echoes in my mind—in the voice of Janus, hushed and tinged with surprise. How could I hear that exclamation? Janus is who knows how far away from here. Yet I heard, or sensed, his verbal fear. Maybe "fear" isn't the right word. "Shock" would be a better term. If only I could contact him…

Why can't I? He granted me his three-sixty vision, and we had a telepathic discussion earlier.

I try sending out a mental message. Nothing happens.

Cyneric, Bob, Ennea, and Janus might simply be too far away for telepathy to work. No, I don't believe that. Janus has vast powers and often tells other beings so, and I'm sure that's why he gets teased whenever he speaks the phrase "vast powers." But it's true. His magics exceed those of any other beings in the Unseen. I just need to try harder to contact him.

So, I squeeze my eyes shut, focus on Janus, and do my damnedest to send a pulse out to him. *Where are you?* Nothing. I squeeze my eyes shut even harder, clenching my fists at the same time, demanding that the multiverse show me where Janus is.

"What are you doing, Felicia?" Ken the oracle asks in his nasal voice.

I peel one eye open. "I'm trying to contact Janus. I felt his shock a minute ago, and it's got me worried."

"Hmm, I see. Let me check." He freezes for a few seconds, then blows out a sigh. "You have good reason to be worried. I felt the anxiety of Janus and his team. They've encountered something evil."

I'm not being paranoid. That's good to know. But I can't hang around in this temple waiting to find out what's wrong. I shove two fingers into my mouth and whistle. The high-pitched noise reverberates through the structure and gets everyone's attention.

"Listen up!" I shout. "Janus and his team are in trouble. Who will take me there to find out what's going on?"

"You shouldn't go anywhere," Ken says. "If something terrible has occurred, you must stay as far away as possible. You're a mortal. That means you could be easily damaged—or killed." He rises onto his tiptoes to survey the crowd, then waves at someone. "Come here, Travis. You too, Max. Oh, and also Sigrun."

I frown at Ken. "Janus ordered everyone to stay here."

But he never said that nobody should go after him.

Ken and three elementals he called over here begin to argue about who should go out there to find Janus and his team. Who knows how long that argument will take. The man I love is out there and in trouble. Screw their discussions. It's time for a command decision.

Can I teleport myself? I'm about to learn the answer to that question. I can sense, though I have no idea how, that the temple is warded. All the beings here will be okay if I enact the plan that occurred to me a moment ago.

My gaze flicks to the gnome who holds the kerkopes in his arms.

The others are still arguing.

I march up to the massive gnome, whose body bears a striking resemblance to a gnarled tree. He stands about ten feet tall, by my estimation, and has arms thick enough to punch through solid rock, I'm sure. Yeah, he'll do.

Brennus, who stands near the gnome and restrains his own prisoner, glances at me sideways. His brows lift a smidgen, then knit together.

I wink at him.

He shakes his head in an "oh, you foolish mortal" gesture.

I clear my throat. "Hey, there, Vandren. You seem like the type who loves to smash bad guys."

Vandren smirks. "Mm, I love to crush elementals. But only if they're evil."

"Good. You and I are going on a mission to rescue Janus and his team. Why don't you set down your kerkopes and let the others take care of them? I'm sure Brennus can handle them. What do you say?"

His lips curl into a satisfied smile. "Let's go, little mortal."

"My name is Felicia."

The gnome tosses the three kerkopes to the raven shifter, who catches them handily. None of those critters try to escape from Brennus's hold. They're still scared shitless.

Vandren bends his knees, holding out his cupped hands to let me climb onto his huge palms. Then he sets me on his shoulder. I wrap my arms around his neck while he whisks us away.

The journey through the abyssal tunnel seems to go on forever. The energies inside it crackle and snap, writhe and whip, their agitation palpable. I can see, feel, and smell it.

Vandren sets us down in a place I don't recognize, where night has already fallen. Back in the temple, it had been daytime. I can't figure out if we're now on the other side of the Unseen, which would mean this realm rotates, like the Earth in the mortal world. But it doesn't matter.

The gnome sets me down on a patch of slimy earth.

Up ahead, I spot a familiar blond head.

I race down the murky, slippery path, tripping twice before I reach Janus and fling my arms around him from behind. He spins around, hoisting me into his arms.

"What are you doing here, *dulcissima*?" he asks. "How did you even get here?"

I nod toward the gnome. "Vandren brought me. It was a wild ride through that spooky tunnel."

"Yes, the Unseen is in turmoil." He brushes a lock of hair away from my face and kisses my forehead. "I wish you had not come to this place. We're in the domain of Kronos."

I scan my gaze over the vicinity. "This looks like the worst place in the universe."

"That is an accurate assessment. The domain of Kronos was never like this before. His fury, simmering for eons, must have infected everything within his kingdom." Janus peers around me. "Why did you bring a gnome with you?"

"Everybody else was bickering about who should go after you and your team. I sensed you were in danger, and I couldn't wait around for a consensus." I nod toward Vandren. "A gnome seemed like the best bodyguard. Maybe he can smash Kronos into tiny little bits."

Vandren lumbers up to us. "I would do that if I could, but it's not within my power." He gently touches my shoulder. "You are a brave mortal. I will fight on your behalf anytime you need me."

Janus's brows shoot up briefly. He seems confused by Vandren's declaration, but he realizes now isn't the right moment to question me. Instead, he takes my hand to lead me over to the spot where Cyneric, Bob, and Ennea are studying a patch of ground. Only when we approach that area do I understand why.

The mangled form of a blue-skinned creature lies limp in a puddle. Greenish stuff oozes from the body.

I lean over Cyneric, who kneels at the puddle's edge. "Is that Kali?"

Cyneric nods. "She is dead."

"But I thought elementals and gods could only die by being destroyed. That incinerates the body." I know that because I watched while Janus relived his destruction. The remains of Kali are still here. They haven't vanished in a cloud of magics. "How is this possible? If we're assuming Kronos did this, why would he bother? He could've annihilated her much more cleanly."

Janus crouches beside me. "That is the dilemma we've been wrestling with."

I make a slower appraisal of the remains and realize that some of the, uh, pieces are scattered further away. It's almost impossible to tell which bits belong to which parts of Kali's corpse. "What should we do now? Search for Dionysus? He's the only one left on our hit list."

"To search for Dionysus might be exactly what Kronos wants. Somehow, he amassed enough power to divert us from our intended destination." Janus frowns and shakes his head slowly. "Since Kali had limited temporal powers, Kronos must have hoped to steal them from her to bolster his own magics. But a goddess with cataclysmic powers should not have been so easy to kill."

The note of confusion in his voice doesn't ease my anxiety.

I stand up and look at Bob. "You're an oracle, right? Doesn't that mean you can foresee shit like this?"

"My foresight isn't unlimited. However, the answer to your question is yes, I should have sensed this calamity coming." He stares down at Kali's body, and I swear his face grows a shade or two paler. "This is completely unprecedented."

"Maybe I should try," Ennea suggests. "I'm not an oracle, but I can cast a myriad of spells including ones to gaze into the past. My magics aren't as good as yours, not by a long shot. Still, I could give it a go."

"Let's combine our magics. Together, perhaps we can find a few answers."

"Sounds like a plan to me."

Janus freezes for a few seconds, then springs upright and whirls around to face Bob and Ennea. "That would be exceedingly dangerous. We're in Kronos's domain."

Ennea rolls her eyes. "We'll be casting spells, not shouting 'hey, Kronos, ya big lug, join the party.' Come on, we're desperate. Might as well try."

Vandren stomps closer to the group. "I have magics too. My outer skin is suffused with them. I cannot cast spells, but I could peel off a piece. When ground up, a gnome's skin has been known to enhance the magics of other beings."

Janus gazes at Vandren with clear confusion. "I have never heard of this before."

"Gnomes don't like to advertise their powers. Did you think we won battles just by stomping our feet?"

"I never considered such things. That is my mistake." Janus sets a hand on the gnome's forearm. "We would be honored to have you participate in the spellcasting, Vandren." He glances at Bob and Ennea. "Do you agree?"

Bob nods, and so does Ennea.

"Very well. You three should begin the spellcasting immediately." He spins on his heels to face away from the rest of us. "I must explore this precinct."

I whirl toward him, seizing his arm. "Not alone, you won't."

"You cannot accompany me. If Kronos—"

"Shut up. I'm going with you."

Cyneric saunters up to us. "I will also go with you, Janus. If nothing else, I can drain the blood from Kronos's body. That should slow him down for a while."

Bob and Ennea have begun chanting. When I glance back at them, I can see the magics coalescing around them as a glittering, semitransparent curtain.

Without warning, they both scream and fall to the ground, writhing in agony.

Janus throws an arm around me, clenching me so tightly that I almost can't breathe. He spins us both around.

Ennea and Bob lie prone on the mushy ground, splattered with mud, their hair a mess. With glazed eyes, they struggle to form words but wind up spluttering instead. A shimmering purplish haze has formed around them.

I try to run toward Bob and Ennea, but Janus maintains his iron grip on me. "Go no closer, Felicia. You might be swept up in the dark magics."

"We need all our friends fighting with us. Can't you summon them?"

"And risk everyone being mired in dark magics? No. Their fight will come later."

Cyneric gazes dispassionately at Bob and Ennea. "They will survive, most likely. We need to find the heart of Kronos's domain."

Janus nods gravely. He keeps his arms around me as we turn away from our friends and gallop into the unknown. Shouldn't Kronos have a castle or something? I don't see any structures anywhere. A magical domain like this one might have ways of cloaking the castle or whatever type of building Kronos has constructed. This place does have a sky, of sorts, though it's dark and lightened only by the occasional shimmering field of bluish clouds. A constant, low rumbling noise makes every hair on my body stiffen.

I've had the strangest sensation of déjà vu ever since we stepped into this place. But I've never visited any precinct like this one. The further we travel, the weirder things get. We tromp through an open area that's full of tall, weed-like plants that sway faintly, though I don't feel a breeze. Every so often, with no regularity, something ticks—like a clock that doesn't know how to count the minutes.

Cyneric throws an arm out to halt us. When Janus opens his mouth to speak, the vampire shakes his head and raises one finger in a gesture meant to keep us quiet.

Janus mouths, "What is it?"

Cyneric stretches an arm out to point at a blurry thing in the distance. He mouths, "We go there."

Janus compresses his lips, a sure sign he thinks it's a bad idea.

The vampire aims a hard look at Janus and points directly ahead of us again. He mouths, "Now or never."

I glance up at Janus. When he veers his attention to me, I mouth, "Trust him."

Janus exhales a gusty sigh, then nods.

The vampire silently tells us, "Quickly."

We step up our pace, walking so fast that it almost counts as running. But Cyneric places a hand on both our backs and urges us to pick up the pace even more. Soon, we're racing toward the blurry shape in the distance. Janus refuses to let go of my hand, though that makes it more difficult to run. When Cyneric races ahead of us, Janus sweeps me up in his arms and as he sprints alongside the vampire.

I'm a human sack of wheat, cradled in his arms and clinging to him.

The blurry thing we'd seen hunkering low to the horizon grows larger every minute as my companions accelerate their pace even more. The surroundings become a blur. The speed of our traveling turns into a gale that blusters in my face, and I have to squeeze my eyes shut.

Abruptly, we stop.

I peel my lids apart. The first thing I see is the vampire standing beside me and Janus. Cyneric is breathing hard, his chest heaving, though I'd assumed an elemental vampire would never get winded. Our trip across the spooky field of grass, or whatever it was, must have been much longer than I realized. No quick sprint would do this to a being from the Unseen. Right?

Janus at last sets me down on my feet, though he still hugs me tightly to his side. "We are here."

"Where?" I follow the track of his gaze, which is aimed directly ahead of us. That's when I see it—a gigantic black structure that has threads of purple pulsing through the walls. "Is that a huge black castle?"

Cyneric grunts. "It's a temple, not a castle."

"The Temple of Kronos," Janus tells the vampire. "A stronghold of the darkest temporal magics."

As I gaze up at the mammoth structure, a chill tingles up my spine and outward into all my limbs. I know what this is. It's sheer horror brought on by the terrifying vision before us—a temple of pure evil.

I huddle closer to Janus, as close as anyone could possibly get. "What now?"

Before he can answer my question, the stronghold begins to groan and grate as if it's fighting against its own walls. Then a crack of purplish light appears just as the hulking doorway grinds open.

Oh, yeah, we are all so screwed.

Chapter Thirty

Janus

By the stars, in all my existence I have never witnessed anything resembling the fortress of Kronos. The edifice that's rising up inch by inch, seemingly from the depths of the multiverse itself, reminds me of the castles in the dragon kingdoms. Yet it's also nothing like that. I have no words to describe the stronghold of my most depraved enemy. Even Kali and Dionysus cannot steal that prize away from Kronos.

The grinding cacophony terminates abruptly. That gateway has opened its gaping maw as far as possible.

Cyneric moves to stand beside me, almost touching me. Never have I seen the vampire behave this way. With Felicia on one side and Cyneric on the other, we've become a sort of trinity—father, mother, son. If they assume I can protect them, I pray their faith in me will not be in vain.

The only light comes from the sallow glow of something I cannot see, something that lies inside the courtyard. I can think of no other term to describe what lies beyond the gates.

"Are we going in there?" Felicia asks.

"I believe we have no choice. Since my powers cannot take us away from here, then we are trapped in the domain of Kronos."

A flapping noise erupts behind and above us.

Felicia jerks. "What the hell is that?"

Cyneric glances upward. "Dragons."

"Oh, terrific. Let me guess. They can breathe fire."

"And speak as well. They're humanoid creatures."

I only half listen to their conversation. A strange sensation prickles the hairs at my nape, warning me that what Felicia and Cyneric believe is incorrect. "That is not the sound of dragons. The Furies are here."

Overlapping shrieks confirm my assessment.

I clamp my arms more tightly around Felicia and Cyneric. "We must run for the stronghold and pray Kronos won't allow the Furies to destroy us."

We race across the remaining distance to the stronghold while the winged creatures descend at high speed like living missiles. One of them grazes the top of my head. I hoist Felicia and Cyneric off the ground so I can run faster in a bounding fashion that I hope will get us to our destination more swiftly and unharmed.

A Fury swoops down and seizes Felicia's arm.

I punch my fist up into the underside of the creature's chin. Her jaw snaps shut with enough force that the sound echoes around us. The Fury gives up—for the moment. But another of her kind swoops down to sink her taloned feet into Cyneric's shoulders.

He sinks his fangs into her feet and begins to suck her blood.

She tries to drag him away, into the sky.

But I slam my elbow into her groin, and the beast flies away.

A third Fury latches onto my shoulders and thrashes until I lose my grip on both Cyneric and Felicia. They tumble to the ground, rolling and rolling.

I throw my arms up behind my head, grasp the back of the Fury's neck, and execute a forward somersault that flips the Fury onto the ground with me atop her. She slashes her talons at me, drawing blood a few times. That will not deter me. I punch her in the face repeatedly until she becomes too dazed to fight any longer.

When I leap to my feet, I catch sight of the other two Furies. One has grabbed Felicia, the other Cyneric, and they are bending their knees in preparation for takeoff, intending to whisk their quarry away.

I bend my knees and launch myself into the sky with far more force and speed than they could hope to achieve. I reach the Fury who has captured Cyneric first and punch that beast's jaw until she loses her grip. Cyneric falls to the ground, but that won't kill him.

The other Fury veers left and swoops downward, clearly hoping to evade me.

My feet strike the ground with so much energy that the earth quakes. I bend my knees and launch myself into the sky yet again. I've aimed for the third Fury, who has Felicia. The moment I ram my head into the creature's back, she loses her balance and her grip on my beloved. As the Fury spirals toward the earth in an uncontrolled spin, I wrap my arms around Fliss and land us on the ground gently.

I'm gasping for breath.

Felicia lays her hands on my chest, her gaze searching mine. "Are you okay? That was…incredible and terrible at the same time."

Cyneric shuffles up beside us. "I have heard of the Furies, but this was my first encounter with them. They're formidable."

I lash my arms around them both. "We must hurry into the stronghold, though I'm not certain we will be safer there. It's our only choice."

We hurry to the gates and rush straight through them. The halves grind closed with almost as much volume as they had when they opened. Fortunately, the act of shutting the gates moves faster.

The courtyard is vacant. The wan yellow glow seems to seep out of every crack in the structure as well as the earth itself. We halt halfway across the space and glance around at our new surroundings.

"At last, you're here," a deep, rasping voice declares. "It took you a very long time to give up the fight and come to me."

Felicia has gone stiff against me.

I swerve my attention to her face. Her eyes have grown wide with shock, and her lips have fallen open. They tremble too. "Fliss, what is it? Why have you gone pale?"

She swallows hard, the movement visible in her throat. Her hands have begun to shake as well. "That's—But it can't be. No way. I'm hallucinating or something."

"What can't be?"

Felicia raises one unsteady arm to point at the being who has just traipsed out of the shadows and stopped halfway to us. "Him."

That single syllable emerged as a whisper.

My brows cinch together, and I veer my focus to the being before us. His reddish skin shimmers faintly violet when the light plays on his flesh. He boasts a large, muscular body that's of a similar stature and physique as mine. Though the beast sports worn leather pants, he has no shirt or boots. This is Kronos, but I cannot fathom Felicia's reaction to him.

I hook my finger under her chin, urging her to look up at me. "Do you know this creature?"

"Yes."

"How could you have met Kronos? He never leaves his domain."

Kronos chuckles. "You are such an innocent, Janus. The truth should be obvious." He winks at Felicia. "Go on, darling, tell him."

She huddles against me. "That beast is my ex-husband."

I jerk my head to stare at her. "He cannot be."

Kronos ambles toward us, head held high, arrogantly certain of his dominance here in the domain he created. The *irrumator* halts inches away and taps one finger on my chest several times. Naturally, he smirks. "The Almighty Janus doesn't know one tenth of what he thinks he knows. How could you not have guessed? Fliss loves a good, thick, hard cock inside her. Only a god could provide the kind of pleasure a sex fiend like her needs on a regular basis."

"Do not speak of her in that manner," I snarl through clenched teeth. "Everything you have said is a lie."

Felicia clears her throat. "Not all of it."

My heart skips a beat, and I swerve my gaze to her. "You have enjoyed carnal relations with this beast?"

"No," she snaps with an indignant tone. Then she winces. "Well, technically, yes. I was married to Blake Vincent for eighteen months, but I had no idea he was actually Kronos, a beast from another world."

Kronos reaches for her hand, but she kicks him in the shin. That doesn't faze him, of course, being a god of the Unseen. But he did wince the slightest bit. "Now, now, Fliss, there's no point in fighting the inevitable. If you don't come with me, you'll die along with everyone else in the multiverse."

Cyneric lifts one brow. "How do you propose to do that? You are not the most powerful being in the Unseen."

"Once, I was not. Now, I am."

"I'm curious about how you achieved that change in status. It must have taken a great deal of time and energy to do so."

Cyneric is luring Kronos into a trap of sorts, convincing him to reveal his methods to us. Yes, the vampire is a clever creature. I'd known that even all those eons ago when Eros created him. His intelligence has only grown since then, particularly once he was freed from the ensorcellment of Eros. I can't deny I'm fascinated to discover how Cyneric means to trick Kronos. His methods might reveal a means of stopping my enemy.

Kronos folds his arms over his chest and smiles with smug certainty. "You are correct, vampire. I commend you for your mental acuity. Achieving my goal did require an enormous amount of energy, both magical and physical. Would you like to know more about my scheme?"

Ah, yes, Kronos just revealed one small piece of his secret. He admitted his plan demanded physical energy—which means it would have drained him for some time afterward. Physical magics are volatile. He would have needed to replenish his magics often to achieve his goal.

Cyneric tips his head to the side, doing an excellent impression of someone who is enthralled by hearing the time thief divulge his tactics. "I would be quite interested to learn more, Lord Kronos."

I just stop myself from laughing. Cyneric would never call any other being "lord" anything. He despises the high and mighty gods of the Unseen, mostly because of what Eros did to him. The vampire is massaging Kronos's ego to get more information.

Felicia whispers to me in my mind. "What are physical magics?"

"Any spell or incantation that requires blood or flesh to become viable."

"That's disgusting."

I agree with her, but we both need to pay attention to what Kronos is about to reveal to us. No more mental conversation, at least for now.

Kronos winks. "I'll tell you all about it, but not out here in the courtyard. Let's retire to my study."

I don't believe for one moment that he has a study, at least not the sort used by beings who aren't evil. This compound seethes with dark energies, though most remain invisible. Every inch of every wall, floor, and stick of furniture is drenched in vile magics that feel viscous on my skin as they spread out across my entire body. It's an illusion, I'm certain. Kronos hopes to unsettle us.

Felicia rubs her forearm, undoubtedly sensing the viscous magics. But Cyneric, naturally, pays no heed, though he must feel what we do.

Kronos sweeps one arm wide in a grand gesture. "Follow me. You'll be fascinated by my living quarters, but we'll begin our tour in the study."

I will allow him to play out his childish farce, but not for long.

As we trudge down a hallway that seems to stretch on forever, Kronos begins his charade in earnest. "Isn't my home impressive? Eons of crafting the magics required to raise this fortress paid off." He glances over his shoulder at us. "Aren't you impressed? Of course you are."

I grind my teeth.

Felicia flattens her lips and narrows her eyes.

Cyneric continues his conversation with Kronos. "How did you acquire the physical magics needed to erect this fortress? Regular magics are simple to acquire if you have the skill, patience, and intelligence to do so."

"I will explain momentarily." Kronos halts and turns toward the right side of the corridor's walls. He waves a hand negligently, then a door materializes and opens with such slowness that it becomes irritating. A creaking sound accompanies the movements as if the hinge is rusty. It's pure artifice. "Come inside, and the answer will be revealed."

His delay tactics are infuriating. I'll give him one more minute, then I'll knock down his entire fortress.

Kronos waits until the three of us have taken seats on magically conjured chairs. Then a much larger, more ornate chair appears. He settles onto that seat, crossing one leg over the knee of the other. And he clasps his hands. "For longer than any human civilizations have existed, I've been plotting my revenge. You, Janus, are the thorn in my side. It's time I yanked it out and set the thorn on fire."

Cyneric lifts one brow. "How do you mean to destroy a god? Considering the fact that you murdered Kali, I doubt the other gods will participate in any sort of destruction ritual."

Kronos leans back, setting his arms on the chair. "I don't need anyone else's help. I can destroy Janus all on my own."

Felicia huffs. "Oh, brother. You're an even bigger jackass than I thought. It took seven gods to destroy Janus. Like Cyneric said, you killed your own lackey, and nobody likes to work with a traitor."

"I crafted this fortress for you, Felicia. We will rule the multiverse together. I'll even conjure a crown for you."

"Keep your scummy crown and your scummy magics. I don't want them. You'll have to kill me, because I will never marry you again."

He chuckles. "Oh, you innocent waif. The deed has already been done. We were joined in unholy matrimony on the first night I fucked you. Nothing and no one can steal you away from me. I need only activate the magics I injected into you."

I narrow my gaze on Kronos. "Injecting magics? I've never heard of such a thing."

Kronos laughs heartily. "My seed, you fool. Every time I came inside my wife's body, I slipped a bit of dark energy into her womb."

Felicia freezes as her face goes pale. Not for long, though. Her shock crumbles away in an instant, and she flies out of her chair, screaming like the Furies themselves as she latches on to her former husband's throat. "I'll kill you for this, Blake! I'll find a way to rip your heart out of your chest and tear your dick off your body too, you evil, conniving, snake!"

While she rages, Kronos casually peels her hands away from his throat. "Settle down, Fliss. You won't be so offended once I've ensorcelled you."

She screams again and reaches for his throat once more.

But he bats her away as if she were a fly.

I spring out of my chair to catch her as she sails backward. While I cradle her to me and murmur soothing sounds, she begins to sob. The anger I'd already experienced now surges into a wrath like none other. When I speak, my voice has grown so harsh that I don't recognize it. Spittle sprays from my lips as I snarl at him. "Kronos, *iuppiter te perdat*! I'm done listening to your patronizing banter. The moment you hurt Felicia, your fate was sealed. Now, we will end this once and for all."

Kronos holds perfectly still for precisely two point nine seconds. Then his affable facade crumbles away, replaced by the ugliest expression of disdain I've ever seen. "You want a battle? Good. No more coddling you and your vampire friend, or Felicia either. I shall rip you apart, Janus the Almighty, but only after I've murdered everyone you hold dear. Every member of your lineage, beginning with Laelia, will be expunged from history as if they never existed."

Felicia lifts her head from my chest. Though her eyes are bloodshot, she's no longer enraged. Her anger has lessened and solidified into steely resolve. "We won't let you hurt anyone ever again, you bastard."

Kronos rises from his chair. "Furies, come to me! Summon the entire horde!"

The stronghold collapses to the ground, vanishing in an instant.

And a horde of Furies descends upon us.

Chapter Thirty-One

Felicia

THE SKY DARKENS, BUT NOT BECAUSE THE SUN HAS SET—IF this evil realm even has a sun. The blackness overtaking the sky is a swarm of winged shrews descending on us like a horde of locusts. The flapping of their wings becomes deafening. What my ex-husband the demonic time lord hopes to accomplish here remains unclear. I don't believe he gives a rat's ass about reclaiming me.

He despises Janus with a fiery passion. All because he couldn't usurp the most powerful god in the Unseen and become the new king of time.

This might be the most epic tantrum in history.

As one, the Furies touch down, keeping their wings partly open to make sure we understand their position. Kronos is the mafia boss, and the Furies are his enforcers.

I still can't wrap my head around the fact that my ex is a supernatural psycho.

Blake—uh, Kronos grins at us and spreads his arms wide. "The god and his vampire have no alternatives. Felicia is already mine, but I will allow you, Janus, to take your bloodsucking friend and leave this place. You'll still die, of course. But rather than being struck down by my sword, you will watch the worlds die and then be destroyed yourself."

"What a generous offer," I say with sarcasm dripping from my voice. "You're a real sweetheart, Blake."

"Do not call me that ever again. I am King Kronos, Lord of Everything."

"I thought you wanted to annihilate the multiverse. You won't have anything to lord over."

"Enough of this." In the blink of an eye, he transports me into his arms, facing Janus, and holds me close to his body. "Alecto, Megaera, Tisiphone, gather your army and enact the orders I issued earlier." As the three Furies fly away, my ex-husband slides his arm up to cup my breast. "You will become the queen of the apocalypse, my darling wife, and mother of the new realm I shall create."

Alecto, Megaera, and Tisiphone are the names of the Furies in mythology. But back then, there were only three of them. Kronos has amassed hundreds, maybe thousands, of those creatures.

Janus tries to throw himself at Kronos, but he can't move. It looks like my ex created a magical barrier around my lover. Cyneric has the same problem, though he gnashes his teeth to express his disgust.

The trio who seem to be in charge of the army of winged shrews fly back to Kronos, taking up positions behind him. He manages to keep me caged with one arm while reaching out to pet the wings of the Furies. "Take flight, my lovelies, and hunt down all my enemies. Destroy them and leave no trace."

Alecto, Tisiphone, and Megaera rocket into the sky and soar away from us.

The rest of the Furies line up behind Kronos. I twist my head around to peer past his shoulder where the army has congregated.

My ex-husband grins again and chuckles. "Let's find out if a vampire and a celibate god can defeat the Dark One, the greatest god of all, the mighty Kronos."

He has no idea Janus isn't celibate anymore. Will the magical energies from our sexual encounters be enough to make him victorious? I pray they will.

Kronos flings me away, and I go rolling across the barren landscape so fast that it makes me woozy. "Catch her, Janus. I dare you."

Janus clearly still can't teleport, so he races toward me. I can barely see what's going on since I'm still rolling across the ground. He leaps on top of me, but even that doesn't make me stop spinning. His weight slams down on me every time he's on top. All he can do to keep from crushing me is to fling himself away.

He unleashes a string of Latin curses.

Cyneric tries to help, racing toward Janus, and I get more glimpses of what they're trying to do. Nothing makes a difference. I'm getting dizzier and sicker by the second while a vampire and a god desperately struggle to end the madness.

Without warning, I stop whirling and fall flat on my back. Just as Janus and Cyneric reach me, I flop onto my side and throw up. Twice. I'm so weak I can't move a muscle, not even my eyelids which have closed of their own volition.

Janus kneels to brush damp hairs away from my face. "Don't worry, *dulcissima*, I will destroy Kronos no matter what it takes." He kisses my forehead. "Cyneric, protect Felicia."

The vampire nods. "At the cost of my own life, I will protect her. She's clearly the key to stopping Kronos."

Janus kisses my forehead again, then stalks over to my ex-husband.

The vampire kneels beside me wearing an expression full of so much cold fury that it gives me a chill. But he isn't staring at me that way. His attention remains rooted to Kronos.

Janus halts directly in front of his enemy with mere inches between them. "Let's end this now. Name your weapon."

Kronos grins like the demon he is. "Gladiatorial combat with endued weapons. My Furies will be the spectators, and all of them will be on my side, of course."

"Conjure the weapons. I assume you're still blocking my ability to do so."

"Yes, but you will have your full powers—during this battle only. You won't save my wife that way."

Kronos backs away a few paces and conjures two long, wickedly sharp swords, tossing one to Janus. "And so it begins, the end of Janus the Almighty."

Janus twirls his sword as if he's testing it.

Kronos wears the most conceited expression I've ever seen, as if he's positive nothing can stop him. He raises his weapon.

For a moment, they both stand motionless.

Then Kronos rushes at Janus, slashing his blade toward my boyfriend's belly. Janus leaps out of range just in time.

I raise up onto my elbows to watch the two gods attacking each other with stunning viciousness and lightning speed. Cyneric stands beside me, his face inscrutable, his eyes flicking back and forth as if he's actually keeping track of every movement. Kronos and Janus become blurs to me, two superhumans determined to annihilate each other. Blood splatters on the ground, turning it crimson, reaching far enough away that it spatters on me and Cyneric.

My heart is pounding. Adrenaline has strengthened me, and I leap up to stand beside Cyneric. "Should we do something?"

"Such as..."

"No idea."

"Even I cannot determine who's murdering whom. Their movements are like lightning, swift and hot and deadly."

I can't just stand here watching. I need to help Janus. Kronos will cheat any way he can, for sure. The love of my life is out there fighting for his own life, for all our lives, for everyone in the multiverse.

Cyneric sets a hand on my shoulder. "No, Felicia. I can't let you go out there."

"But I have to—"

He shakes his head slowly, almost sadly. "I can't let you do it. Janus would never forgive me, though perhaps I can assist him." He squints at me. "But you are not to leave this location unless it becomes unsafe. Agreed?"

"Yes."

Cyneric sprints toward Janus faster than any human, but he skids to a halt before he even gets to the battling gods. I want to rush over there and punch him. But then I see why he stopped. The gods have slowed their warfare just enough that even I can tell Janus is losing. Blood covers his entire body and soaks his hair. He's breathing hard, so winded that his sword hand is trembling.

How is that possible? He's a fucking god.

Kronos pulls his sword backward and thrusts it straight at Janus's chest.

"No!" I scream, and I forget all the reasons why I'm a goddamn moron for doing this. My soul mate is in dire trouble. "Stop it, Blake!"

Hearing his earthly pseudonym distracts him for only two seconds, three at most, but it's enough.

Cyneric tackles Kronos. The bastard's blade goes flying. That gives the vampire a chance to do something. He sinks his fangs into the evil god's throat and rips it open. Blood gushes out, flooding down his chest and arms, forming a puddle on the ground.

A chorus of angry shrieks echoes across the wasteland.

Janus scrambles to his feet and staggers toward the vampire and the evil god. "Back away, Cyneric. You might be entangled in the destruction magics."

Cyneric pulls his fangs out of Kronos's neck and staggers backward several yards.

The Furies launch themselves into the air and speed toward us. We have seconds, at most, to finish off Kronos.

Janus raises his sword, slamming it downward toward Kronos's chest.

But a mob of Furies descends on him before he can sink the blade into my ex-husband's chest. They claw at his flesh with their talons. Janus is forced to back away along with me and Cyneric. The winged bitches have swarmed Kronos. How do we break through that kind of protection without getting ourselves cut to ribbons?

Abruptly, the Furies fly up into the sky and begin circling the area around the four of us as if they're awaiting instructions.

Janus tries once more to skewer Kronos, but he still can't do it. The other god's flesh has begun to shimmer with unearthly shades of scarlet, greenish yellow, onyx, and olive green which seem to act as a protective barrier. Every time Janus thrusts his blade, the colors that surround Kronos pulse and brighten briefly.

And he laughs.

The deep, husky tone of his voice rankles. It's riddled with sarcasm and rife with loathing. "You will never defeat me, Janus. And it's time to prove that to you." He glances up at the squadron of Furies, then smiles with smug superiority. "This is the end of time, the end of everything."

He flings his arms straight out toward Janus. But instead of hurling him away, Kronos wraps him up in a bubble of sickly yellow and scarlet. Janus grimaces as he struggles against the barrier, to no avail. The sky mutates into roiling shades of scarlet and greenish yellow, the same shades as the protective bubble Kronos created for himself. A circular void opens up directly above us, and it begins to absorb the hues, drawing them deeper and deeper into the black emptiness at the center of the void. The blackness consumes the colors.

Oh, shit. That's a black hole.

Janus tips his head back to stare at the sky. "What have you done, Kronos?"

"I've initiated the apocalypse. The only ones who will survive will be me, the Furies, and Felicia. She will bear my depraved children."

Like hell I will.

I sprint up to Kronos and pound on his chest. "Stop this, you lunatic!"

"Stop? No, my darling, you will be a witness to the destruction of time itself." He grasps my chin and drags me closer to mash his mouth to mine. "At last, I will get rid of Janus forever."

He lashes me to his body with one arm.

While Janus thrashes inside his confinement bubble, Cyneric rushes at Kronos. His enraged cry is nearly drowned out by the racket that just erupted overhead. That black hole is doing more than sucking up light. It's vacuuming up the Unseen realm. I watch as earth and trees get ripped out of their roots and swirl up into the black hole. Soon, this entire world might vanish.

And then Earth.

If he intends to destroy the multiverse, that means countless beings and planets will become...nothing.

Cyneric slams into Kronos, but the impact barely nudges the evil god. Instead, it makes the vampire bounce off an invisible shield. Kronos must have just thrown that up around himself and me. But Cyneric won't give up. He hurls his body at the shield that confines Janus, only to bounce off that one too, smacking onto the ground backward. Just as he scrambles to his feet, a Fury snags him by the shoulders.

I need to do something. What? My soul mate is about to get sucked up into a cosmic vacuum cleaner along with all my friends.

Soul mate. I go still as a strange composure overtakes me. My pulse no longer thunders in my ears. Of course. It's obvious. I should have figured this out so much sooner, but it's better now than never. Janus is my soul mate. We're connected in more ways than I can describe, but there's one truth I believe with complete certainty.

We are bound by love and magics.

Janus had shared his powers with me, and he never rescinded those magics. We've communicated telepathically. I know, deep in my soul, that our love has bound us in every way. I can free him. Right now.

But first, I need to shake off my evil ex.

Cyneric struggles to his feet, clearly preparing to leap on Kronos. But I cast him a sideways glance that my evil ex doesn't notice. He's too focused on Janus. So, I give a minute shake of my head aimed at Cyneric. He freezes, tilting his head slightly to the side, then he gives a barely perceptible nod.

The vampire understands. He won't fight, not yet.

Now comes the dangerous part.

I muster all my acting skills, praying I'm good enough to pull this off, and I clear my throat. "I'm confused. What will eradicating the multiverse get you, Blake?"

"Don't call me that," he snarls.

Bingo. I've hit the jackpot. "I didn't mean to upset you, Blake, but—"

He wraps his hand around my throat. "Stop using that name, or I'll destroy Janus and the vampire."

"I honestly didn't mean to make you feel bad. It's just that I'm wondering where you and I will live after you've annihilated everything in the multiverse."

"Shut up, Fliss."

"Sure, Blake, whatever you say."

Kronos flings me away from him, then stalks up to me so he can glare down at my face. "You stupid cow, shut your fucking mouth. I'm busy right now."

Wow, I can't believe my plan actually worked. Kronos really does not like to hear his mortal name, the one he invented so he could seduce me.

The roiling colors that surround the black hole have slowed their motion. That must be a good sign. Good magics are gathering inside me.

I tip my head back to see Janus, who hasn't stopped pounding on his see-through cage, and pretend to be confused. "Um, does it look like he's weakening that force field or whatever it is? Might want to check on that, Blake."

He fists his hands and roars at me. The veins in his arms and forehead bulge.

I throw a quick glance at Cyneric, rolling my eyes toward Kronos.

The vampire leaps onto the evil god's back and wraps his arms around the bastard's neck. Then he buries his fangs deep.

The amethyst necklace Lindsey had given me appears in my hand. I think I summoned it. Not sure why, but I know Janus needs it.

And I fling myself at Janus's cage. The force field shatters.

Janus is free—to destroy Kronos.

Chapter Thirty-Two

Janus

I HURL MYSELF AT KRONOS, ROARING LIKE AN ENRAGED hell beast. An amethyst pendant materializes in my hand as magics of the same color unfurl around me in a cloud that glitters with tiny, jewel-like particles. I have never seen such a thing before, but I swear the protective magics come from Felicia. Cyneric yanks his fangs out of Kronos's neck and leaps backward several paces. He's getting out of the way of the destruction magics.

Before Kronos realizes what's happening, I've summoned his sword.

Kronos remains fixated on Felicia.

I plunge my sword into the chest of Kronos, sinking it in so deeply that its tip emerges from his back. Blood pours out of his nostrils and his chest. I hoist my blade upward, then down again, slicing Kronos in half. The halves of him fall to the ground. While the black hole goes on whirling and sucking in more and more pieces of the Unseen, the body of Kronos shudders violently. The agonizing energies of the destruction process have begun to sizzle over his flesh, and yet he manages to scream.

Though his body has been rent in half, his head remains intact. Blood pours from his nostrils. The sizzling of his flesh grows louder as a curtain of pure white energy enshrouds him, devouring his body one molecule at a time. I understand the agony of destruction. Perhaps I feel an iota of regret, but that sensation vanishes quickly. Kronos would have annihilated the multiverse, and perhaps he will have his wish after all. The black hole remains intact, still spinning, if slower than before.

A blood-curdling scream explodes out of Kronos.

The magics make it difficult to see how his body is being melted and disassembled one atom at a time. His cries abruptly stop. A cloud of residual magics rises from the spot where Kronos had lain, drifting away until it dissipates completely.

Felicia rushes to my side. "Kronos is gone, but our problems aren't over yet. Am I right?"

"Yes. We must return to our friends, then whisk ourselves into the mortal world. I pray my worst fears will not come true."

"What is your worst fear?"

"That the black hole is only the beginning, and the spells cast by Kronos might devour the entire multiverse if we can't stop them." I plaster Felicia to my side, then call out to the vampire. "Cyneric, we must leave now."

He hurries over to us, and I wrap an arm around him as well. I sense that the magics Kronos had used to trap us here are faltering. That means we can teleport to our friends.

Our first stop is the location where Kali's corpse lay.

We find Bob and Ennea squatting on the muddy ground, their gazes fixed on the remains of Kali. Vandren stands behind them, also staring at the ground.

Bob raises his head. "There you are. We wondered if you'd forgotten about us. I take it Kronos is gone?"

"Yes. But the magics he initiated remain active. Before we can fix the problem, we must know the extent of the damage. You might have noticed the black hole above us." I point up at the roiling sky. "We must work quickly and remain together."

"Duh," Ennea says. "Thanks for stating the obvious. By the way, how did you kill Kronos?"

"With my sword. Cyneric and Felicia distracted him while I cleaved the *irrumator* in half."

"Ouch. He deserved that."

I gesture for Bob, Ennea, and Vandren to come closer, then fold my arms around them as well as Felicia and Cyneric. The abyssal tunnel seems to have broken down, yet my powers allow me to transport us anyway. I have never traveled in this manner before, and I had no idea it was possible. All the elementals and gods transport themselves via the tunnel.

But now, I am different. My love for Felicia has changed me.

We touch down inside my temple in the Unseen where our friends await us. The three kerkopes and Theo are huddled on the bed as if they need comforting.

All our friends, including Sigrun and Anthea, have remained here. Even Gundisalvus did not flee. The magics that Kronos had invoked must have sent my temple wards tumbling down, yet everyone waited for us. Perhaps this team isn't as irregular as I'd believed.

Travis crosses his arms. "Forgot about us, didn't you?"

"I forget nothing. We were assaulted by Furies. Kali is dead, by the way."

"You mean she was destroyed."

"No. I said she is dead, and that's precisely what I meant." I raise a hand to stay his objection. "Kronos invoked unusual magics to kill her. We found Kali's desecrated corpse lying in a mud puddle in his domain. He undoubtedly hoped that sight would deter us."

Tris jogs up to us and begins to speak.

I silence him with one raised hand. "Discussion must wait. The black hole is still churning, and I fear the entire multiverse is imperiled. We must return to the mortal world now."

Since I can't reasonably hold all of these beings in my arms, I ask them to gather in the center of the temple. They must also remain touching each other, though a simple shoulder-to-shoulder stance should do.

Then I whisk us away.

We land in the garden of statuary behind the rock shop in Michigan. Above us, the sky has mutated into a roiling mass of blood red and sickly yellow. The patrons of the shop are fleeing as quickly as possible, some shrieking, some shouting vulgarities at the sky. Parents rush to collect their children and drive away.

No vehicle made by man will shield them from this apocalypse.

"Remain here," I command our irregular army. "We must check on Lindsey."

I grasp Felicia's hand as we race into the shop.

Lindsey and Nevan stand alone in the barren building, huddling behind the counter. Nevan clings to Lindsey, who in turn clings to their child, Liam.

"What the bloody hell is going on, Janus?" Nevan demands. "No one warned us about an apocalypse."

"Are you three unharmed?"

"Yes. I suspect we won't be for long."

Should I leave them here? Will they be safer that way? No one can say for certain. "You might as well stay here. I doubt anywhere in the multiverse will be secure."

"All right. We'll wait here."

For reasons I can't fathom, I rush behind the counter to hug the babe and Nevan, then drag Lindsey into my arms to give her a firm embrace. And I kiss her cheek. "Whatever happens, Lindsey, know that I love you."

I glimpse her stunned expression as I turn away.

Felicia and I race out of the shop, holding hands. As we sprint across the rock garden, I shout, "Follow us. No time to explain."

The gang doesn't object. They hurry after us.

Felicia and I lead the group to the clearing beside the waterfall and its pool. At the wooden railing, we halt and face our friends.

"We must prevent the black hole from consuming the multiverse," I tell them. "Kronos essentially employed the same destruction magics used to eradicate a god like me. The black hole seems as if it's not expanding, but that is an illusion. The magics are being sucked into the multiverse."

"How do you know that?" Pendi asks.

"Because I can feel it. My temporal powers are rooted in the multiverse."

Riley raises her hand. "So, what are we going to do?"

"Stop the apocalypse, obviously. We have no time to discuss the problem, so you will all need to trust me." I scan the group. "Does anyone have an issue with that?"

Every head shakes.

The sky darkens to blood red.

An explosion above our heads makes the forest convulse, and the action generates rippling waves in the earth beneath our feet. The movements cause the water from the falls and the pool below it to spill over into the clearing, inundating it. Fortunately, no one is swept away.

But we have run out of time for discussion.

"The apocalypse is nigh," I shout. "We must split into two groups. One will head for the point in the mortal world that is furthest from the earth's core. It's a mountain called Chimborazo in Ecuador. I will transport half of our group to that location, and the rest will teleport with me and Felicia to The Eternal Plane in the Unseen. Bob will go with the first group. He knows the destruction ritual, which we will perform in reverse."

Bob's eyes widen. "In reverse? I've never done that."

"Ken will go with you. Together, you should be able to complete the ritual. You can do this, Bob."

The oracle nods. "I trust you, Janus. We'll get it done."

"Larissa is mortal, therefore she should go to the rock shop to ride this out with Nevan and Lindsey."

A massive pine tree is ripped from the earth, along with its roots, and flies up into the sky. Our time has run out. We must do this right now.

I teleport Max, Harper, Bob, Ken, Pendi, Sigrun, Anthea, and Gundisalvus to Mount Chimborazo. Just as I'm about to whisk us away, the earth beneath our feet heaves upward, splitting apart, creating a fathomless cavity. We all begin to slide toward it. But I whisk us away just in time.

Now, we stand atop The Eternal Plane. The mountain trembles faintly, a clue that we don't have much time. The destruction ritual normally requires precisely seven gods or elementals, but I've chosen eight in each of our groups. Though I can't explain why, I believe we need an exactly even number of individuals to ensure success.

"Form a circle," I exclaim. "But do not link hands yet."

I grasp Felicia's hand. Magics zings through me, and I know she felt it too. We've connected with each other, but now I must connect the others as well. My plan is more belief than evidence, but I know deep in my soul that it will work.

So, I clasp the hand of the being on the other side of me—Cyneric. "Take hold of Travis's hand, continue to link our hands to form a circle."

One by one, my friends do as I commanded. With every new link, the power grows and sizzles, though not in an unpleasant manner. Instead, this connection is reassuring. When the last link is connected, an audible buzz lets us know the circle is complete.

I chant the destruction spell backwards, one syllable at a time, taking it slow to ensure I haven't made a mistake. One tiny error might speed up the process of the black hole devouring the multiverse. Just as I felt our hands connecting, now I feel the words I speak as if they aren't coming from me but from a benevolent force beyond myself. I sense what it is, yet I can't believe it's true.

The Oversoul has assisted me.

As the last word tumbles from my lips, the sky above us begins to lighten. The grinding and growling racket of the apocalypse gradually winds down to nothing. A beautiful silence falls over the worlds. The Unseen and mortal realms have returned to normal, and no one on Planet Earth will remember what transpired on the two mountaintops. I've made certain of that. Every creature in the Unseen will retain the memories of this near calamity, yet humans will forget in an instant.

Except for the ones who already knew about the Unseen before Kronos tried to annihilate the multiverse. That includes Lindsey and her family as well as Larissa and a few others.

"It is done," I pronounce. "All is as it should be once again. I have teleported the others away from Mount Chimborazo and back to the rock shop."

"Can we go home now?" Travis asks. "I need to hug my wife and daughter for an hour or two."

"Yes, you may all go. I will teleport you back to your homes."

With a single thought, I send them away. Felicia and I are alone here on The Eternal Plane. She stands perfectly still, gazing straight ahead, as if she's in shock.

I turn toward Felicia and pull her close, cupping her chin with one hand. "Are you unwell, *dulcissima*? Has the apocalypse that almost occurred frightened you so much that you can't speak? Or perhaps you wish to leave me."

Felicia swerves her gaze to my face, and her posture softens. She smiles in the sweetest manner. "I will never leave you, Janus. Never. We're bound by more than the powers we share. You and I are soul mates forever, so you might as well get used to being stuck with me. Even if I die, I'll still be here with you."

"Do not speak of death. If I lost you—"

A throat clearing draws both of our attention to the two beings who just materialized a short distance away. Bob and Ken amble closer.

"What are you doing here?" I ask the oracles. "Has the black hole not been fully neutralized?"

Bob sighs. "Why do you always assume the worst when you see us?"

Ken tries to stifle a chuckle but only partially succeeds. "Why else would they do that, Bob? We rarely come out of our lairs, and I don't recall us ever playing a game of gin rummy with our friends or starting a soccer match."

"Football, Ken. Those of us who speak with British accents know the correct term for that sport is football."

"Let's not relive that tired old debate. We came here to reassure them and deliver some news."

"Of course. I do apologize, Janus and Felicia. Ken can be so tiresome." Bob brushes a hand over his hair as if he's smoothing it out. "For the first time ever, Ken and I have experienced identical premonitions. Our foresight has shown us that you have nothing to fear. For as long as you live, Janus, Felicia cannot not die and will continue to share your powers."

"That's right," Ken says. "She is neither an elemental nor a god, yet she is as indestructible and almighty as you are."

I stare at him, stupefied, unable to do anything except shake my head slowly for a moment or two. "How is that possible? I don't understand."

Bob twists his mouth into an odd slant. "Well, you see, when you and Felicia were in the time stream temple getting frisky, your, ah…carnal activities altered her. Your powers began to sift into her. That was the moment when you two became indivisible, spiritually speaking."

"Are you saying Felicia is now also the god of time and portals and—"

"No, not quite. She is something in between, though her powers might grow into godliness." Bob glances at Ken. "We've done our due diligence. Let's party with the others in the copper fae village."

"You're both welcome to join us," Ken says. "But we assumed you and Felicia would prefer some alone time."

"I need no foresight to understand what our immediate future holds." I kiss Felicia's forehead. "As for what comes after that, we will deal with it together."

Bob clears his throat deliberately. "One last thing before you whisk your true love away to your time temple for more spicy shenanigans."

"What is it now?"

"Ken and I have foreseen two surprises that will rock your worlds quite soon. Ta-ta."

The oracles vanish.

I frown at the empty space where the oracles had stood. "What was that nonsense?"

"Oh, don't get grumpy yet. I have a feeling the surprises will be good ones." She lashes her arms around my neck. "Whisk me away for more spicy shenanigans in the time stream temple."

"Anything for you, *mea lux.*"

EPILOGUE

Felicia
Two months later

JANUS AND I AMBLE DOWN THE PATH FROM THE WATER-
fall to the garden of whimsical statues and pause at the periphery. I never get tired of having his big, warm palm clasping mine. I
never tire of anything related to the man I love more than anything in the multiverse. Our friends have orchestrated a massive
blowout to celebrate…well, everything.

Life is unbelievably good these days.

Thankfully, with some help from a few fae witches, Bob and
Ken were able to rid me of all the dark magics Kronos had im-
planted inside me. I'm free of my ex for good. I'm free, period.

"They're here!" shrieks Dani, the adopted daughter of Travis and
Larissa. The eight-year-old might be the happiest kid I've ever met,
though Lindsey's fifteen-year-old brother Ash comes in a close second in that contest.

Janus and I trot into the statue garden.

Dani meets us halfway, throwing her arms around my waist. "I'm
so happy you're here." She twists her head around to glance over her
shoulder. "Mom! Dad! Janus and Felicia are here!"

That's how the revelry begins.

Max and Tris had set themselves up as DJs, and now they take turns
choosing which songs to play. Every song is a happy one, of course.

I have one task to accomplish, and it might be the hardest thing I've ever done.

Janus is talking to Riley and Tris.

I barge in and grab my honey's arm. "Come on, sweetie, it's time."

"For what?"

"Your first dance lesson."

He throws his head back and moans in a very ungodlike manner. "Not now, Fliss."

"Okay. When? Give me the exact time down to milliseconds."

Tris grins and laughs. "Janus dancing? I'll bet you ten bucks you can't get him to do the electric slide."

"Isn't betting a no-no in the Unseen?"

"Sure. But we're in the mortal world."

"Well, in that case…" I tug on Janus's arm. "Your first lesson starts now. No whining, no bitching, no excuses. Dance with me, sweetie. Unless you'd rather treat everyone to a harp concert."

"No. I play the harp only for you."

"Then it's time to boogie. That means dancing."

He bows his head, scratching the back of his neck. "I suppose we should practice. Dancing is required at weddings, or so Max told me."

"Whose wedding? Is Quin getting hitched?"

"No." He lifts his head to study me for a moment, then drops to one knee. "I've been debating when to do this, but I cannot wait any longer. Felicia Marie Lagorio, my soul mate and queen of the time stream, will you be my bride?"

I gape at him for seven point one seconds. Yeah, I can count that way too now. But I've left him hanging, so I bend over to cup his face with both hands. "Yes, of course I'll marry you sweetie."

He flings his arms around my waist and leaps to his feet, hoisting me high above his head while we both grin and laugh.

After a while, Janus and I retreat from the party and grab a couple glasses of champagne. Then we settle down on one of the stone benches that flank the healing vortex. Just as we begin sipping our bubbly, Tris and Cyneric sit down on the bench opposite us.

"Why so dour?" Janus asks. "You two look as if you're expecting another apocalypse at any moment."

Cyneric lifts one brow. "That is not the case. But we are wondering if there have been any sightings of Dionysus."

"None at all. Perhaps the black hole dragged him into its maw and consumed him."

"Shouldn't we be trying harder to find him?" Tris asks. "He was number one on our list of baddies."

Janus knocks back his entire glass of champagne. "Cease your worrying, Triskaideka. For all we know, Kronos devoured Dionysus."

"But even the oracles can't find him. That's weird."

Cyneric nods. "Quite strange, indeed."

My hubby-to-be rises and gestures for me to do the same. "This is a party. Fliss and I just became engaged, and we want to celebrate. No more worries about Dionysus. When the time is right, the answer will come. Besides, no one will ever again breach the portals without my consent or Felicia's."

His new Zen attitude has infected me too. I can't manage to worry about anything today. *C'est la vie*, as the saying goes.

Naturally, the party kicks into high gear again in celebration of our engagement news. Janus does learn the electric slide, much faster than I do, actually. I predict he'll become a fabulous dancer. But as the festivities wind down, for good this time, we say goodbye to our friends and head for the clearing beside the waterfall. Lindsey and Nevan have come with us, and their secretive expressions make me wonder what they've got up their sleeves. As far as I know, they came long strictly to wish us goodbye before we retreat into the Unseen.

"Stop right there," Lindsey instructs us. "This is the perfect viewing spot."

"What are we meant to view?" Janus asks. "We have both seen the waterfall many times."

Lindsey wags a finger at him. "Shush, Janus. Just watch."

We're both standing at the railing, facing the clearing, but I don't see anything unusual.

Then a ghostlike being materializes in front of us. The female wears flowing white robes, and her hair flutters in a nonexistent breeze. Just as she smiles at us, more beings begin to appear behind the first. They're all female and dressed in the same fashion. The last being who materializes walks up to us and smiles at me and Janus.

My fiancé gapes at the woman. His jaw drops far enough that I think a hummingbird might fly in there.

Since Janus can't speak, I'll do it for him. "Who are you?"

The woman smiles with a serenity that seems completely genuine. "I am Vita."

Now it's my turn to gape, but I recover faster than Janus. "Vita? As in the woman Janus loved back in Roman times?"

"Yes. And you are Felicia, his true soul mate. I'm pleased he finally found the perfect woman for him."

Janus finally shakes off his shock. "Vita…Who are these women who have come with you?"

"Your descendants, of course." She glances back at the crowd of ghostly women. "We couldn't fit all of us in this clearing since many thousands of your descendants have been born since Laelia. She lived a long and happy life with her husband and daughter. The Janusite lineage began with our daughter, and it will continue forever. The birth of two sons—first Ash, now Liam—has changed things. We are all anxious to find out precisely how those changes will unfold."

Janus skims his gaze over the crowd, and tears begin to gather in his eyes. "All my daughters…I truly am blessed and honored to meet all of you."

Another woman approaches us, halting beside Vita. "Hello, Father."

Janus hesitates only for a second, then hauls his daughter into his arms. Tears roll down his cheeks, and he gets choked up. "Laelia, my Laelia. Never did I imagine I would have the chance to hold you in my arms."

Laelia starts to cry too, and soon Vita and I join in.

Once the happy cry-fest ends, Janus walks among the ghostly crowd to hug and kiss the cheek of every single descendant. Well, not quite all, not yet. We watch the spirits of the Janusite lineage fade away one by one. Laelia hugs her father again, then blows him a kiss as she vanishes. Then he hugs Vita once more and kisses her forehead before she too fades away.

Janus wipes the tears away with the heel of his hand. Then he straightens, clears his throat, and marches over to Lindsey. "I hope you haven't thought I'd forgotten about you."

Lindsey smiles, clearly about to speak. But she doesn't get the chance.

Janus drags her into a bear hug before kissing her forehead. "I know I shouldn't have a favorite, but I can't help it. You, Lindsey, are the brightest light in the Janusite lineage. And I cannot wait to meet the next generation of beautiful, strong, incredible women."

"But I have a son. Did Bob tell you I'd have a daughter sometime?"

He taps a finger on her nose. "You are not the mother-to-be."

"Huh?"

Janus pulls me close. "Felicia is with child."

Lindsey shrieks with joy.

My journey from loser in love and museum tour guide to powerful time queen was a rocky one, for sure. In a way, I need to thank Blake aka Kronos for my happiness. He triggered the chain of events that would lead me to my true love. And soon, we'll have a child of our own—a little girl who will be as amazing as her father. I used to scoff at fairy-tale endings, but a scorching-hot time god gave me the happily ever after I never knew I needed.

And I can't wait for our future to unfold.

THE UNDERCOVER ELEMENTALS SERIES WILL CONTINUE.

Did you love

THE

IMMORTAL FALLS?

Visit

AnnaDurand.com

to subscribe to her newsletter
for updates on forthcoming books in this series
&
to receive exclusive content!

ANNA DURAND IS A BESTSELLING, MULTI-AWARD-WINNING author of contemporary and paranormal romance. Her books have earned bestseller status on every major retailer and wonderful reviews from readers around the world. But that's the boring spiel. Here are the really cool things you want to know about Anna!

Born on Lackland Air Force Base in Texas, Anna grew up moving here, there, and everywhere thanks to her dad's job as an instructor pilot. She's lived in Texas (twice), Mississippi, California (twice), Michigan (twice), and Alaska—and now Ohio.

As for her writing, Anna has always invented stories in her head, but she didn't write them down until her teen years. Those first awful books went into the trash can a few years later, though she learned a lot from those stories. Eventually, she would pen her first romance novel, the paranormal romance *Willpower*, and she's never looked back since.

To get exclusive content, join Anna's Facebook group, Anna's Romance Addicts, or sign up for her newsletter.

VISIT ANNADURAND.COM TO SIGN UP.

.